IN THE ⟨...⟩ mighty and ancient ba⟨...⟩ial Navy protect mankind fr⟨...⟩ic enemies, charged with the safet⟨...⟩ mperial space lanes. First Officer Ward, ⟨...⟩ the Imperial Navy vessel *Relentless*, is less than pleased when a new commander, hardliner Captain Becket, is appointed. To protect his own corrupt schemes and ambitions, Ward ruthlessly arranges to have Becket assassinated. Unbeknown to him, the new captain manages to survive, and embarks on a campaign to fight his way through the ranks to seize back command of the ship and claim his revenge. Yet, while the battle for control of the *Relentless* rages, a sinister alien presence draws ever closer...

Action and adventure with the Imperial Navy in the cold reaches of the Eastern Fringe.

· GAUNT'S GHOSTS ·

by Dan Abnett

*Colonel-Commissar Gaunt and his regiment, the Tanith
First-and-Only, struggle for survival on the battlefields
of the far future.*

The Founding
Omnibus containing books 1-3 in the series:
FIRST AND ONLY, GHOSTMAKER and NECROPOLIS

The Saint
Omnibus containing books 4-7 in the series:
HONOUR GUARD, THE GUNS OF TANITH,
STRAIGHT SILVER and SABBAT MARTYR

The Lost
Book 8 – TRAITOR GENERAL
Book 9 – HIS LAST COMMAND
Book 10 – THE ARMOUR OF CONTEMPT
Book 11 – ONLY IN DEATH

Also
DOUBLE EAGLE

· THE ULTRAMARINES OMNIBUS ·

by Graham McNeill

(Contains the novels NIGHTBRINGER, WARRIORS
OF ULTRAMAR and DEAD SKY, BLACK SUN)

· ROGUE TRADER ·

by Andy Hoare
ROGUE STAR
STAR OF DAMOCLES

A WARHAMMER 40,000 NOVEL

RELENTLESS

Richard Williams

For Eumenides de Valence

With thanks to Jules, McCabe and the Gnome

A BLACK LIBRARY PUBLICATION

First published in Great Britain in 2008 by
BL Publishing,
Games Workshop Ltd.,
Willow Road, Nottingham,
NG7 2WS, UK.

10 9 8 7 6 5 4 3 2 1

Cover illustration by Dominic Harman.

A CIP record for this book is available from the British Library.

ISBN 13: 978 1 84416 501 8
ISBN 10: 1 84416 501 9

Distributed in the US by Simon & Schuster
1230 Avenue of the Americas, New York, NY 10020, US.

See the Black Library on the Internet at
www.blacklibrary.com

Find out more about Games Workshop
and the world of Warhammer 40,000 at
www.games-workshop.com

IT IS THE 41st millennium. For more than a hundred centuries the Emperor has sat immobile on the Golden Throne of Earth. He is the master of mankind by the will of the gods, and master of a million worlds by the might of his inexhaustible armies. He is a rotting carcass writhing invisibly with power from the Dark Age of Technology. He is the Carrion Lord of the Imperium for whom a thousand souls are sacrificed every day, so that he may never truly die.

YET EVEN IN his deathless state, the Emperor continues his eternal vigilance. Mighty battlefleets cross the daemon-infested miasma of the warp, the only route between distant stars, their way lit by the Astronomican, the psychic manifestation of the Emperor's will. Vast armies give battle in His name on uncounted worlds. Greatest amongst his soldiers are the Adeptus Astartes, the Space Marines, bio-engineered super-warriors. Their comrades in arms are legion: the Imperial Guard and countless planetary defence forces, the ever-vigilant Inquisition and the tech-priests of the Adeptus Mechanicus to name only a few. But for all their multitudes, they are barely enough to hold off the ever-present threat from aliens, heretics, mutants – and worse.

TO BE A man in such times is to be one amongst untold billions. It is to live in the cruellest and most bloody regime imaginable. These are the tales of those times. Forget the power of technology and science, for so much has been forgotten, never to be re-learned. Forget the promise of progress and understanding, for in the grim dark future there is only war. There is no peace amongst the stars, only an eternity of carnage and slaughter, and the laughter of thirsting gods.

PROLOGUE

'GENTLEMEN!'

The silver knife with the rorschbone handle rapped against the cut-glass flute. The noise rang around the grand table, still laden with the remnants of the final course of the banquet, and the hearty conversation hushed.

'Gentlemen officers of the *Relentless*,' the portly speaker said, rising and commanding the attention of his guests. 'Thank you for joining me this evening for this most special occasion. It has been my singular pleasure to captain this ship and its indomitable crew for twenty-one years now.

'Twenty-one years? I hear you say. Never!' A few of the braver officers chuckled. 'But I tell you that it is far worse than that, for it has been no less than forty-five years since I first stepped aboard. Yes, I was a junior midshipman once, just the same as the young lads who have been waiting on us this evening. The captain then

7

was an iron-hearted fellow, I can tell you. He ran this ship tighter than an inquisitor's arse!'

The officers all laughed hard. Many of them had called in a considerable number of favours to be at this dinner, for the speaker had the power to make, or break, their careers aboard ship.

'There were some tough times and a lot of good men who aren't here today. The *Relentless* was a feared name indeed. Of course, we've seen some adventures ourselves, haven't we? More than once xenos raiders have taken to singe our bow, before we sent them running with a bloody nose!

'And Commander Ward down there,' the speaker said, gesturing towards his first officer at the other end of the table, 'he can tell you a thing or two about coming face to face with the enemy, or face to fist if you prefer, eh commander? Eh?'

Ward smiled dutifully, and the guests enjoyed the rare opportunity for fun at the expense of the daunting first officer.

'To be serious, though, the *Relentless* has had much to be proud of in its past, and I know that between myself, the commander and all of you, comrades and friends, it will have much to be proud of in the future.

'So, gentlemen, charge your glasses and join me in a toast. Come, stand up! Stand up! Gentlemen: to the glorious traditions of the *Relentless* and to the future.'

'To the future!' the assembly replied.

With that, the purple wine at his lips, a look of consternation crossed the face of the old captain of the *Relentless* and he fell down stone dead.

SOME TIME LATER and far, far distant this incident became the subject of discussion of another, more sober, gathering.

'Moving on to the next order of business, sir,' the aide said as he respectfully passed another set of data-slates around. 'As you all know, we received this communication from the Imperial Warship *Relentless*, a Lunar-class cruiser currently on extended patrol through the outer sub-sectors. Their communication stated that their captain had found the Emperor's Mercy.'

'In action?' one of the vice admirals piped up.

'No, sir, it appears it was natural causes, over dinner.'

The vice admiral scoffed, though he was far more likely to meet a similar fate than ever have the chance to fall in battle.

'Most unfortunate,' the commodore chairman smoothly interjected and turned to the aide. 'I've looked at the summary you prepared. Some discrepancy over the transmission notes of the communiqué?'

'On further investigation, sir, some relay inhibitors caused a delay of some seven months in the communiqué reaching us. Nothing of significance. The *Relentless* has continued with its duties in the interim with the first officer in command.'

'Yes, and this is the man your report recommends to take over the captaincy.'

'That's correct, sir. Commander Ward has served aboard the *Relentless* for eighteen years, five of them as first officer. I understand that he is capable in the position and well respected by his fellow officers. As you know, sir, the recent conflicts have left us short of senior line personnel.'

'He will be our recommendation, unless anyone has anything to add?'

'Unacceptable.'

'Yes, admiral?' The chairman strained to hear the rasping words distorted by the vox-enabler that had been used to repair the admiral's throat.

'Commander Ward… unacceptable as captain.'

'In what way?'

'Three occasions in the last ten years… *Relentless* assigned to battle groups… three times assessments are good, yet enginseer reports a fault and the *Relentless* delayed... unable to reach conflict zone in time.'

'She's an old ship, overdue for refit, perhaps.'

'Incorrect... ship is sound... crew is not.'

'What are you saying? The *Relentless* has a fine history.'

'History, yes... present, no... *Relentless* has lost its spirit... promote from within... present will be future... history will be history.'

'Then do you have an alternative suggestion? The other officers available are hardly appropriate.'

'This one.'

'Him? I thought the *Granicus* had been lost with all hands.'

'There were a few survivors.'

'Yes, sir,' the aide said, bringing up a new file on the chairman's data-slate. 'The captain survived. He is returning for his court martial.'

'Formality only.'

'Begging your pardon, admiral,' the chairman said, 'but he lost his ship, a ship that had served for over five hundred years and which had been vital to the defence of its sub-sector. No tales of valiant defence can change the situation. If we reappoint him before the court martial sits–'

'We have a ship without a captain... a captain without a ship... and enough spirit for both... the decision is obvious.'

'Very well, I will put both choices before the lord admiral to decide–'

'Will agree... my assessment... this one will be the new captain of the *Relentless*.'

'So, if we can now move on.' The chairman looked pointedly at the aide.

'Yes, sir, the next order of business is the request from Battlefleet Iulium regarding the xenos incursion in the Segesta sub-sector. I've drawn up the following schedule of local assets that can be coordinated with their effort.'

ONE

'AUDITOR? EXCUSE ME, auditor?'

The auditor, entombed within the master aggregatum, swivelled around and regarded the young watch officer.

'What is it, son?'

'It's your animal, it's… er…'

'His name's Thengir, son. Better get used to it, he doesn't like being called an animal.'

'Yes, auditor. Your… Thengir, it's interfering.' He shifted uneasily, trying to dislodge the oversized snow-white canine with its muzzle across his lap.

'He's just curious, bat him away if he's bothering you.'

'Er… yes, auditor.'

He looked for somewhere to grip its head so he could push the thing away without losing a hand, or something worse, in the process. Above them, the auditor gave a sharp whistle and the canine instantly sat up and padded back up to its master.

The watch officer sighed, settled himself back at the aggregatum console and focused once more on the glowing lines crawling across the screen. Each line represented the feed from one of the many servitor bays embedded all around him in the wall, and spiralling down into the deep well over which central command was perched. His first year of service at the Imperial listening post C-157 *Exaudiare Veritam* had not gone as he had imagined. *Exaudiare Veritam* was a new outpost, the first in the Pontic sub-sector. It represented the very beginning of the full integration of these worlds into the Imperium. Over the following decades more would be built and the network would be expanded. Finally, the coverage would be sufficient for the Imperium to bring a proper level of direct supervision to the sub-sector, not only curbing the aggression of pirates and xenos races, but also providing a greater check on the local planetary rulers acting as Imperial governors.

Until that network could be created, however, *Exaudiare Veritam* stood alone, listening in the dark. He had anticipated the hard work and tedium, to labour for the Emperor is to love the Emperor, and comprehending the mass of barely decipherable fragments of information they received was labour indeed. But he had most definitely not anticipated the auditor's pet.

He knew that the commanders of listening posts were often indulged in their eccentricities as long as they produced results, and there was none so highly regarded in the sector as the auditor. However, surely this animal pushed that indulgence beyond the pale.

There was a sharp bark right by his ear. The watch officer jumped nearly clear out of his skin.

'Auditor!' he looked up to the highest station imploringly. The auditor opened an eye and it rotated in his direction.

'Caught you napping, did he?' The auditor's eye closed and his brow knitted in familiar concentration. 'Get back to it, son. Check the feed from Gamma Zircon, there's something interesting there. Boy's already seen it, haven't you, boy.'

The dog barked twice as though in acknowledgement, and then trotted up the steps to the top station, where his master sat installed within the master aggregatum. The watch officer spared a final look at the monstrous figure above him. The master aggregatum was a massive machine that near fully interned the human form. Little could be seen of the auditor except his face. His body was encased in the life sustaining casket, and his head was crowned with a forest of thick tubes plunging into the sockets in his skull. Through them, the auditor absorbed every piece of information harvested by the post's battery of strange surveillance devices.

The watch officer knew that insanity or addiction, and often both, were the inevitable consequence of such exposure. Over the last few months he had seen the auditor outside of the master aggregatum less and less. He knew that, one day, the auditor's body would finally give out, and they would have to empty the machine of his remains and install another. Perhaps it would be his turn to take that place of honour. Having worked so close to it for so long, he no longer looked forward to that day with pleasure.

The animal had taken a seat by his master's side and rubbed its fur against his cold fingers. A brief smile flickered across the auditor's face before it swivelled and fixed the watch officer with a commanding gaze.

'Gamma Zircon, son.'

'Yes, auditor,' the watch officer replied, fastening his connections and reintegrating himself back with his station.

Gamma Zircon was a station assigned for the local ambient. The only intercepts it normally made were the dust clouds that floated in the area, occasionally impeding their work, but, more importantly, helping to conceal their position. At first glance, the item the auditor had indicated appeared to be the same again, a cloud drifting by, but as the watch officer aggregated more lines, he started to discern what the auditor had seen from the start. There was something inside it.

Gamma Zircon read it simply as a mass inside the cloud. An active probe would garner far more information, but it would also spotlight the post's location. Instead, he reassigned the Theta Orizon and Epsilon Roba bays to ambient local to triangulate the mass's position and vector.

With barely a flicker of interruption, the servitor bays switched from one configuration to another. New lines tumbled out of the aggregatum console. The watch officer read them, checked them, and then checked them again. The mass was not moving with the cloud at all, it was moving through it, straight at the post.

'Permission to go to active measures–'

'Permission granted,' the auditor cut in, his voice tight.

The watch officer quickly signalled Zeta Radia bay where the mindless servitor activated the pulses. From the viewpoint of any sensor within a million kilometres the station suddenly bloomed with energy in the depths of the black space. Moments later, detailed information flooded across the screen.

'Minimal engine readings, auditor. It's a Mule-class frigate, it looks like the *Piadore*.'

'If that's the *Piadore* then, fumes and vapours, why is it a month late? And why is it not broadcasting its merchant ensign?' The auditor paused for a moment. 'Is that the only unaccounted mass object in local?'

'Yes, auditor. Active confirms no intercepts.'

'How long until it reaches us?'

'Five hours, auditor.'

'Fancy a trip outside, son?'

IT TOOK AN hour to prepare one of the station's launches and assemble a party of neophytes and assault servitors, and then a further hour at full burn to cover the distance to the dust cloud that still blanketed the approaching frigate. As the launch plunged through it, its protective void shield fought to maintain its integrity. The watch officer knew that, back at the post, initiates would be scurrying to prepare the cannon batteries, mighty naval lances and the other, less conventional, weaponry with which the post was defended. The ship was already within their kill range, and if given the go order they were fully prepared to obliterate it, irrespective of whether the launch party was on board or not. The station had continued its active scans and was signalling the *Piadore* on a tight wave, but there was still no response, nothing that would indicate that anyone was alive on the ship, least of all in control.

There were several reasons why a vessel might be in such a condition. Contagion was one; battlefleet maintained strict quarantine regulations, but the merchant fleet was notoriously slipshod in the matter. Accidental or deliberate damage to air or water redux systems, likewise, could kill the crew whilst leaving the ship undamaged. Damage to something as small as a thermoregulator could have left the crew as frozen corpses. There were worse things, though, for any ship that travelled through the maelstrom: mass hysteria, warp madness, possession. The watch officer flexed his fingers within his deactivated power glove. There could be no prediction of the nightmares that might infest the *Piadore*, even as it silently slid towards them through the dust.

'Primus to Beraka launch, status.' The vox crackled into life with the voice of the auditor.

'Beraka launch, unidentified's readings constant, will shortly be entering dead proximity. Acknowledge.'

'Acknowledge, son. Mechanicus Deum.'

'Mechanicus Deum, Primus.'

They were close to dead proximity, although still a long way from being able to see the vessel with the naked eye. The watch officer received the inputs from each of the launch's sensors directly into his brain.

Each of them was straining to pick up as much as they could about their target and transmitted their findings back to the post. Based on their readings, they constructed an image in his brain that clearly showed the derelict Mule, only recognisable from its dampened engine signature.

As he watched through the sensors, the body of the ship began to flicker. The engine signature was beginning to break down. Perhaps the plasma generators were finally collapsing.

'Beraka, full shield!' the auditor's voice blared over the vox.

Before he could even think, the watch officer obeyed the command and the void shield gorged on the redirected energy, even as it struggled against the dust that surrounded it.

'Turnabout! Turnabout! Burn full!'

'Acknowledged, Primus, acknowledged!' The watch officer's heart caught at the urgency in the auditor's voice and the barking of his animal in the background. Even as he gave the orders, the readings flipped.

'Energy spike! An explosion?'

It was not. The engine signature of the ship had split and shattered, and then re-formed into something entirely different.

'Deus mortem, not enough.' The auditor's words tumbled over the vox. 'It's not. I should have seen it, son. I should have seen it–'

Coursing energy beams burst from the mysterious ship, blew the failing void shield out in an instant and burned through the launch's hull within a split-second, and then out of the other side. The mortally wounded launch faltered and fell, the atmosphere inside pouring out through both front and back for a minute before the engines cascaded and blew the launch apart. In their last act, its sensors constructed one single image of their attacker for the watch officer's mind: an image of insanity and evil that he took with him, even as he raced into the Emperor's Grace.

'STAY ON HIM, Mister Crichell, bring us up as close as you can. We shall not lose him. Mister Kirick, keep that battery on target. If his warp engines even flicker then take him down. If he escapes, I will have your hide, Mister Kirick. Mister Aster, ensure they're still receiving our command, "Surrender or be destroyed".'

A chorus of acknowledgements resounded across the command dais. Commander Ward leaned forward in the captain's chair of the *Relentless*. In front of him, his four bridge officers were intent upon their consoles. Below him, many more officers and crew worked busily at their stations. Above him, above them all, hung the massive symbol of the Imperial aquila, its wings stretching from one side of the command deck to the other.

'They're turning, sir, coming to a new heading.'

'Get those hexameters working and plot an intercept course! Now!' The icons flashed on the consoles, and a new line burned between them.

'They're coming to bear.'

'Mister Aden,' Ward said, turning on the bridge auspex officer, 'your assessment was that the target vessel was unarmed, correct?'

'That it had no significant weaponry, commander.'

'One day, Mister Aden, I will have to try out some non-significant weaponry upon your skull and assess your reactions to it.'

'Yes, sir.'

'Mister Kirick, you'd better have that ship marked or I will toss you out there myself.'

'Battery ready to fire, sir.'

'Communiqué from the target, sir,' Lieutenant Aster, the vox-officer, reported. 'They're standing down.'

Ward allowed himself a smile of satisfaction and stood up smartly.

'Match velocity and relative distance. Mister Kirick, don't let our gun crews relax a fraction. Mister Vickers?'

Senior Armsman Vickers, standing at his usual post beside the dais, stepped forward. He raised a hand in a salute.

'Sir.'

'Take your men across. You know what we're after; make sure you find it.'

'A pleasure, sir.'

Vickers returned the commander's smile, saluted again and marched away smartly. Ward turned back to the merchant vessel that cowered under his guns and felt a thrill of excitement. What bounty might they find this time?

As Vickers departed, another figure arrived on the command deck and approached the dais; this one was far from welcome, however.

'Commissar Bedrossian, to what do we owe this honour?'

'This is today's catch, is it?' The commissar took his place upon the dais, the silver mask he wore gleaming in the light.

'That's correct, commissar.' The first officer did not look at him. 'The *Ruffleigh's Wealth*, registered as part of the merchant fleet, but you know how little that means out here.'

The commissar had already stepped away and seated himself beside the captain's chair. The serious young cadet-commissars accompanying him retreated to a respectful distance and stood formally at ease. The commissar leaned on the armrest and rested his chin upon his fist.

'Very well, commander, carry on.'

THE INSPECTION OF the *Ruffleigh's Wealth* proceeded with every success. The armsmen's entry was unopposed, their assault transport safely latched onto the vessel's hull, and the few crew they had encountered had been more than courteous. Of course, the senior armsman recalled, this was not the first time the *Ruffleigh's Wealth* had received the *Relentless*'s attentions. Evidently, their crew had learned from their experience. Every hatch and portal they met as they travelled down the primary dorsal transit corridor was unbarred and open before them. Yes, all went as well as it possibly could, until they reached the tramp's command deck.

Vickers led his squad from the front; he always did, irrespective of whether it was on parade or into a contested breach, as the tapestry of burns, scars and shot trails that mottled his hide testified. He was the first onto the freighter's bridge, and therefore the first to be confronted by the unforeseen nuisance.

'This seizure is intolerable! This cargo is the personal property of the governor of Hayasd, and I, as his personal envoy,' the opulently garbed popinjay flapped, 'demand that we are immediately released with a full reckoning and an immediate apology from your captain.'

Vickers paused a moment to allow the terrified fop the opportunity to appreciate fully the expression on his face, the gun in his hand and the dozen other armsmen that were stepping onto the bridge and targeting the command crew. The envoy, though, being blind or terminally stupid, rattled on.

'Furthermore, I shall have your name and the name of every man here, and you will all be included in my summation to the governor. He will ensure that you are strung up high if you continue behaving in this... in this...'

'Intolerable?' Vickers supplied.

'Yes, in this intolerable manner.' The envoy's voice broke as his desperation finally exhausted itself. 'What have you to say to that?'

Senior Armsman Vickers gave it a moment's experienced consideration, and then smashed the butt of his shotgun into the side of the envoy's head. The weight of the

unconscious body made a considerable thump as it hit the
deck. Vickers brought himself up to his full, considerable
height and addressed the freighter's command crew, none of
whom had moved to help their fallen passenger.

'Now, which of you is the master of this scow?'

'THEY ARE COOPERATING, commander.'

'Excellent work, Mister Vickers. I shall expect your
inventory within the hour.' Commander Ward flicked off
the vox-receptor in the chair's headrest.

'The operation goes well, commander?' the commissar
said from beside him, his mask still turned and fixed
upon the smaller vessel hanging in space. Ward glanced
over at him, caught sight of his own reflection in the
mask's cheek, and looked away.

'All goes as anticipated, commissar. Mister Vickers is
exceptionally effective.'

'Yes.'

The word hung in the air between them for several
moments, Ward waiting for the commissar to continue.

'And thorough.'

'Yes, commissar, Mister Vickers is very thorough.'

Another moment.

'Yes.'

'Perhaps I could ask, commissar, if there were any concerns–'

'Keep me informed of progress, commander,' said the
commissar, rising, without warning, and stepping away
from the captain's chair. His cadets fell into step behind
him.

Ward made to open his mouth to reply and found that
he had been grinding his teeth.

'Of course, commissar,' he called down, as the black-
coated figures disappeared from view.

Ward sat back and fixed his gaze on the officers stationed before him on the command dais, all of whom
were immediately intent upon their consoles and crystal

screens. The commander tried to settle back in the captain's chair, but found it suddenly irksome. Instead, he walked down to the front rail of the dais and looked out onto the command deck proper where a hundred crew and officers bustled and laboured. Like insects, the commander thought.

One of the insects was approaching, and was certainly not one that either bustled or laboured. It was Confessor Pulcher Purcellum, or as his acolytes sometimes referred to him 'Sulphur' Purcellum because of the stench of stale incense and unguents that wafted with him. Ward had been more than usually generous to the informant who had given him that piece of information.

Orbiting around the rotund figure of the confessor were his pair of blue-skinned cherubs, alternately flapping ahead a few metres, turning around, and then returning to clutch and grab at the loose folds in the priest's clothes, to help him continue his climb up the side of the bridge to the dais. The commander watched this absurdity, until finally one of the cherubs flew straight up to him, caught a look at his face, gave an infantile squawk and swooped away. It took cover in one of the logistician banks embedded in the wall where its fellow swiftly joined it, leaving the confessor quite alone in his struggles.

Unwilling to have the corpulent priest ascend to the dais and then, no doubt, have to take his ease there, Ward strode down to meet him half way.

'Confessor.'

'Ah, commander, I am glad I found you here.'

'Where else did you expect to find me? We are engaged in a combat situation, confessor, and your presence was neither requested nor required.'

'Ah, are we?' He peered at the main view-portal. 'In that case, I should be here. I should have my choirs here. We should be praying and entreating the Emperor for a victory today.'

'Confessor, I do not think we need to trouble Him today.'

'We all need Him, commander, and those who think they do not, need Him more than any.'

'Yes, confessor.' Ward nodded at the two junior officers who had appeared nearby and they each gently took one of the priest's arms. 'But as you can see, the enemy is defeated. He has provided us with victory already.'

'In that case, we should sing our praises and thankfulness to Him.'

'Of course, confessor, you must lead the crew in a service as soon as the danger is over, but for now we must attend to His will just a little longer.'

'Ah, yes, the crew. That is the reason I came here. The situation is critical.'

'What? What is?'

'The situation with the crew, as we discussed.'

'Yes, yes… we must discuss it further,' Ward said, although he could not, for the life of him, recall which of the dozens of apparent tribulations Purcellum was referring to. 'But not now, confessor.'

'Amorality, godlessness, even heretical worship perhaps, who knows the extent it has reached?'

'Pardon me? I can assure you that all here are true in their faith.'

'Not here, not here. I did not say here. No, the crew down below, the indentured workers, the conscripts. You may stand in the captain's stead and rule their bodies, but I am responsible for their immortal souls. I know what happens down there. Have faith, commander, I know. Those decks must be cleansed. Better they die and face the Emperor's judgement now, before they cannot be redeemed, than let them continue on and have them lost.'

'Confessor, we must continue this later, my duties demand my attention. But I am sure, down there, they will die soon enough.'

* * *

THE SHIPMASTER OF the *Ruffleigh's Wealth* was far more obliging than the governor's envoy. Vickers had had no trouble extracting a complete ship's log and manifest from him. Despite this ostentatious cooperation, the senior armsman knew better than to drop his guard. Hayasd merchantmen had a well-deserved reputation for two things: a theatrical obsequiousness when you had the upper hand, and rapacious extortion when you didn't. Vickers counselled his men to keep their weapons high.

He transmitted the log back to the *Relentless* for analysis, and dispatched Officer Kjohn and half his force to check the cargo holds and verify the manifest. To try to ward him off, the shipmaster had produced some impressive sheaves of gilded parchment to prove that they traded under the governor's protection. It was clear to Vickers, though, that this was not a shipment destined for the governor's own hands. They carried luxuries, to be sure, 'But none nearly fine enough to interest the Grand Punzhar personally, eh senior?' Kjohn had remarked.

'For everything they say about the Hayasd, Kjohn, it's nothing but a tenth of what's true for the governor. This scrap isn't going to grace his table, it'll just be flogged off to those that don't know better.'

How Vickers did know better, especially considering his background, was something he did not dwell on. He merely gave thanks that the angels had found him before the daemons.

After three hours, Kjohn returned with the verdict that the manifest was accurate.

'I wouldn't put it past the scunners to be hiding something. A Hayasd wouldn't make this run for just what's down there.'

There would be more. There wasn't a Hayasd shipmaster who didn't slip a few crates into a 'smuggler's berth' as they were known, and there wasn't much else in the galaxy that they guarded more jealously. No doubt, with time and patience, he could have forced its location out of the shipmaster, but the only way he would be able to remove it from the freighter was over the bodies of the shipmaster and every crewman to whom he had granted a stake. And that was something for which the commander simply hadn't given him the time.

Despite Kjohn's poor opinion of the cargo, there were a few items that had caught Vickers's eye. He only hoped that the commander would let him keep one of them.

'You take this? You take all this?' the shipmaster had spluttered in his broken Low Gothic when he had been presented with the confiscation list. 'This is too much. Surely, this is too much?'

Both he and Vickers knew that it was a pretence, but if he thought that Vickers was here to barter then he was much mistaken.

'Have it recovered from the hold. Make it ready for transport. It will be inspected before we leave, I tell you now.'

'It's too much. The envoy spoke the truth. This cargo is personal for Governor Hayasd. You take this much, it will be your head.'

'It'll be your head first, scunner. The governor knows the way things work out here, and so do you. Just give thanks to your Emperor that you're getting off lightly this time.'

He plucked the list out of the shipmaster's hand and then shoved it back into his chest. The Hayasd stumbled away.

'Get that cargo out and ready,' Vickers bellowed, raising his shotgun and firing it into the shipmaster's vacant chair for emphasis. 'Let's get it moving!'

ON THE RELENTLESS, the commander scrolled impatiently through the *Ruffleigh*'s decrypted log. The minutiae of their squalid shipboard life was not of interest to him, but their auspex records and notes of the ships they had encountered along the trade route could be gold. The merchantmen of the fleet were as obsessed with discovering their fellows' cargoes and

destinations as they were with their own. A single mer-
chantman gathered a wealth of information far in
excess of any battlefleet warship, and every ship they
noted down had the potential to be another inspection
and another successful haul. The only obstacle was
deciphering their infernal encryption, but that was
something at which the cogitators of the *Relentless* had
had considerable practice over the last two years since
the old captain had entered the Emperor's Grace.

There! The commander halted the log and used a wand
to activate the detail of the entry. Another target awaited.
He strode over to the vox-officer.

'Mister Aster, connect me through to the Navis dome:
Lord Principal Menander.'

'At once, sir.'

This target was a prize catch. He had read references to
it in several logs before, but never recent enough to make
it worth tracking it down. This time the location and vector were fresh. The *Relentless* could overhaul them.

Ward noticed that the vox-officer beside him had
stopped working.

'Well, Mister Aster?'

'The... the... they deliver their regrets, sir, but Lord
Principal Menander is not available. They offer instead
one of his seconds.'

Ward's good cheer soured. Not available? Menander
and his three-eyed freaks did nothing but idle in that
bubble, sitting on their hands. Well, he would be hanged
if he was going to be palmed off onto one of his inbred
flunkies.

'Then have them contact the lord principal and have
him attend upon the commander of his vessel,' he replied
frostily.

The vox-officer busied himself at his station again.
Ward waited one minute, two; by the third, he saw the
sweat spring from Aster's brow.

'What is it, Mister Aster?'

'They say they do not know when the lord principal will be able to attend. He is indisposed for an… uncertain duration.'

'And what is the lord principal doing for this uncertain duration?'

The vox-officer gulped, and then forced the words out.

'Meditation, sir!'

Meditation! He was being rebuffed because the primary Navigator of the *Relentless* was asleep? Ward bit down on his irritation. He knew that it was not the way the old captain would have done things. The Navigators were the only members of the crew without whom they could absolutely not continue. Without their ability to pilot the *Relentless* through the currents and tides of warp space, their trips between systems would take months instead of weeks. Though they were nominally under his command whilst aboard, they were in effect independent, and they lost no opportunity to assert their status.

Ward cleared his throat. 'Inform the Navis dome, that the commander of the *Relentless* will require their service in ten hours time. That is all.'

'Aye, commander,' Aster replied, but yelped as Ward grabbed his ear.

'Deliver the same message to the magos majoris, and deliver it to the magos himself, or I will send you down there personally with orders that you be grafted into a servotomaton. That is all.'

THE COMMANDER STAYED on the dais for several hours, and only retired after he received word that the boarding party's assault transports and their cargo lifter had returned safely. Then, he handed the bridge over to the officer of the watch and made for his chambers.

As he walked, he examined a list of the inventory the boarding party had brought back. Vickers had done well. Merchantmen often carried much that was of value to them, but little that was of use on the *Relentless*. Exotic foodstuffs and mild intoxicants were ideal to reward the junior officers as it kept them amused and in line. Older officers often had their women and retinues to provide for, and so appreciated trinkets, ornaments and fabric. The commander certainly knew that a bolt of fine sunweave was going to be delivered to his quarters, and would keep his women amused for days. The most senior officers had varied tastes, but always desired easily tradable gems and precious metals, anything they could use at the ports of call to allow them to purchase what they desired from the dirtfeet.

He reached the door marked with the letters 'CC' engraved in heavy script. It had not been long after the old captain's death that the first officer had moved into his chambers. It had not been the result of any disrespect, but sheer practicality. The old captain had kept an entourage of women as commensurate with his rank, and, when he passed away, the first officer, as his duty demanded, had taken them into his own retinue. Not all of them, of course, as to be frank the old captain had obviously kept some of the more mature specimens around out of sentiment rather than for any other qualities they possessed.

The first officer had no room for the old captain's women in his existing chambers, and he could hardly leave them unsupervised where they were. So, it had occurred quite naturally that he had moved residence from the first officer's chambers on the starboard side of the upper deck to the captain's chambers on the port side.

In truth, it was no more than he was entitled to; he was the captain in all but name. After the fateful banquet that had taken the old captain from them, Ward had been so busy quelling the anticipated panic amongst the officers and men that there had been no time to write the dispatch back to battlefleet informing them of the loss. When the rigours of his duties had finally eased, he had, with all justification, delayed its composition further. The *Relentless* was committed to its patrol route, and the governors of those worlds relied upon its visit. Out here, in the great expanse of the Bethesba Sector, they might see a battlefleet warship no more than twice a decade, which made it all the more important that those appointments were kept. They and their people could not be allowed to forget to whom they owed their loyalty, even out here.

What would those high-hats back at battlefleet have done anyway? Their best decision would have been to leave him in command in any case. His delay merely prevented them making a foolish error. Irrespective of the demands of their situation or of simple common sense, they might have called a halt to the *Relentless*'s patrol, throwing his authority into doubt, and making the ship impossible to control. Worse, the *Relentless* might even have been recalled to the Central Command of Battlefleet Bethesba on Emcor for reassessment. Some outsider might have been appointed to the chair. That would have been an absolute disaster; an outsider was the last thing the crew wanted at such a time. They needed authority, a familiar voice to obey. The *Relentless* was a venerable ship, a ship that had had her own customs and practices, her own structure, for hundreds of years. A transferred captain would never understand.

As it was, besides the acknowledgement of his eventual report, battlefleet had been silent on this matter. They had kept him waiting far longer than he had done them. However, he was no longer concerned about their decision. The longer they had delayed, the more comfortable he felt. Obviously, they had concurred with his judgement in taking command and continuing with the patrol, and, though it were poor taste to say so, with the distant war, the Emperor was rapidly robbing them of any qualified alternatives. He did not even like to think it, but each and every report from the front of the death of a senior commander made him feel a little more secure.

It could only be a matter of time before the dispatch runner arrived with his new commission.

As he stepped through the portal into the captain's… into *his* chambers, he felt the weight of the day lift from him. The room was empty, but for the dish and wine he had ordered. His women knew better than to disturb him immediately upon his return; they would come when he desired. They would have learned that there was a new shipment aboard and would be especially attentive to him as a result, each hoping he would grant them the choicest items from the portion that he had earmarked for his own use.

It had been a good day, and it would only get better from here.

'COMMANDER.' THE TINNY voice from the intravox disturbed his slumber. 'Commander. Commander,' the voice repeated.

The many shocks and perils of naval life did not allow for sloth. Ward snapped awake.

'Ward here,' he croaked, the prior evening's indulgence returning to punish him. There had better be a damned good explanation for this.

'Commander, ship in proximity.'

Proximity? They had left the *Ruffleigh* behind hours ago.

'What ship?'

'From battlefleet, sir, transmitting ident Benedictus Lentonius.'

Ward threw himself out of the bed. It was a high-speed messenger straight from battlefleet. Finally, it must be his commission.

'They're sending a communiqué.'

'Tell them they can bring it aboard.' He needed his dress uniform. He needed his aides. He needed to get out and meet them as soon as they docked.

'Sir, they've brought the new captain.'

TWO

CAPTAIN BECKET STOOD squarely on the bridge of the command deck of the *Relentless*, his gaze fixed upon the stars before the ship's prow. He had stood there since concluding his first assembly with the senior officers of the ship, and had not shifted for the past three hours. To passers-by, he might have been installed there when the ship was first commissioned, which, the first officer suspected, was the effect he was trying to achieve.

At the start, the first officer had stood beside him, treating it as a test of fortitude. After an hour, though, he was grateful to have been called away to deal with another matter. He was not keen to return, but he could only spin out a minor adjustment to the ancillary curatium procedure for so long. Sub-Lieutenant Keister approached with a worried look upon his face.

'Sir?' he said hesitantly.

Ward rounded on him with gusto.

'Yes, Mister Keister. You had a question?'

Momentarily taken aback by the enthusiastic response, Keister's face went blank. He recovered and continued to speak in hushed tones.

'It was to do with the captain's… belongings, sir. The handlers were wondering where best they might be placed.'

Hang it all, Ward thought, if the situation wasn't bad enough he was going to have to move back into his old quarters.

'Yes, I suppose. Please arrange for my belongings to be packed and transported back to…'

Ward trailed off. Lieutenant Aden had walked straight past him and was presenting a report slate to the captain, who received it with a curt nod. The smug expression on Lieutenant Aden's face inspired a new determination in the first officer. Ward took Sub-Lieutenant Keister aside.

'Mister Keister, you hope to have a long and distinguished career aboard this ship, do you not?'

'Certainly, sir,' Keister replied.

'It occurs to me, Mister Keister, that the type of man who will have a long and distinguished career aboard this ship is the type of man who can, in the next two hours, remove all erroneous references to the captain's chambers being on the port side of the upper deck, when it is well-known that they have been on the starboard side of the upper deck for as long as anyone can remember.'

It took several seconds for Sub-Lieutenant Keister to reply. Obviously not command deck material, Ward concluded.

'Yes, sir. I think I understand.'

'All erroneous references to it being on the port side, Mister Keister.'

'Yes, sir, all erroneous references.'

'Excellent. I imagine you will want permission to leave and set about it straightaway.'

'Yes, sir.'

'Permission granted.'

'Yes, sir. Thank you, sir.'

'Thank you, Mister Keister.' Ward sighed as the sub-lieutenant beat a hasty retreat.

'Mister Ward.' The command came from high above him.

'Mister Ward.' It took the first officer a moment to react; he had not been addressed as such for two years.

'Yes, captain?'

'Join me please,' the captain's measured voice instructed.

The first officer mounted the dais and walked briskly to the captain's side, his mind racing. He couldn't possibly have overheard that brief exchange. He would have to have the ears of a bat. He approached and stood to attention. The captain raised the data slate that Aden had given him.

'Mister Aden's report on your recent encounter with the *Ruffleigh's Wealth*, Mister Ward.'

The first officer reached out to take it, but the captain kept the slate in his hand.

'Your inspection did not uncover any illicit goods on their vessel?'

'No, sir, they were clean. There was nothing of interest to us, sir. In fact, the shipment was accompanied by an official of the Imperial governor of Hayasd, and was fully authorised by that government, sir.'

'Yes, that is noted here, but you did find a matter of interest in their ship's log, detailing the location of an alleged smuggler, whom we are now pursuing.'

'Yes, as we discussed, sir. I know it takes us slightly off our route to Pontus, sir, but in my assessment it was worth the diversion.'

'Not if it results in another clean inspection, commander. I assume you corroborated the information from the log. After all, it may be a trap; it may have been intended to deflect us from our course so that we do not discover something else. It may simply be wrong.'

'I am afraid that out here, sir, there simply is not the same infrastructure to confirm information we receive as you may be used to. The exigencies of the situation sometimes demand that we act immediately.'

'You have their present course, commander. You can check their likely last ports of call to ascertain if they were actually there. You can check their likely destination to ascertain if they are due to arrive. There is a listening post in this area that you could have contacted to coordinate with the information at their disposal. Something to consider for the future. As it is, I have complete faith in your judgement in this endeavour. I am sure it will be successful.'

Ward was lost for words. Though the captain had kept his tone light and informal, he had made a damning indictment of the first officer's decision. Ward wanted to say that it was not the way things were done here. The *Relentless* was by far the biggest vessel operating in the sub-sector. Merchants and smugglers did not lay traps, they did not stand and fight, they put their heads down and ran when they saw the *Relentless* coming.

'The senior staff assembly was very well attended, don't you think, Mister Ward?' The captain cut into his thoughts.

'Yes, sir.' Indeed it had been, almost every officer who could be there had attended, all come to stare at this strange animal that was their new captain.

'I did not notice a representative from our Navis Nobilite, though.'

'No, captain, I believe the Navigators sent their apologies. They were indisposed.'

'Indisposed? For what reason?'

'They did not specify, sir.'

'I think if even the venerable magos majoris was able to attend in person then there should be no difficulty for the Navis Nobilite. Are they regularly absent from such assemblies?'

The first officer paused; the Navigators' inexplicable withdrawal from life on the ship over the last few years would not reflect well on him.

'I have always endeavoured to keep them fully involved in all appropriate procedures, sir.'

'I understand, Mister Ward. Thank you. I think I will pay a visit to them personally.' The captain, finally, shifted and stepped off the dais.

'Very good, sir.'

'Oh and Mister Ward. That listening station, the *Exaudiare Veritam*, I noted from your encrypts received today that it is well past its last reporting deadline, and that a Mule sent to resupply it has also not been heard from. It is not officially being treated as a cause of concern yet. However, I am more cautious. Once we are finished on Pontus we will stop over there to ascertain its status. Make the necessary arrangements, commander.'

DEEP IN THE mechanical heart of the *Relentless*, within its most sacred altar forge, Magos Majoris Nestratanus was gently lowered back into his socket. He recoupled with the machine-spirit with an audible click. The straining attendants around him released their breath with a communal sigh of relief. The magos settled himself comfortably as the familiar data inputs flowed through his brain. It was hard, harder than it had ever been before to detach and attend the assembly, but it had been worth it. At last, a new captain. The magos had had high hopes of him since he had heard the news, and he had not disappointed. Nestratanus considered that this Captain Becket might be just the man to tackle the rot.

For years, Nestratanus had been the last record, the surviving link to the *Relentless*'s vigourous and glorious past. He had tried to impart that vision to his priests, had tried to keep them separate from the new breed of officers and hold them true to the faith. His efforts had been fruitless. For all their training and devotion they were still men, and men could be tempted from the path when they were allowed to forget the full majesty of their god.

This captain though, the words he said, he would show them all the machine at its greatest once again; Nestratanus could feel it through the circuits.

Someone was speaking to him. It was his denunctator, informing him that the magos minoris craved an audience. Well, in that case, an audience he must give.

Magos Minoris Valinarius contained his impatience as the majoris emerged from his commune with the machine-spirit. Now of all times, the antique had chosen to lever himself out of his altar and attend the senior officer assembly, which he had known was the perfect opportunity for Valinarius to establish himself with the other command crew and the new captain. When he had been selected as minoris, Valinarius had known that Nestratanus had felt that the choice had been forced onto him, that Valinarius was simply too popular and respected for any alternative candidate to stand a chance at commanding the necessary authority amongst their priests. Despite Nestratanus's initial misgivings, however, the two of them had reached a tacit agreement. Valinarius as minoris would lend his support to Nestratanus in public, but in private the two of them would be equals. He should be more than equal in truth, as the majoris barely emerged from his communion anymore. As a result, Valinarius had long since taken up Nestratanus's responsibilities, and yet the relic still clung to the trappings of his position, including making the minoris wait for an audience.

'You may approach,' the denunctator finally announced.

Valinarius did so, and bowed his head in formal reverence. Hidden beneath the hood and rebreather the priests invariably wore, no one could see the expression on his face.

'Exalted magos, our priests and the common artificers of the crew have completed their labours in the tertiary aft generatium. We only require your blessing upon our work to proceed.'

There was silence. None of the majoris's attendants moved from their stations as Nestratanus's mind reached out through the machine-spirit.

'There is an impurity within,' the majoris announced. 'The labour was not done with pure intent, and it carries that mark.'

'Exalted one, the labour was exacted in accordance with all scripture. I cannot see how such an impurity may have occurred.'

There was a rustle from the attendants; they thought him impertinent.

'Do you doubt my word, magos? An impurity lies within. It must be consecrated again.'

'Your word will be done. I will arrange a consecration.'

A consecration, Valinarius fumed, the generatium functioned perfectly, he had overseen the testing himself. This was nothing more than the majoris flexing what little power he had left because he could. Consecrating it would take hours, a day perhaps, and Valinarius would lose the time of the several initiates who would be required to perform it.

'Arrange?' Nestratanus said. 'No, magos, you must perform it yourself.'

'Exalted one, surely that is hardly necessary?' Another rustle rose from his attendants at his question.

'It is most necessary. Evidently, the original consecrators did not have the faith required. We must enjoin our most faithful servant to perform the task to ensure its success.'

'You honour me, exalted one. It shall be done as your word.'

'Mechanicus Deum, magos.' Nestratanus dismissed him, and with that Valinarius removed himself from the altar forge. The new captain had obviously instilled renewed fortitude into the majoris's creaking old body, Valinarius realised. It was now clear to him that Nestratanus was intent upon rebuilding his old authority over their priests. The equal partnership between them was most definitely at an end.

* * *

THE CAPTAIN WAITED in the antechamber to the Navis Nobilite's dome. He had given his name to the automaton who had requested it, and he had been left to wait. He had served with Navigators in the past, had even grown to respect a few, but he had never been entirely at ease around them. Most humans weren't. Navigators carried an innate air of confidence around with them, that of a human so alien that he could stare into the heart of the maelstrom and survive. It provoked caution and outright fear in normal men who had all learned as doctrine that any mutant, any deviation, was heresy beyond redemption.

The Navigators were coveted pariahs, and they knew it. The Imperium could only exist because of their talents, yet such service provided them only partial reprieve for the sin of being different. The Navis Nobilite, the noble families of the Navigators to whom all their kind belonged, were a closed community, inbred and intro-verted. The third eye they bore, their warp-eye, ensured they could never blend in with humanity, and so instead of hiding it, they revelled in their difference.

The Navigators aboard the *Relentless* had gone to every effort to ensure that no visitors could possibly be mistaken that they were entering a foreign domain. The antechamber was decked out with ornaments, carvings, paintings and tapestries, all of a bizarre, angular, intricate design. The cap-tain could not discern whether they were of Imperial or xenos in origin, but any human mind that could create such things must surely have dabbled with the unholy.

The antechamber's crowning glory was the full dome above his head: so clean, so pure as to be invisible. Mov-ing from the corridor into this chamber felt as though one were stepping out onto the hull of the ship, and the vast expanse of the infinite bore down from all sides.

For the captain, who stared at space every day through the command deck's view-portal, it was bearable. For a crewman who, despite a life in space, might never see it, it would drive him mad. In this way, the Navigators declared their distinction from those who were not of their kind.

Becket had been taught to hate and fear the mutant as much as anyone else. Once he became captain, though, he felt the root of that caution change. A captain was an unquestionable ruler, lord and master of his ship. The control he wielded over his crew was greater than any other, save for that of the Emperor. A captain had total command over his ship at all times, except when it traversed the maelstrom. There, a captain became nothing more than one of the thousands of helpless mortal hosts that were the prey of the nightmare denizens of that dimension. His fate, his crew, his ship, were entirely in the hands of the Navigator.

A face appeared through the portal before him, tall, thin, preternaturally aged, its forehead mercifully bound to shield the third eye upon its brow.

'Speak,' it said.

'Are you Lord Principal Menander?'

'Speak,' it repeated.

'I am the captain of the *Relentless,* and I will speak only to Principal Menander.'

The face considered this for a moment and then faded. Another face appeared, much like the first, but the captain could see the authority within its eyes.

'Lord Menander, I am Captain Becket and I am the new commanding officer of this ship. Earlier today, I held an assembly for the senior personnel aboard. I noted that you did not attend.'

The face continued to stare, eyes unblinking.

'I wanted to ensure that you received the message,' Becket continued, 'and that you were fully aware–'

'Your message has been received,' the face interrupted, and then promptly faded.

And that was all there was.

'MOVE! MOVE! MOVE!' the chief petty officer boomed as the artificers scrambled around him.

'Station One!' the cry went up as the area went bright.

'Station Two!' followed.

'Station Six!'

'Station Three!'

The chief waited for the remaining acknowledgements with growing infuriation. They had already been made to do this drill eight times, and they had been dogged by problems on each occasion. These were all this new captain's order, these constant drills, tests and assessments. The chief resented it bitterly, Commander Ward had never interfered so with the proper running of the ship.

'Station Five!' The chief could hear the relief in the artificer's voice.

The chief turned towards the only station outstanding, Station Four, where a petty officer and a senior artifex were in the middle of a blazing row, while ripping the guts out of an overloaded console. The chief knew that the first officer didn't support all this. He had trusted them, but this captain insisted on having every single drill run and timed, and if it wasn't what he thought was up to snuff then they had to do it again and again, everything from readiness drills, bracing exercises, damage control alarms to barrack inspections. It was ridiculous!

'Station Four!' the shout finally went up.

Despite his iron posture, the chief felt his shoulders sag a fraction. He looked up at the lieutenant monitoring the drill. The lieutenant shook his head.

'Right!' He drew himself up. 'Again!'

The men uttered a collective groan.

'Stow that mouth, you dirtfeet fraggers! Again!'

THE CAPTAIN SLAMMED hard into the floor. He rolled away from the heavy hands reaching for his head and staggered to his feet. There was no escape, Becket realised as the fists flew at him again. He was finished. The first blow hit his elbow and sent jangling pain shooting up his arm; the second went low, below his guard, and landed squarely on his kidney.

His guard fell, and the third and fourth thudded straight into his solar plexus. He staggered back, his vision clouding, and felt his wrist being seized and twisted. His body arched and twisted in agony, and his legs were kicked out from under him. He hit the deck again, and this time he could not resist the steel grip around his throat, squeezing hard, closing his windpipe. In desperation, Becket raised his arm off the mat. The pressure on his throat eased, and he collapsed exhausted, breathing in great gulps of air.

'Apologies, captain,' said a deep voice above him. 'I thought even trapped in that skiff you would have kept in shape. Still, not bad considering. You should be proud of yourself.'

'I will feel pride...' Becket gasped, 'as soon as I can feel anything again.'

His opponent gave a great belly laugh. Becket rolled onto his back, and looked up at the smiling, heavy face of Officer Warrant.

'If you have breath left to joke then you still had some fight left in you,' Warrant said, as he hauled the captain to his feet.

'I'll thank you, sir, to let me be the judge of that.' Becket winced as he limped off the padded palesta mat towards the water basins at the centre of the row of columns. The columns were spaced across the wide, deserted deck, and adorned with all manner of equipment: ropes, nets, staves and weights, long unused.

Becket would never have normally been so informal, even when sparring in the officers' gymnasia, but Warrant was the only one of the survivors of the *Granicus* that had come with him to the *Relentless*. They had gone through much together, and Warrant had long ago earned his familiarity with the captain. Perhaps Becket should have left all those old ghosts behind, but Warrant had proved his worth aboard the *Relentless*. In the couple of weeks they had been aboard, his relaxed and disinterested manner had already earned him many easy acquaintances amongst his own rank. The non-commissioned officers were a great deal franker with one of their own than they would ever be with their captain. Added to which, Warrant had the speed and strength to lay any man out flat who mistook his geniality for weakness.

'When you're on the command deck, captain, you can be the judge. When you're here, I am the judge,' Warrant retorted.

'I should watch your step,' the captain replied with a smile. 'That's insubordination. Some people might consider it mutiny.'

'Alas! No witnesses.'

The captain conceded the truth of that, as he pulled down the top of his singlet and washed the sweaty dust from his bruised arms and chest. The gymnasia had obviously once been well stocked, but neglect had reduced much of the equipment to premature dilapidation. Certainly no one had interrupted them in the hour or so that they had been here.

'They must be soft, these officers,' Warrant said, 'to let this all go to waste.'

'The whole ship is soft, Warrant. I could not believe it before, but now I am here it is all too plain to the eye.'

'The crew has not seen a real battle in some time.'

'The crew is not my real concern. They take their lead from their officers. They are the body, and the body follows the mind, whether it knows it or not.'

The men did not concern him, but their attitudes to their officers did. There was no better barometer of a man's ability to lead than the condition of those he commanded. Becket did not mean whether the men flattered and praised their officers, a good officer was often cursed more than a bad one, but there was a vitality to a man who was effectively led, a sense of focus and trust in those around him. Good commanders did not make friends, but they garnered respect, and in a crisis they were obeyed instantly and willingly, as they were trusted to know what was best.

'So,' Warrant broke into his thoughts, 'what do you want?'

'How do you mean?'

'I assume you didn't call me here just to demonstrate the flaws in your pankration technique. What do you need from me?'

Becket considered for a moment.

'I need to know everything about this ship and its crew that is not written down in a log or listed in an inventory.'

'Ha! You ask for little.'

'But you know something, don't you? You have some piece of advice to give me.'

'Are you going to do the same as you did on the *Granicus*? The standing orders?'

'Yes.'

'Good. They could use it.' Warrant finished wiping down the palesta and moved over to the washbasin. 'You think too much about the system sometimes. You think if you can find the perfect system then everything will work as well as it can do.'

'I cannot be everywhere, Warrant. There are ten thousand men aboard the *Relentless*. I cannot counsel every rating on how best to swab a deck. I cannot advise every petty officer how best to crew his post. All I can do is give them rules that give them the best chance to make the right decisions. That is what happened on the *Granicus*. The *Granicus* did not become the ship it was because I made a single right decision, but because everyone onboard made a thousand right decisions every second.'

'What did you think of the officers there? Did you think they were good men?'

'Of course they were good men,' the captain said, a little harsher than he had intended. He bit his tongue. 'Are you saying these are not?'

'On the *Granicus*, the officers were good men who just needed a leader, which you became. Here, these officers, I do not know what they are, but I do know that they already have a leader.'

'Commander Ward.'

Warrant nodded, and then towelled himself dry and started to head out. 'Just don't forget the people, captain. Even the strongest fortress will not stand if its stones do not wish it.'

Becket watched Warrant disappear, and then sat to pull on his boots. The situation with the first officer was always going to be difficult. He had hoped battlefleet might have sent out a message ahead, giving the *Relentless* forewarning of his arrival. However, it was clear from Ward's reaction that he had been taken completely by surprise. Becket had still not settled on his opinion of the first officer. From the very beginning the man had tested him, even more so than the strange commissar who did little and said even less. In those first few days Ward had pushed a few low priority decisions across the captain's desk. Matters simple enough to an experienced captain, but that might trip up the ignorant or slapdash. When they were both on the bridge, the commander had sometimes anticipated the captain's orders a little too readily, to see if Becket was so insecure as to countermand them simply out of contrariness. Of greater annoyance was that the logs that Becket had requested had been archived without priority and content tags. It was impossible to use them for quick reference unless you had written them yourself. He had set three logisticians with erasable memories to work on the logs full-time to add the missing notations.

The other members of the senior staff had tested their new captain's limits as well. The magos majoris had put in a request to perform certain testing when they reached orbit around Pontus, which he had provisionally granted, and the confessor had lodged an appeal for squads of armsmen to support his missionaries' attempts to instil the proper worship of the Emperor in the lower decks, which he had categorically refused.

Becket had also called in Commissar Bedrossian to quiz him on his assessment of the officer corps and the ship. Despite the inevitable tension in the relationship between any captain and the ship's commissar, Becket had developed a certain affinity with this quiet man. The silver face mask that Bedrossian wore and that unnerved so many, worked in quite the reverse manner on the captain. The injuries it concealed marked the commissar as a man who had seen the war, and had experienced some of the worst it had to offer. In this, he and Becket were the same. Unlike the first officer, whose closest brush with full-scale conflict had been an inconclusive engagement with some wandering xenos pirates who had taken to attack a merchant convoy.

The captain had a certain degree of patience for his first officer, it was a difficult situation for a usurped commander to stay on under another's direction, but that patience was wearing thin. Battlefleet was not known for its consideration of human ego. They had given Becket a job to do, and by the Emperor that job would be done. The first officer was testing him; that was not necessarily a problem. The critical question was, why?

There was the testing that every first officer should do of a new captain: to determine his personality, to ensure he was not stupid or weak or tainted, and to discover how best to work together. The ship was all, and if its greatest vulnerability sat in the captain's chair then it was the first officer's duty to take action.

Then there was the other kind of testing, the testing that a predator might do to assess a prey's weakness and bring it down. If it were that then serious action would have to be taken.

So was the first officer merely a motivated, capable officer judging his new captain just as Becket judged him, or was he something else?

In either case, the introductory pleasantries were over. It was time the *Relentless* met its new captain properly.

'I HOPE YOU were as appalled by these results as I was, commander.'

'Well, I–' Ward began, before realising he had to admit to being either negligent or incompetent. 'With all respect, sir, there was not much warning given.'

'Warning? The enemy will not give you a warning, commander! If this ship were on the front line, this performance would have her consigned to escorting scuttle trawlers!' the captain remonstrated. 'Still, I do not hold you accountable, Mister Ward, given how long you had to wait for battlefleet to send you a new commanding officer. Some deterioration was inevitable. Here.'

Becket threw a document down on the desk. Ward snatched it up, bridling more at the captain's mitigation than at his original condemnation of the crew's performance.

'New standing orders, commander,' Becket continued. 'What we need to turn this ship around.'

Ward flipped through them. There were fifty-seven in all. From the titles alone he could see that they covered new training, new punishments, longer shift hours, greater supervision, restrictions on behaviour, curfews and many other disciplinary measures. He flipped back to the front.

STANDING ORDER 1

> *Each man onboard is expected to know, obey and be*
> *able to recite the Principal Measures of the Imperial*
> *Navy Articles of War.*

'These are the starting point. More will be added as required.'

'Captain, I would strongly recommend that if you want to introduce these to the men you take a more gradual approach. Half a dozen perhaps–'

'I will not be implementing them, commander. That will be the job of their officers. They will announce them, implement them and enforce them. You or I should not be the face of authority for the men, all of their officers should be. We command our officers, they command their subordinates, and their subordinates command the common crew. That is how it should be, and that is how it will be.'

'As I say, sir, the men will not take to it.'

'The men will be inspired by the examples of their officers.'

'You don't mean...? These will be applied to the officers also?'

'To the officers most of all! Every man aboard this ship needs to pull together. The men will take to it because their officers will take to it, and they will expect them to obey it. There is no choice in the matter. The ordinary crew outnumber the officers a hundred to one aboard this ship, more even than that. If it ever came to it, it would not even be a contest, it would be a massacre. Have you ever seen a mutiny, commander?'

'No, sir.'

'Neither have I, and I do not intend to see one aboard this vessel. Discipline will not be achieved by pandering; it would bloat the men with self-importance and lead them down a path that ends in execution or damnation. They must not be allowed to conceive the idea. They must not be allowed to believe they have the power. They must know their place in the order of this ship, and they must not be given the opportunity to question it. If we are without discipline and activity, then the Emperor have mercy upon us, because they certainly will not.'

Ward retreated. He reasoned that it was inevitable that the new man would want to make his mark, and the captain was acting well within his rights. If this was all there was, then Ward could deal with it; a few month's diligence and then they could be quietly forgotten, once Becket had become more amenable. Becket would calm down in time, and Ward was confident that his grip on the officer corps was still tight enough to control their outrage at the issuing of these new orders, just as long as the captain did not make a habit of it.

* * *

STANDING ORDER 63

Officers may not gamble or game for monies or anything over nominal value. All existing gaming debts must be declared to the purser or be nullified.

Ward read the latest missive from the captain.

'Our officers need to be completely focused on their duties, commander,' Becket had said. 'We cannot have them distracted by gambling debts at their posts, or worse, be vulnerable to undue influence because of them.'

'And this is just for the officers, not the men?'

'The men have little of value to gamble with, and no one would be prepared to lend them significant sums with nothing to stand as surety. They risk what they can afford to lose, unlike some of our junior officers.'

Ward considered his words carefully. Certain of those officers owed him considerable debts and that helped to ensure their obedience, but he certainly did not want to declare that interest publicly.

'The officers work exceedingly hard, sir. A little gaming is just their form of relaxation.'

'I am sure if gaming with tokens is not to their liking they will find other ways to relax. I am told there is an officers' gymnasia that goes quite unused.'

'Yes, captain.'

STANDING ORDER 70

No officer promotion or privilege may be granted without the express authorisation of the captain.

'I am afraid I have to disagree with you, commander. Sub-Lieutenant Keister simply is not ready for further promotion at this time. I realise from your sign-off that you think he is a promising candidate, but it is clear to me that whatever promise he does have has not yet manifested itself in actual ability above his current grade.'

Of course, Ward had fumed, Keister had been the first one caught by the captain's new standing order, and now he looked like a fool for approving him. Ward made sure to tear a strip off Keister, and tell him that it was his own incompetence that made him impossible to promote, but still, he knew word would get around that the first officer's favour was not the boon it used to be. Patronage and preference were essential tools for a commanding officer to ensure the loyalty of his subordinates and now the captain, with his insistence upon evaluating them by ability, was tossing that away, and he didn't even realise what he was doing.

'Yes, captain.'

STANDING ORDER 88

> *No officer may be excused duty on grounds of ill health without medicae dispensation. All dispensations must be lodged with the captain's office.*

'I HAVE NO problem with one officer standing shift for another, but, I think you will agree that we should know exactly which officer has been responsible for a certain duty. Also, we really must take care and monitor our officers' health. We cannot have them suffer in silence if there is a risk of contagion.'

The first officer, who had had several officers stand shift for him after heavier evenings, merely nodded.

'Yes, captain.'

STANDING ORDER 112

> *All maintenance work must be inspected and approved by the officer responsible for the relevant area before any of the work detail can be dismissed. Any deficiencies subsequently discovered in the work will be the personal duty of the officer responsible for that area to make good.*

'Did Acting Sub-Lieutenant Baisan enjoy scouring the ancillary boiler in his area?'

'He did not comment, sir.'

'But what was your impression?'

'Probably not, sir.'

'Do you think he will fail to inspect his men's work properly in the future, commander?'

'No, captain.'

WARD STOOD IN his bedchamber in front of the full-length mirror, fiddling with a clasp on his dress jacket. The clasp refused to close and, despite Ward's elegant attire and noble countenance, he fair turned the air blue with language that he had learnt as a midshipman.

The recalcitrant clasp, along with every other of his present troubles, was the captain's fault. Ward had never been quite so infuriated as he was with recent events. No one doubted that the captain was out of control, penning new standing orders every day, requiring each and every member of the crew to know them and be able to recite them back. Ward had tried to calm him down, and had even deliberately ignored a few for the sake of the crew, only to have the captain haul him over the coals. It was quite clear to him that the captain needed to be taken down a peg or two. It was for his own good, after all, to learn that the *Relentless* was her own ship with her own ways. Ward had certainly not had any difficulty finding accomplices amongst his fellow officers, who felt that they were bearing the brunt of Becket's disciplinary excesses.

He had delivered the traditional invitation to the captain to dine in the senior officers' mess. A captain was absolute ruler aboard his ship, but on some occasions the rules of decency and protocol took precedence. The senior officers' mess was the domain of the first officer, and the captain was as much a guest there as the commander had been on his visit to the captain's table.

Becket had accepted, though in Ward's opinion he had not indicated any great enthusiasm for it, and had dutifully arrived at the appointed hour.

Becket, Ward and the senior line officers had sat and dined off a magnificent service. The same service, Ward recalled, that the old captain had used at his last meal; alas, fate did not choose to repeat itself. The mess gastromo had taken full advantage of such an audience to dazzle them with an array of his most succulent and most exotic dishes. Becket had dined and conversed politely. The officers were able to elicit from him some tales of his time as a junior officer and as captain of the *Granicus*, though he had carefully deflected any questions around the circumstances of its loss.

At the end of the meal the diners, enjoying their heavy liqueurs, had leaned back in their chairs so as to better listen to the conversations at the head of the table. The mood was most comfortable, and Becket had appeared a little heavy-eyed. It had been the perfect time to begin. At a discrete signal from Ward, Lieutenant Commander Guir had launched into a racy anecdote about the legendary Rear Admiral Borega of the *Torteen*, who had won his place in Battlefleet Bethesba's lore, not by great victories or cunning stratagems, but for his sheer number of wives. Lieutenant Kirick had then chipped in with another. Lieutenant Crichell had then begun bemoaning his lot with his own wife, to the general groaning of the company. Who amongst them had not already heard Crichell's endless tales of the affable native girl he had brought aboard, who had turned swiftly into an ironclad tyrant just as soon as she had installed herself in his quarters? There was no duty tougher, the sub-lieutenants joked, than the one Crichell returned to every night.

Ward had laughed along, but his eyes had been fixed on the captain. Becket had smiled well enough, but had there been an edge of discomfort there? A weakness? Time to tell.

'So, captain,' Ward had begun, drawing all attention around the table towards them, 'You did not bring any "companions" along with you back from battlefleet command?'

Becket had not been surprised at the conversation being turned upon him. He had been waiting all evening for Ward to test him now that he was on the first officer's home turf.

'I am afraid not, commander.' Becket had replied. 'You will have to content yourself with the ones you already have.'

This predictable comeback had spurred a few chuckles, but most at the table were intent on what they knew was to be the climax of the evening.

'Oh, I have more than enough women to keep me warm at night.' The twinkle in Ward's eye had provoked a far larger laugh from the company. 'But you are our guest! You must have some companionship tonight. Choose one of mine or, if you trust my judgement, let me choose one for you.'

The company had watched and listened hard. It was time to close the trap.

'Unless, of course, none of my women are worthy of your consideration.' Ward unsheathed the steel in his voice. 'In which case, take your pick of any! Is there any man here who would not offer his woman to the captain?'

'Nay!' they had replied, and at a stroke Ward had unified them all against the outsider. The captain was alone.

Becket said nothing, but Ward could be patient, knowing that there was no escape from the choice the captain faced. Becket could play the prude, stammer out a polite rejection, tuck his tail between his legs and run, and the officers would laugh at him together after he left. Or he could play the lech and bend to the pressure to take up the offer.

The prude would, at least, have kept the shreds of his dignity, but he would have faced his men united, and fled, and they would never have taken him seriously after that. The lech would have had an even harder time, as he would have taken as an intimate companion a woman loyal to the first officer, and would therefore have placed himself entirely within Ward's power.

Becket had furrowed his brow as if in careful consideration, playing for time.

'And you are all agreed in this? Any I might wish?' he had ventured.

'Aye!' they had cried back, eager to see him break.

'In that case,' he conceded, 'I accept.'

The company had cheered. Excellent, Ward had congratulated himself, a little social pressure and the captain had yielded. He had turned out to be far more mundane than Ward had given him credit for.

'So, captain, which one?' Ward had called over the merriment.

'He can take mine!' Crichell had cried to general laughter.

'Which one, captain?' Ward had repeated, not willing to release his victim.

'Why,' Becket had drawled, the officers quietening to hear, 'all of them, of course.'

That cheer had been even louder. Ward had even found himself joining in before he froze.

'All of them?'

'Yes, all of them!' Becket had stood, his eyes no longer smiling, but those of a righteous god staring down upon sinners.

'Every single companion, courtesan, wife and whore on this ship; each and every one will report to the medicae deck tomorrow morning for a full examination,' Becket ordered crisply, his voice clearly heard by the stunned assembly. 'You may not care what infestations you pass between yourselves, but this is the Emperor's ship and to endanger it is to betray Him. That is a crime for which there can be no forgiveness.'

At that, the captain had left the mess. No one had laughed.

The order had been issued first thing the next morning.

* * *

STANDING ORDER 139

> *All dependants and other persons onboard, who are not Naval personnel, must submit to full medicae examination at least once every two months. Any person who does not present themselves within this period will be confined to the brig until next landing, when they will be ejected. First examination to be carried out on the date of this order.*

None of the other officers had dared say anything to Ward, but they were talking behind his back. A medical examination was bad enough, but the situation was aggravated a thousandfold by the captain's additional orders that all the women on the ship were to attend at the same time. For alongside the clear-cut command structure of captain, officers and crewmen, there ran the complex hierarchy of the female.

Quite properly, Ward considered, the first officer's own companions were well-established at the top of said hierarchy, above the herd of women attached to the lesser officers, midshipmen, and that strange female population that survived a rank below those formally attached to an officer's entourage and yet above the mass of indentured conscripts in whom gender was unimportant and, in many cases, indiscernible.

Ward had made it quite clear to his household that the alternative to presenting themselves on the medicae deck was being dragged there kicking and screaming by a squad of armsmen. Such a threat was enough to force his companions to acquiesce, while inflaming their outrage even more. For Ward, however, his authority should have been enough to settle the matter. Of course, as it seemed with everything this new captain did, nothing was ever settled before it had caused Ward the maximum possible public embarrassment.

His companions had arrived typically late, their dress carefully calculated to overawe their inferiors, and they had then proceeded to sweep past the long line of women who had been waiting. At least, they did until they were confronted by a group of the medic's burly orderlies, who had refused to let them pass. The captain had left precise instructions that the women were to be seen strictly in order of their arrival, with no exceptions.

Feeling humiliated and not a little exposed, the first officer's women raised merry fury, alternately attempting to berate or beguile the orderlies until finally word had come back to Ward, just as he was standing beside the captain on the command deck receiving the watch report.

Excusing himself with as much dignity as he could muster, he voxed straight to the medicae and demanded to know what was happening. The medicae replied that he would have been more than happy to prioritise the first officer's gentlewomen, Ward noted the stressed 'gentle' over the screeching argument that he could hear in the background, if only the first officer would provide the captain's authorisation.

Ward had no desire to display any weakness to the captain, least of all an inability to control his retinue. He barked at the medicae to do his duty, closed the vox, and pushed the whole matter to the back of his mind as he returned to the more trivial matter of ship security.

So, his women could do nothing but wait, fume and design increasingly vicious methods of expressing their dissatisfaction at his neglect, which included, at present, refusing to help him with this thrice-damned clasp! Ward gave it a last frustrated twist and it finally buckled. The first officer took one last look in the mirror, and strode out of his quarters.

The women, however, were the least of the problems that the captain was inflicting on him. Ward had assigned two junior officers to Becket to be his adjutants, and he had impressed upon them the value that he would place on receiving detailed reports on the captain's actions: where he went, who he spoke to, and every piece of information that he requested.

What they reported back was not at all comforting. The captain was snooping around the cargo bays.

The cargo bays were vast, the different compartments stretching over a kilometre long. Somewhere in there was absolutely everything that the ship needed to stay in space, and everything the crew needed to stay alive and sane: machinery, fuel, hundreds of tonnes of rations, water, textiles, and replacement parts for virtually everything onboard, because in the void if something breaks ten light-years away from the nearest outpost then you could be dead. However, a tiny fraction of the bays' contents, scattered throughout these necessary staples, was the first officer's personal cargo, lifted from every merchant fleet hauler and skiff that they had inspected. He had been adding to it his entire career. He trusted one master chief down there, whom he paid staggeringly well to keep it dispersed and hidden. Now, the captain was involved, and just this morning, he had issued the latest standing order.

STANDING ORDER 142

> *All goods considered illicit under the Navy Articles must be declared and will be confiscated. All goods acquired as the result of seizure must be declared and will be confiscated. All goods held in quantities in excess of the limits within the Navy Articles must be declared and will be confiscated. Any officer found in breach of the above orders will be subject to immediate sanctions.*

Ward's choice was simple: declare the haul as Naval property and lose it all for certain, or say nothing with the risk that if it were found his career and probably his life would be over.

For Commander Ward, the last true champion of the spirit of the old *Relentless*, given the choice between losing his riches and losing his life, the decision was clear.

The captain had to die.

THREE

THE GOVERNMENT TROOPERS threw Framir into the back of the armoured truck and slammed the heavy doors shut behind him. Framir spat the blood in his mouth onto the floor, at least he had given as good as he got. He didn't even know why they had taken him; for the first time in a month he'd actually been minding his own business, but the troopers hadn't cared. They just grabbed him on the street, no questions, no nothing.

'Prisoners! Secure yourselves for transport!' The announcement blared in the cabin.

'Scrag yer!' Framir shouted back, clambering to his feet.

Framir felt a hand take hold of his shoulder in the darkness, and he batted it away.

'Get off me!'

'Easy, friend, easy,' a voice whispered. 'It won't make a difference. Just sit down before–'

The engine snarled under their feet and the truck jerked forwards. Framir lost his balance, tumbled back and fell on his behind. His fellow passenger reached for him again, and this time Framir let him guide him up onto a bench.

'Epitrapoi's arse, what is this?' he asked, as the truck started to race away.

'This, friend, is the end of the line.'

'They didn't tell me what they were taking me for. They didn't even ask my name!'

'Names are not important, friend, not to them.'

'Yer talking like a spacehead, yer know that? Troopers have taken me plenty of times, never like this though.'

The truck belted around a corner and Framir clung to the bench to stop himself sliding off.

'It's the Imperials. The Imperials have come for us. You must have heard of the troopers who come in the night, take who they want and those they took you never see again.'

'The Imperials ain't interested in me,' Framir muttered, but he had heard of them: government troopers, the Epitrapoi's own, driving into a suburb slum and hauling people away.

'Not just you; dozens, hundreds, maybe thousands, all taken in the last few weeks, from Sinope, from all over Pontus, but our great Epitrapos does not allow anyone to speak of it. It's the tithe, the tithe of men he pays to the Imperium.'

The spacehead suddenly gripped Framir hard and whispered fiercely.

'But we know, friend, the word is out. We will strike back and be rid of the Imperium for good. The time is chosen.'

Framir tried to push him away, but he would not relent and said one last word, so close that his lips nearly brushed Framir's ear.

'Concordia.'

The truck screeched to a halt; Framir shook the spacehead off and stepped to the other end of the cabin. He heard doors slam as the troopers dismounted and hurried off. Another engine, further away, rumbled and then receded into the distance. It was then that Framir noticed that there was no other sound. They weren't in the slums of Sinope any more. The troopers had driven them out into the desert and abandoned them, but why? Framir did not understand.

Suddenly the whole truck started to shake and rock from side to side. The doors swung open and the cabin was flooded with bright light. Framir clutched at his eyes and squinted into the light at the figures there, coming to collect them. The spacehead fell to his knees chanting 'The Emperor, the Emperor,' but Framir could see that they weren't any kind of Imperial that he'd ever seen. They weren't even human.

'TARGET SHIP HOLDING steady.'

The smugglers' ship hung dead in space, an assault transport from the *Relentless* clinging to its side. The alleged smuggler, Becket corrected himself, as there had been no proof of it carrying any illicit cargo of any kind.

He had allowed Commander Ward to lead the inspection party. It was not strictly protocol to risk such a high-ranking officer on such a mission, but Becket could not refuse him when he volunteered. They both knew the stakes that were riding on this inspection. If it came back clean then Ward would have led them on a wild goose chase that had taken them a fortnight off their route to Pontus. If it was as he claimed, however, perhaps there would still be a role for him in future strategic decisions.

Becket stood at the rail at the front of the bridge and looked down. It was busy on the command deck, as was proper for a potential combat situation. The Gunnery Imperia was abuzz as crew monitored the readiness of each of the cannon of the batteries, and passed down sighting corrections based on the relative movements of the two ships. The neighbouring Imperia Ordinatus was quieter, but still with a full complement of artificers slaved into their consoles. They were ready at a moment's notice, should he so command, to prepare the *Relentless*'s torpedoes for launch. No less expectant were the scutatum clusters, the officers stationed at each one striving to maintain the perfect balance so as to minimise the constant energy drain of the shields, but to have them ready at a moment's notice, which is all they might ever have, should this be an elaborate ambush. Sunk deep into the floor, the gravitarium and curatium pits were dark and quiet, whilst scattered around the auspex and cartastra arrays chattered between themselves in their intricate language. Finally, embedded into the walls, all the way to the roof twenty metres above his head, were lodged bank after bank of logistician and cogitator rows. Between them, they were tracking and sustaining every single piece of data being disseminated on the floor. It was a sight that had always filled Becket with a sense of wonder and of humility on every ship that he had served upon. There was something more to it when it was a ship he commanded, something he had felt upon the *Granicus* and now he felt it here as well.

At that thought, the captain stepped back up onto the dais and sat lightly back in his chair. The crew's improved performance, however, had not translated into an improved relationship with all of his officers, especially those who had enjoyed an easy life and profited under the old regime. Those who had been less successful under the leadership of Commander Ward were quick converts to Becket's cause, but he kept a distance even from them. Becket did not want to encourage sycophancy, nor could risk the appearance of favouritism. He was not the captain of a faction amongst the officers, he was the captain of the whole ship, damn them!

There was a hump approaching in the officers' attitude towards him. It had happened on the *Granicus* and it would happen here. Their frustration with him would peak whilst the benefits that his orders were bringing were still not discernible. Once they made it over the hump, they would feel the difference in the atmosphere, they would feel their pride returning, and their frustration would recede. They would still not like him, but they would work with him to bring the *Relentless* back up to fighting standard. He just hoped that they could all get over that hump before he had to lose too many of them.

He was not alone on the dais. Though the first officer was off on the inspection, Commissar Bedrossian sat in his usual place with a cadet in attendance. The captain had exchanged pleasantries with him, but the conversation had lapsed. The one ubiquitous characteristic of naval commissars, from Becket's experience, was that they were utterly convinced that their black caps gave them the ability, instead of merely the authority, to command the staggeringly complex bio-mechanical organism that was one of the Emperor's warships. It was refreshing to meet one at last who did not carry around the air that he was the rightful occupant of the captain's chair. As such, they sat in companionable silence while they awaited the inspection party's report.

'It's not looking good, commander.'

'Come with me, Mister Vickers.'

Aboard the ship, which had identified itself as the *Tarai's Challenge*, Ward took the senior armsman into a corner where they couldn't be overheard.

'Now, report.'

'The shipmaster's commission appears legitimate. So far, our inspection teams have not found any discrepancies between his manifest and the storage bays.'

Ward took the news calmly. He had felt remarkably calm over the last few days, despite the fact that the captain had discovered his collection amongst the cargo and impounded it, pending investigation of the master chief responsible for that area. Perhaps it was because he had found his ultimate solution, little the captain did fazed him at all. It was only important that he stay close enough to Becket to put his plans into effect, the lengths to which he had to go to retain that position no longer really mattered.

'Is there anything at all?' he asked.

'One thing, sir. One of their storage bays is completely empty and depressurised.'

'So they dumped whatever was inside?'

'Possibly, sir. Their story is that they've had seal leak on the exterior hatch. That's why they kept it depressurised.'

'So, suspicious, but not enough for him.'

'Probably not.'

Ward took a long moment, and then turned to Vickers sharply.

'Senior armsman, I am appalled at your negligence.'

'Sir?'

'Why, I found illicit goods on this ship almost as soon as I stepped upon it. I placed them back on the assault transport for safekeeping and to ensure that none of the crew might find them and then conceal them. Please go and collect them, and ensure that they are properly included on the inventory report for this vessel.'

'Ah… I understand, sir. I will do so right away. If I am asked who found them, sir?'

'Please, please… I am just an observer in this party. All credit should go to you and your squads.'

'Yes, sir. Right you are, sir.'

BECKET STUDIED WARD's face carefully in the view-portal. It was completely expressionless, professional, with no trace of the relief or the vindication that he must be feeling.

'Congratulations, commander. It appears your information about this vessel was correct.'

'Thank you, captain. We have confiscated the illegal items and are ready to return to the *Relentless* at your order.'

'Hold your position, commander, and take the shipmaster and his men into custody. As you will recall, the Navy Articles expressly require that any vessel used for illegal transportation will be instantly forfeit, and it and its crew delivered for judgement and sentencing. I will assemble a prize crew to take command of the vessel and send them across directly.'

There was a commotion off-screen as he spoke. Ward backed away as several of his armsmen rushed across the view. After shouts and several heavy thuds, there was finally peace again.

'A problem, commander?'

Ward edged back into the centre. 'Just the shipmaster, sir. I believe he thought that the full enactment of the Navy Articles was rather unjust for a minor offence.'

Ward was, as openly as he could be, questioning the captain's judgement. So, this was how he had run this ship: 'tithing' the smugglers rather than upholding Imperial law. No wonder the master chief had had so much contraband. He must have sliced off a share from every ship they had inspected.

'Major offences are committed because minor ones have been indulged in the past, commander. Keep your station until you are relieved. That is an order. *Relentless* out.'

The bridge around the captain was quiet after his curt words. Well, Becket decided, he was having none of it. Warrant had warned him that they still thought of the first officer as their leader. It was high time that belief was shaken. They had a new leader now.

'Lieutenant Aden,' he ordered, 'get me a list of the men you want for your prize crew, no less than fifty men.'

'Yes, captain.' Aden shone with pleasure at such a privilege, his fellow bridge officers looking on with envy.

'I want you all assembled and ready to transfer within the hour, lieutenant.'

'Yes, captain.'

'Lieutenant Aster, contact the lord principal and the magos majoris, and request that each send a representative to the prize. Have them coordinate with Lieutenant Aden.'

'Yes, sir.'

He would have dearly preferred to leave Ward over there and enjoy the rest of the journey to Pontus without him, but it would be simply inappropriate to consign him there. A first officer's duties could not be relieved with the same ease as those of a bridge lieutenant. In any case, Becket wanted to keep him where he could see him.

It was an unexpected turn, Ward considered, as the assault transport crossed back to the *Relentless*. If he did not know that captain as well as he did, he might almost have thought that Becket was an even more grasping opportunist than he had been. Even he had never had the gall to seize an entire ship and its cargo, for he knew that it was far more profitable to shear a flock than to flay it.

As the captain had issued his orders, Ward had thought for a moment that he might be left there. It would have forced him to put his plans on hold, since he could hardly arrange them at a distance, but an hour later he had greeted the sickeningly enthusiastic Lieutenant Aden, who had so quickly become Captain Becket's toady. Once the captain was out of the way, Lieutenant Aden would soon learn the folly of his change of loyalties, as would all those who had forgotten what they owed him. Equally, the seizure of the personal collection did not matter. No matter how tightly Becket locked it away, Ward would soon hold the keys.

Even as Ward anticipated his future success, back on the *Tarai's Challenge*, Officer Warrant completed another part of the captain's orders and bade Lieutenant Aden a good journey as he stepped back aboard the prize crew's transport to head back to the *Relentless*.

Within the ship, the dark world of Lorcatus of the Adeptus Astra Telepathica was one of little sensibility. The sounds he heard were never more than mundane; the taste of his food, nothing more than ashes; and his vision had been taken so many years before, blinded by the beauty of the Emperor's soul.

Though he treasured that memory, the hollowness of his existence thereafter only stood in starker contrast. There were only the words, the coded messages that he passed between other minds far distant among the stars and yet had no meaning for him.

'Greetings, honoured astropath.'

It was a voice he knew well, a voice that could gain access to the Telepathica sanctuary without requiring admittance.

'Commander?'

'Yes, Lorcatus.'

'We are alone.'

It was not a question. Lorcatus felt the presence of the executioner who normally stood over him too well, not to recognise its absence.

'Yes, Lorcatus. I thought it better we speak in private. You recall when we spoke privately before. You remember what I arranged? The rewards I gave you for your loyal service?'

Lorcatus's heart quickened. How could he forget? It had been an explosion, a revelation. Touch was the only sense he retained and to feel, to hold, to be enveloped in hot, female flesh... for that short time, it had eclipsed even His wonder.

'I have need of such service again, and if you accede you will be rewarded ten times as greatly.'

The astropath realised his mouth had gone dry. Ten times as greatly? What could possibly be the experience of ten times epiphany?

'You have my service, commander,' he spluttered, 'but recall, I can only guarantee dispatch. The receiver must also–'

'Do not concern yourself with its receipt. If they are sent then they will find their destination. It is only your discretion of which I am uncertain.'

'Then be uncertain no longer, commander, for you have it complete and total unto death!'

Possibly, possibly, Ward considered, but perhaps that death could be accelerated should any doubts emerge, a thought for the future.

'Where do you wish your words to go?'

'To Pontus, astropath, to the Epitrapoi's palace. My contacts will need some time to prepare what I have in mind.'

'How GOES IT, Mister Guir?' Ward asked the second officer.

'The matters for the landing party are in hand, commander. I can assure you they will be in line with your… suggestions.'

'Thank you, Mister Guir. Unfortunately, our hosts do not share your efficiency. There will need to be a delay to allow them to prepare.'

'A delay? I am not sure that anything that I could do–'

'Just turn your mind to it, will you, lieutenant commander?'

'YES, COMMANDER,' THE magos majoris beamed, 'you may report back to Captain Becket that we have no further requests. You may also add our congratulations to his most successful assumption of command of our ship.'

Ward bowed deeply before the altar forge. 'He will be overjoyed to hear such compliments from one of your standing.'

'Yes, I am sure he will.'

'I shall convey them to him immediately.' He bowed again and the magos nodded back.

The denunctator boomed, 'You are dismissed from the exalted one's presence.'

The self-aggrandising grease-scunner, Ward thought. He should have brought the priests of the Mechanicus to heel more thoroughly while he was still in command. Their sheer arrogance was unbearable. The magos's words 'our ship' had not slipped past him. Despite their pomposity, however, they had always been quiet and obedient, and more trouble than it was worth to subjugate. It was the captain's fault that they felt this new dominion. Ward had never even seen the majoris out of that machine frame on his altar, before Becket had arrived, and now he was regularly in attendance on the command deck. Before, he had always had to deal with one of his subordinates, who had been far more malleable.

As the thought occurred, Ward grabbed the arm of a hooded priest passing by, who recoiled at such brusque treatment.

'Take me to Magos Valinarius. I have business with him.'

THERE HAD BEEN no indication of the problem on the bridge until the curatium pit had suddenly burst into life and started feeding information into the captain's chair. The loss of power to one of the warp engines was eventually tracked down to a malfunctioning regulator. The Mechanicus report did not say as much, but from their words it was not hard to infer that it had occurred because their regular maintenance routine been interrupted by the tests and drills the captain had forced upon the crew artificers.

Becket did not want to give orders for a jump back before the Mechanicus was certain that the strain on the engines could be controlled. He made the decision to allow the *Tarai's Challenge* to go on ahead whilst the *Relentless*'s Navigators plotted a more conservative route to Pontus. If, Becket reflected, Lieutenant Aden had completed his instructions by the time the *Relentless* arrived, it would also considerably reduce the time he would have to spend in orbit.

AFTER A CAREFUL journey, the *Relentless* jumped back to normal space and burst from the warp at the edges of the Pontic system. The communication channels lit up instantly as the automated stations in the area sent interrogatives and the ship replied with its ident configurations. Such defences and early warning systems lay around the entry beacons to every developed system in the sub-sector, forcing unwelcome traffic to take measures to maintain a convincing bogus identity or attempt to use the riskier 'pirate points' that littered the systems out in the wilderness.

Once the automated systems were satisfied, the *Relentless* burned in-system and, as it approached its destination, it was met by further challenges and demands for identity, human, as well as mechanical. Conventional communication between the ship and the planet became feasible for the first time, and the *Relentless* and the naval station on Pontus began to trade immense amounts of information back and forth. With interstellar communication only practical through the psyker astropaths, there was an immense bulk of information deemed not critical enough for their use, and so was physically delivered by the fleet's ships. Each time ships met or arrived at a naval base all communiqués for distribution were copied and swapped. The logisticians all over the *Relentless* buzzed with feverish activity as every item in their communications dump was compared with the headers being sent by the naval outpost, and marked each one for receipt, for transmission, as a duplicate, or for deletion. Privacy for non-sensitive communiqués was assured by the sheer mass of the data that each message was buried in.

In this way, the orders of battlefleet, and every other Imperial organisation that had a presence in the sector, flowed from the central base on Emcor to every outpost and vessel under their command, and the galactic Imperium was able to survive.

There was an item in one of those communiqués that was the culmination of all of Ward's efforts, and which would have a grave impact on the existence of the *Relentless*. It was a personal invitation from the Epitrapos of Pontus to Captain Becket.

WORD OF THE invitation travelled fast, and it was not long before Commander Ward received a personal call from the provost-arbiter of Pontus. He was not happy.

'You are not listening to me, commander.'

'Believe me, arbitrator,' Ward said, leaning forward in his chair, 'you have my full attention.'

'Then why haven't you cancelled your visit?'

'Arbitrator, since we received this invitation, we have had contact with over a dozen members of the governing body, including the Epitrapos governor. None of them have given any indication of the extent of the public unrest to which you allude.'

'I have done more than allude to it, commander, I have come out and said it. The approach of the concordia reaffirmation ceremony has been the perfect opportunity for the anti-Imperialists to whip up their support, worse than it's been for years.'

'The Epitrapos said that Captain Becket's presence at the ceremony would calm tensions,' Ward said, 'and show the people on the streets of Sinope and all across Pontus that he has presented the official petitions direct to the Emperor's representative. I believe that representative is normally you, is that correct?'

'It falls to the most senior Imperial official, which on previous occasions has been the provost-arbiter, and it was to be so on this occasion, until this invitation for your captain came from the Epitrapos.

'What better symbol, the Epitrapos told us,' Ward remarked, 'of the distant God Emperor, than a warrior who travels the stars. Surely, I think the people of Sinope will appreciate the distinction between you and him.'

'Irrespective of any symbolism,' the provost bit back, increasingly riled, 'if your captain is foolhardy enough to set foot on the ground for the concordia, I cannot guarantee his safety, and the Epitrapos certainly cannot.'

'It was my understanding, provost, that it was your responsibility to ensure security, not to find excuses for why you cannot. If it is simply a matter of manpower then the Epitrapos will be calling out his personal guard, the Thureoi, unless of course I should tell the Epitrapos that the chief arbitrator on his world considers his personal guard so ineffective that the representative of the God-Emperor cannot rely on them for his safety.'

'I make no judgements about the effectiveness, or otherwise, of the Thureoi, commander, but Captain Becket should not consider them a replacement for Imperial arbitrators. I have only a small precinct-house here and only a few hundred men–'

'Then they should be more than sufficient to protect the life of one man, which is all you are being asked to do.'

'ONCE YOU HAVE taken the scroll of grievances, you and the Epitrapos will be presented with the concordia for reaffirmation,' the protocol officer continued. 'There will be a quill there for you to sign your name and rank as Imperial representative. You must sign first–'

'How big is it?' the captain interrupted as his dresser fussed with his epaulettes.

'How big? How big is the quill?'

'No,' Becket said, trying to concentrate despite the dresser's fiddling. 'How big is the scroll? What am I supposed to do with it while I am signing the concordia? Is it small enough to hold in one hand? Do I give it to someone? This is ten years of one planet's grievances with the Imperium, am I supposed to shove it in my belt?'

'I do not have any info… I will find out.'

'Will you, please?'

The portal opened and the first officer gave the captain the nod.

'You will have to send it to the shuttle,' Becket stated as he moved out of his dresser's clutches. He went to the vox-unit in the wall and activated it, 'Captain to the bridge.'

'Bridge here, Lieutenant Commander Guir reporting.'

'Mister Guir, we are about to leave. You have command until the first officer and I return.'

'Yes, sir,' the tinny voice rattled back.

'Commander,' Becket nodded at Ward as they set out.

The two of them stepped inside a transit pod. Becket waved back the junior officers following, and so, when the doors closed, he and Ward were quite alone.

'Lieutenant Aden is back with us, did you know, commander?'

'I saw his report, sir.'

'Yes, I spoke to him as well. It seems his trip was quite uneventful.'

'Yes, sir.'

'More uneventful than ours in any case.'

The two stood silently for a few moments. Becket did not want to launch into it, here and now, when there was limited time, but he simply could not contain himself.

'You have been to Pontus before?'

'Several times, sir. Obviously as the central system for this sub-sector, many patrol routes stop off here. Battlefleet command believes it's important, especially this far from Emcor, to keep the Navy high in the thoughts of the Epitrapos and his court.'

'So you know some of the people we will be meeting.'

'A few, sir. Obviously, personnel can change over a few years.'

'What is your opinion of the provost-arbiter?'

Aha, thought Ward, he could see where this conversation was heading. 'I have never had the occasion to meet the man in person–'

'I was contacted by the provost not long ago. He had wanted to talk to me directly. He said that he did not believe that you had taken proper account of his concerns.'

Ward stayed silent. The captain had not asked him a question.

'What do you say to that, sir?' Becket continued.

'I would say that I made a full assessment of the security of this party, sir, in communication with a variety of sources, including the provost, and in my judgement, sir, there were no additional matters to draw to your attention.'

'The provost-arbiter on a planet expresses his concerns over the wildfire growth of anti-Imperial sentiment within the capital city, and in your judgement it is not something to draw to my attention?'

'It is the provost's job to have concerns, sir. It is mine to use my judgement with a view to the overriding objectives of the Imperial Navy in this system. I gave the provost's concerns full consideration, but the evidence he presented was not sufficient to compel this mission's cancellation, as you would agree, sir.'

'As I would agree?'

'As you would agree, for as you said, you have received the provost's concerns and yet you are continuing on. If I had made an error of judgement then you would have cancelled it yourself.'

'The reason I am continuing, commander,' Becket began, 'is not because I agree with your judgement, quite the reverse. Ever since I stepped aboard this ship, you have done nothing but try to conceal the truth from me: the truth about the ship, the truth about the crew and the truth about your conduct, and now I fear you are concealing the truth of the situation on Pontus.

'You have served aboard this ship for eighteen years, sir,' he continued, unable to prevent himself from underlining the first officer's dereliction. 'In that time, it has stopped at Pontus on no less than nine occasions, and yet despite that you have never met the provost-arbiter responsible for the maintenance of the Imperial Order here. You were a representative of the Emperor, and one with far greater influence than he. If heresy or treason has taken root on Pontus then you, sir, are as culpable as him.

'The reason I have continued with this mission, in spite of his warnings,' Becket thundered within the confined space of the transit pod, 'is to assess the true depth of the consequences of your negligence of this world, and the Navy's interest here. I am doing it as part of my basic duty as an officer, sir, irrespective of why I was sent here in the first place!'

The captain had blazed at him, and Ward, shocked, could do no less than return fire.

'You were sent here, sir,' Ward flared, 'because you were so negligent as to lose your ship, and so you had to be given mine instead!'

The captain's heat suddenly switched to ice.

'I was sent here, sir, to ensure that should the call come this ship is ready for war.'

'With all due respect, it is ready for war, sir!'

'It is not, sir!'

'Why not, sir?'

'Because you, sir, are a coward!'

The words whipped out and struck Ward full in the face. He reeled as though he had been slapped. To a man of his status, of his background, there could be no graver insult from one officer to another. Becket eyed him carefully, and then spoke in low tones.

'If you plan to use that, commander, then draw now and we shall finish it as men.' Ward looked down and saw that his hand had instinctively gone to his sabre hilt.

'Otherwise,' Becket said, 'make to draw on me in the future, and I shall have you condemned as a mutineer and strap you to the outside of the hull.'

Ward could not think, his mind was numb, but his hand moved away on its own. The captain arched an eyebrow, and then buckled his gauntlets.

'In that case, commander, we shall say no more about your action. The rest,' the captain said as he stepped out of the pod into the landing bay lined with his honour guard of armsmen, 'we shall save until we return from this pantomime.'

BECKET STARED OUT of the shuttle window at the great city of Sinope stretched lazily out below. The early morning fog that rolled in from the coast had been burned off by the sun and the city lay baking in the heat. The square buildings, washed in light colours, were piled one on top of the other all the way to the horizon, none of them taller than a few storeys. The structures around their destination stood haughtily out of the landscape, as giants amongst ants, against the rising tide of the shanty dwellings. The majestic sweeps and curves of the massive House of the Epitrapos radiated authority and control. The dark snub-nosed fortress of the arbitrators loomed conspicuously beside them. Dwarfing them both, the mighty Cathedral Concordia, the very foundation of the Imperial faith on this world, towered over the cityscape. Some would describe the city as a beautiful tapestry, others as a squalid fleapit, depending on their perspective. To Becket, it was yet another problem.

The passengers in the shuttle were quiet. The captain's black mood curtailed anything but the necessary operational reporting. Ward at least was not on board. Battlefleet protocol demanded that where both the captain and the first officer were required at the same location, they should not take the same transport in case of accident or attack. For once, Becket found that adhering to battlefleet protocol was a relief and not a burden.

'Officer Warrant, would you join me, please?' He had thought it prudent to add Warrant to the landing party, since he could rely on his companion in any situation. A moment's doubt could be fatal. Given the current atmosphere, he was doubly grateful to have included a friendly face.

Warrant settled into the seat next to Becket and leaned across to look at the view through the portal. Becket noticed for the first time that his uniform had been altered, and now bore the insignia of the *Relentless*.

'You know what you're getting yourself into?' Warrant muttered in low tones, his words swallowed by the noise of the engines.

'I think so,' Becket replied.

He had read, in as much detail as time allowed, the *Relentless*'s archive of their dealings with Pontus, and the provost-arbiter's own reports on the current status. The truth about Pontus's entry into the Imperium had been lost in the distant past. Their legend held that the Emperor had visited them at a time of great climactic upheaval. He had calmed the seas and raised the skies, and, in awe and gratitude, the Epitrapos of that time had signed the concordia with him. It was that agreement, along with its countless subsequent amendments and reinterpretations, that governed Pontus's role in the galactic empire of man.

'So the Emperor trod these lands, did He?'

'So they claim.'

'A billion worlds, and each one says that the Emperor came to them. I guess the Emperor must have been a Navy man, just like us.'

Becket smiled. Though their scholars endlessly debated the substance behind the story, one aspect was never in dispute, and that was that the concordia granted the people of Pontus the right to deliver their grievances direct to the Emperor's representative in the hopes of redress.

The petitioning had long ago devolved into a token demonstration, but now it had become a banner that those of an anti-Imperial sentiment could rally around.

'These protesters, captain. What do they actually want?'

'Most just want to be heard. Some want their petitions to be granted. A few are using it as an excuse to leave the Imperium altogether.'

'That's treasonous talk.'

'Naturally, but it shows how bad things have become if such sentiments are not instantly suppressed. They're fools, little fools with their little lives. They enjoy the privileges of the Imperium: the protection, the order. Yet still they rail against it. If they had seen what we had seen, Warrant, out there, the Imperial yoke might suddenly seem much more tolerable.'

'Some things, captain, cannot be described in words; they can only be experienced.'

The engine tone rose as the shuttle slowed for landing.

'Watch my back, Warrant.'

'As always, captain.'

The shuttle dropped down low, the lines became streets; the dots, vehicles and animals; and, in the last few seconds the ground turned into a dark sea of angry, shouting faces.

THE WELCOME FROM the Epitrapos and his court out in the great, enclosed garden within his house was effusive, lavish and utterly unconcerned with the angry crowds congregated not a few hundred metres away. After the captain and his party were ceremonially presented, there began a vibrant exhibition of peoples and traditions from all over the planet. There were musicians from the islands of Trimmissa, colourful dancers from the hills of Asabara and the old cap-ital Amaseia, choreographed fighting artists from Toutalugoae, and pomp and luxury by the boatload. The Epitrapos was clearly not about to be hurried into the ratifi-cation of the concordia. Becket though, could not keep his mind on the entertainments and neither, from his sidelong glances, could most of the *Relentless*'s party.

Commander Ward tried to maintain a demeanour of polite interest, but Becket could see him shifting his weight uneasily. Confessor Purcellum, who had insisted on coming down to the planet, appeared most flustered by the whirling bodies and flying fabric before them. Only Senior Armsman Vickers seemed genuinely intent, but perhaps that was no surprise. Vickers was a bull of a man, whose every move-ment spoke of the brutal power at his command, and yet Becket had learned that the senior armsman also possessed a considered aesthetic taste, and had acquired a small but carefully chosen collection of rarities. Becket knew that he was exceptionally competent at his duties, but, equally, he was Ward's right hand, which brought Becket back, once again, to what had happened in the transit pod, and what the consequences would be.

The Epitrapos was a man of noble face and sharp eyes, who was dressed in ornate, but not unwieldy, flowing robes. He had greeted Becket with a smile, and had maintained the same benevolent expression since. The court instantly responded to each small gesture he made, providing him

and his guests with food or drink, or moving from one performance to the next. Even as the dancers gave way to stunt
performers using swords, fire and animals, the Epitrapos
remained the central focus of the room.

At length, the exhibition came to its finale, and Becket
and his men were ushered out of the building. As they
walked onto the street, they were hit with the wall of heat
and sound. The crowds were out of sight, held back several streets from the house of the Epitrapos, but the hot
air did nothing to muffle the din.

The provost was there with his grey-suited arbitrators and
their grey vehicles, and they parcelled the Navy men into a
convoy of identical low-slung land crawlers, as heavy and
fearsome as tanks. Becket ensured Warrant rode with him.

From the air the Cathedral Concordia and the House of
the Epitrapos appeared nestled together. On the ground,
however, the distance between the two monolithic buildings was a lot more imposing. The provost's concerns
were justified. Even with his arbitrators and the Thureoi
there were not enough men to keep the mass of people
far from the route, and they packed the cathedral's
square, so that the guards could only throw a close protective noose around the building and its entrance.

Becket peered through his shaded window. He tried to
catch sight of individual people, but they passed in a blur
behind the gold and purple barrier of the Epitrapoi's
Thureoi. He could not even read the signs and banners as
they were written in a local language, only a few words
recognisable in Low Gothic. Warrant looked out through
the window on the other side.

'What do you think?' the captain asked.

'Impractical uniforms.'

'Who?'

'The Thureoi.'

The Epitrapoi's guards had their backs to the convoy,
holding back the crowds. Becket had not given them
much thought.

'I meant the crowd.'

'Never watch the crowd,' Warrant dismissed. 'Every Thureos and arbitrator is watching the crowd. I'm not going to see anything they're not.'

'So where are you watching?'

'Everywhere else.'

The land crawler came to a halt just before the cathedral's postern. The rare green stone used in its construction, shot through with ivory veins, glowed brilliantly in the light. The captain waited while a squad of arbitrators formed around the exit hatch with their power shields, and stepped out.

His boot crunched against real dirt for the first time in the year since he had left Emcor, no, it had been even longer than that. He looked up and saw a blue sky, and he felt the warmth of the sun direct upon his cheek. The air was hot and fresh, without that taint of recycling. The clamour of the crowd stretched free. A shoulder jolted him in the back.

'Apologies, captain,' Warrant muttered. The arbitrators edged out and moved forwards, escorting the captain onto the steps and up towards the portico within the emerald walls.

THE CAPTAIN TOOK the thick parchment scroll proffered by the Epitrapos, with great solemnity. The Epitrapos then gave the deepest bow. The captain, as avatar of the Emperor of Earth, was the only one to whom the Epitrapos of Pontus would show such homage.

'Hoi Anaforae!' the pronouncer's voice with its strange Pontic dialect of High Gothic boomed across the heads of the ten thousand kneeling supplicants in the cathedral's nave.

The captain placed the scroll in the hands of the specified bearer, a noble youth who had been judged the wisest of his generation.

The Epitrapos straightened, and he and Becket took a step forwards to the symbolic concordia agreement.

Becket took the long striated quill and signed his full
name, rank and title.

'Ho Emperatos Gi!'

The Epitrapos took the quill from him and did the
same on the other side.

'Ho Epitrapos Pontoi!'

The Epitrapos then stepped before Becket, and knelt
before him as a symbol of his people, pressing his temple
to the captain's feet.

'Concordia!'

IF THE EPITRAPOS had hoped that the ceremony would quell
the disturbance outside then he was to be disappointed. As
Becket emerged within his ring of arbitrators, the bedlam
was even greater than when he entered. The chanting was
stronger, and the men and women who thronged against
the line of Thureoi shouted together, using the beat of their
cry to push against the barricades in unison.

Becket saw the provost-arbiter realise the potential danger and reach down to activate his vox, but at that
moment an almighty crack splintered across the square as
one of the barricades broke. The Thureoi manning it
dashed aside. The protesters at the front struggled
through the breach, pushing away the bodies of those
who had been crushed before them against the barricade,
and being pushed in turn by the jubilant subjects behind
them. Whether the frontrunners intentions had been
peaceful or otherwise didn't matter, they couldn't stop
themselves barrelling towards the captain.

The arbitrators around Becket reacted without hesitation.
He felt them step back into him, pressing in, their power
shields completely encircling him to ensure that nothing
could get through. The provost, though, was caught for a
moment with the split-second decision of whether to dash
for the land crawler below or bundle the captain back
behind the solid walls of the cathedral, potentially trapping
them all. While he took a moment to make the decision

that might save or kill them all, some of the Thureoi from
the broken barricade rallied around the arbitrator cluster
and instinctively moved in close to support. As the provost
ordered his men to grab Becket and dash for the land
crawler, the arbitrators' shield broke slightly as they moved.
In a flash of gold and purple, Becket saw the concealed
pistol that one of the Thureoi had drawn.

A force shoved him hard in the back as he heard the
phut of the tiny shot.

'Apologies, captain,' Warrant muttered as he took the
bullet.

The sound of the shot did not carry for more than a few
metres, but the arbitrators heard it. Their power mauls
lashed out, first at the Thureoi with the pistol, and then
at the others around him wearing the gold and the purple. The arbitrators turned on the Thureoi with
indiscriminate ruthlessness; whether each guard might be
a co-conspirator or an innocent, the arbitrators could not
take the risk. They were too close. They had to be taken
down. The Thureoi further away, though, saw the grey
arbitrators attacking their own. They saw the captain
down in the middle and, distracted, faltered in their
efforts to keep back the crowd.

The provost was screaming into his vox, and the captain was dragged up bodily, the fallen Warrant slipping
from his grip. He was near-carried towards the land
crawler whose hydrocannons were firing at the crowd in
the breach. The last thing he saw before he was thrown
into the land crawler's hatch were the bursts of red
exploding from the chests of the struggling protesters, as
the arbitrators' shotguns found their marks. The hatch
door slammed shut. The land crawler's engine roared. All
the captain could hear was a voice in the cabin shouting
Warrant's name. It was his own.

'I'M TELLING YOU, captain. He's fine.'
'Are you sure?'

'Yes!' the provost replied, flustered. 'Officer Warrant got out with the second crawler, along with the rest of your crew.'

'Thank the Emperor.' Becket sighed in relief in the crawler's cabin.

'If I may say, captain, he's a tough bastard, that one.'

'More than you know, provost-arbiter,' Becket said, his thoughts flicking back to the last days of the *Granicus*, 'more than you know.'

BECKET SAT QUIETLY in his shuttle seat. For all the provost's hurry to get him out of danger and off this world, some things could not be rushed, and one of those things was shuttle launch preparation. He had already contacted Lieutenant Commander Guir and Commissar Bedrossian back on the *Relentless* to confirm his safety. The battlefleet did not traditionally take kindly to having the lives of their senior officers threatened. In darker days in the past, entire cities had been levelled from orbit for the offence. In any case, the would-be assassin was dead. He had died lying unconscious on the ground. The cause wasn't certain yet, but the provost thought it was most likely poison. Whether he took it knowingly or not was another question.

The Provost, too, was in a significant amount of trouble. He had not circulated the information that the attacker was one of the Epitrapoi's personal guard, or had at least disguised himself as such, since it would be certain to escalate the situation even further. It would be a charge against the Epitrapos. On the other hand, stories of arbitrators attacking the Thureoi without provocation were being repeated far and wide. The arbitrator precinct would be under siege by the mob by nightfall. The precinct, however, was designed for that very purpose, and Becket had no doubt that after a week or so the mob would be broken, and the provost would retake the city. Whatever aid the *Relentless* could offer him would be his.

Becket glanced at Officer Warrant beside him, a tear in the man's uniform and a bandage around his middle the only evidence of his earlier heroism. Becket opened his mouth to say something, but the main shuttle engines fired, and his mind turned back to the matters of the *Relentless*, and his first officer.

'COMMANDER, LISTEN TO ME.'

'No, confessor, I will not. Mister Vickers, will you please escort the confessor to our shuttle?'

'But wait! Listen! What are we going to do?'

Commander Ward waved Vickers back as the captain's shuttle launched and soared across the baying city. The confessor was falling to pieces, Ward shook his head in wonder. How could a man who poured such fire and brimstone from the pulpit each day turn to jelly so easily?

'We do nothing, Pulcher.'

'But your man failed!'

Ward cut him to the quick. 'Listen to me very carefully, confessor, or I will be the last thing you hear. I would have nothing to do with such a sloppy attempt. That was not my man. Everything is in hand.'

'But I thought–'

'The Emperor did not make you to think, Pulcher, he made you to pray. Confine yourself to that.'

That seemed to give the confessor some comfort. 'Yes, yes, I shall pray for our souls, commander.'

'Oh, confessor,' Ward interjected, an admonishing tone in his voice, 'do not pray for our sakes. There is another who needs it far more.'

'Who?'

Ward did not reply. Instead he watched, a small smile on his face, as far above their heads the captain's shuttle exploded.

FOUR

THE CAPTAIN STRUGGLED to open his eye. The blood had congealed in the socket and glued it shut. The noxious smell of shuttle fluids, burning hair and the underlying stink of human effluence burned in his sinuses. His chest, his waist, his legs, his arms all ached, but, Emperor's Teeth, at least he could still feel them. His ears still rang from the crash, but underneath there was a crackle; fire, and something else: screaming.

Boom! The memory of the explosion flashed back into his mind, the black smoke pouring into the passenger cabin from the front of the shuttle blinding him and filling his lungs; the smoke whipped away; the pilots hanging limply from their harnesses; and the shouts of the Navy men.

Before, on the ground, Becket had looked into the eyes of the Thureos assassin and had frozen, but when a ship, any ship, was in danger, a true Navy man could not help himself. The captain had moved.

He pulled himself up from his seat and called for Warrant. He could barely hear the sound of his own voice against the roar of the dive. Another officer, bleeding from a head wound, had joined them, but he had been knocked from his feet as the shuttle lurched to one side, and had tumbled to the rear. Then the shuttle had flipped, and Becket and Warrant had slipped and slid along the carpeted deck down into the cockpit. Warrant had torn the bodies of the unfortunate pilots from their harnesses as Becket pulled back on the controls. The city still lay beneath them, the suburb slums stretched out in every direction. There were no gaps, no space, nowhere to go except straight into the flimsy houses and people-choked streets.

Their dive had flattened, but it had been too late to recover. One of them hit the sanctuary pods. The pod had closed around Becket and he had been blown out, into the air.

The blood cracked, and his eyelid opened a little way. All he could see was a blur, his vision swimming for a long minute before it settled back and he could focus. There was not much to see: only, a few centimetres in front of his face, escape instructions written in formal Navy lettering. He was still in the sanctuary pod.

Becket carefully eased over onto his side within the confined space. The pod didn't shift or rock beneath him. At least whatever he had landed on was solid. The pods were built to protect their occupants from the void, for a short time at least, long enough for a parent ship to mount a rescue. They could also withstand high orbit drops, with grav-chutes and stabilisers to slow a descent. As low as the shuttle had been, however, there had been precious little time for any of those measures to have worked. He should not have survived.

Overruling the protests of his body, Becket started to work on the exit hatch. He had to find out what had happened. He had to get out of the pod, and the sound of fire outside spurred him on all the more. He tried a deeper breath. His chest ached, but it was only bruised. Perhaps a rib was cracked. The pod had held on impact, so his torso had taken the worst of it where his harness had had the weight of his body slam against it. He had kept his neck still, fearing whiplash or worse, but his preliminary explorations were greeted with nothing more than tender stiffness.

The sound of the fire was muffled through the hull of the pod. It sounded distant, but no less threatening. The pod could protect him from the heat, but it would become his tomb if he ran out of air. He cracked open the pod's hatch, and for a second caught a glimpse of his surroundings before the flames burst in. He jerked the hatch back, his face and hand seared. He clamped down on his cry, fighting the shock and pain. He bit down on his cheek, buried his uninjured hand in his armpit to stop it instinctively pawing the burns, and took slow breaths, as deep as he could, until his control returned to him. He wriggled out of his heavy coat and wrapped it over his head, keeping it clear of the tender wound. He cracked the hatch again and, muttering a prayer, he launched himself out into the fire.

THE CROWBAR LEVERED open the rupture in the side of the sanctuary pod with a heave.

'Commander,' Senior Armsman Vickers called, still holding the pod open.

The first officer peered inside at the crushed and crumpled body.

'Lieutenant Aden.' Ward recognised the corpse of the ambitious former bridge officer. He nodded at his adjutant, who made a small notation with a stylus on the pad in his hand.

Senior Armsman Vickers beckoned a couple of other armsmen to him to help free the body, and Commander Ward wandered back towards the fuselage, while, around them, the slums of Sinope burned.

The fire had sparked up immediately after the crash and spread quickly. The shuttle's fuel tanks had been full, to power out of the planet's gravity. Those tanks had been ruptured in the initial explosion and further stressed in the terminal descent. The densely packed slum was a powder keg and, if there had been a strong wind that evening, the entire southern half of the city might have been at risk.

The remains of the captain's shuttle lay in the centre of a circle of blackened devastation, carved out of the ramshackle sheds and housing blocks by the laser-beams of the first officer's shuttle in order that he have somewhere to land.

Many of the slum dwellers had already run, either from the fire or from the shuttle's lasers that destroyed their homes. Some, however, insisted on returning to the wreckage to pull possessions or family members from the rubble. Ward had ordered the two-dozen armsmen with him to establish a perimeter around the crash and keep the slum dwellers clear by any means necessary.

It was the smell that Ward detested the most, not of the bodies, but of this place. It had that mixture of rotting foodstuffs, waste chemicals and human effluence. It was the stench of squalor. He could not wait for Vickers's armsmen to find the captain's body. Then he could get out of this pit for good. Ward and the party from the *Relentless* were certainly not welcome guests. His shuttle had been almost ready when the captain had taken-off and so they had been first to the scene, eight kilometres west of the House of the Epitrapos in the outskirts of Sinope. It had taken them a mere twenty minutes to get to the main crash-site: a hundred-metre long furrow scored through the crowded shacks and tenements of one of Sinope's suburban slums.

As soon as they landed, they claimed the area in the name of the Navy. Ward had already contacted the *Relentless* and ordered Lieutenant Commander Guir to despatch the stand-by shuttle full of armsmen down to the surface. Ward did not expect to find anything that tied him to the shuttle crash in the wreckage, but this was not the time to be taking chances.

The provost-arbiter, who might, under normal circumstances, have taken charge, was still fighting a running battle against the protesters in the middle of the city. Ironically, he subsequently praised the first officer's quick response and assumption of ownership of the situation as a 'textbook example of rapid incident deployment'.

Once the reinforcing armsmen arrived, the Navy was in full control of the area around the main crash site. These suburb slums were virtual no-go areas for local emergency services in any case. Without proper roads, and with the streets choked with slum dwellers, the region was near impassable. Those few Sinope rescue crews and peace officers who made it to the crash site were confronted by the *Relentless*'s armsmen, and firmly told to limit their attentions to the general populace and leave the Navy's interests to the Navy.

Secure in their perimeter, Commander Ward started to send expeditions beyond it towards the shuttle fragments and sanctuary pods that had hit ground elsewhere. Even with the aid of a second shuttle overhead, identifying where the pods had fallen amongst the dilapidated and derelict shanties was difficult. The smoke from the fire obscured entire neighbourhoods and that, and the heat generated, made close flying treacherous.

Once a pod was spotted, the expeditions still faced the challenge of how to cross the intervening distance from the perimeter. The fire had moved away from the crash site, and the inhabitants who had initially fled began to return and assemble in a loose ring enclosing the perimeter, sometimes shouting, sometimes chanting. They had been helpless, as death and destruction had been wrought on them from above, but their destroyers had come to ground and could be seen and touched, and revenge could be taken upon them.

Vickers would have none of it. He personally led each and every sally out from their lines, his shotgun burning hot with use. As he and his armsmen went out, they aimed high, catching the foul natives in their chests and heads. On the way back, they aimed low, catching their chasers in the legs and feet so that they fell, and entangled others who ran after them. Each time Vickers went out, he brought back another name for the first officer's list of the dead, but it was never the one that Ward so fervently wished to hear.

BECKET SHRANK BACK into a doorway as another narrow cart thundered past, laden with a family, their belongings and their screaming, mewling children. He had crashed straight through the roof of a tenement, the flimsy roof and cheap floorboards breaking his fall until his pod had become embedded in the ground. He had no idea if any of the floors he had smashed through had been occupied. A fire had started somewhere in a middle storey, perhaps a light, or a cooking flame had been broken out of its crude container. The fire had driven any survivors away and turned the block into an inferno. He had only just escaped when the building collapsed, burying his pod, and nearly himself, under the rubble. Now, he was alone and adrift in a city baying for Imperial blood.

His coat lost to the fire, his face blackened by the soot, he had covered himself in a flea-ridden blanket and huddled in a gutter. He did not even have his pistol. He had to hide until he could find his men. He had crawled into a murky drainage channel behind the street and there, as the crowds trampled back and forth above the captain of the mighty *Relentless* had collapsed, exhausted, waiting for rescue.

The rescue had not come. He did not see one armsman or one arbitrator, not even a single local trooper to whom he could have identified himself without risking being torn apart by the mob. He had wrapped his head in a dirt encrusted rag that he had found, and had staggered back into the street, hunching down, hiding his face. He had

originally made for the largest plume of smoke rising above
the constricted alleys, reasoning that that was the crash site,
that his rescuers would be there, but his progress had been
so slow through the thick crowds that the column had
shifted as fire sought fresh material to consume.

He was turned around and lost. There were no signs, no
maps, and the buildings were all the same sandy brick
and gnarled wood covered with a patina of grime. The
pain in his chest and in his face and hand was beginning
to tell. He squinted up again at the smoke, silhouetted
against the setting sun, trying to get his bearings. His legs
were like lead, and he had been knocked to the ground
time and again as people forced past.

The air was stifling, the dirt and dust kicked up by the
refugees choked him. The crush in the streets was terrible.
He had never been packed so close with other bodies,
never had so little room to move or to gasp for air, not
even leading assault transports, crammed together with a
platoon of armsmen, waiting to smash into the side of a
target or to be instantly vaporised by defence turrets.

Then he heard the distinctive boom of a shotgun a
street away. The crowd screamed and ran for any exits they
could find. Spurred by the sound, Becket plunged through
the mass. He took a blow to the side of his head and was
knocked to his knees. He rolled aside from the kicks until
he hit a wall. He looked up and caught a glimpse of a
Navy uniform flash past along a side street. He struggled
to his feet and stumbled after it. It was a squad of armsmen and an officer, running. One of the armsmen had a
body over his shoulder. A mob was chasing them, hurling
stones, calling after them. The officer turned again and
fired wildly. The pursuers cried, and Becket was dragged to
the ground as the shot passed harmlessly overhead. Then
he was lifted up with them as they carried on the pursuit
all the way back to the crash site.

* * *

'COMMANDER, WE'VE GOT a survivor.'

Ward felt his stomach freeze. Somehow he had known that the scunner would survive. He turned to Vickers, who held the heavy body on his shoulder without apparent effort. The rest of his squad had hunkered down at the perimeter, and the slummers that had followed them were calling and throwing missiles, hiding behind the rubble.

Vickers gently rolled the body off his shoulder and it folded out before the first officer. The heavy face was dented and bleeding, and the hair was matted with blood. The gunshot wound in his side from earlier in the day had reopened and the blood had soaked through his uniform.

'This is not Captain Becket.'

'No, sir, it's Officer Warrant. He came down in a refuse tip. Bloody lucky to do so, sir.'

Commander Ward held out his hand to his adjutant, who passed him the stylus and pad. Ward then dismissed him with a nod and turned back to the senior armsman.

'This is the man that the captain brought from the *Granicus*, is it not? His personal aide?'

'Yes, sir.'

'This is a man who took a bullet for the captain earlier today, is it not? On the steps of the cathedral?'

'Yes, he did, sir.'

The commander's pistol appeared in his hand.

'If he can take a bullet for the captain, Mister Vickers, he can take a bullet for me.'

Warrant's eyes fluttered open, and the first officer fired a single shot to the head.

Out in the crowd, a figure watching the scene, fighting to get through, suddenly stopped struggling. He disappeared back into the mob.

Ward strode away, making one final sweep with the stylus. Vickers did not move.

'Pick the body up, Mister Vickers. We cannot leave anything behind. This was all a terrible tragedy: our captain's body lost to the fire, so many fine promising officers gone, but we have searched for as long as we can, and there were no survivors, Mister Vickers, no survivors.

'The *Relentless* was mine before, and it is mine again. Recall, Mister Vickers, the service I have done for you. Remember what you owe me. Pick it up and let us go. Do not worry, everything will be as it once was.'

THE NAVY MEN left in their shuttles, leaving the gutted neighbourhoods in the hands of their original occupants. Some of the slum dwellers returned in dribs and drabs, either looking for friends or relatives, or just to scavenge whatever they could find. Many who had lived there had had so little, and had lost even that, and they had not bothered to return. They took whatever they still carried and set off to a different part of the suburbs to try to set themselves down there. Others, mainly young men, who had been denied their retribution against the Navy men, set out in groups instead to get revenge wherever they could.

As the night deepened, it was the turn of other neighbourhoods nearby to suffer their toll of violence, as the gangs crossed their borders and began to loot and steal whatever they could. The occupants resisted and defended their homes. In the shadows, under the cloak of just retribution, countless rivalries were tested and old scores settled. The local troop commanders were unwilling to send their men into the labyrinthine back streets and so settled on containing the unrest within the slums, keeping it from the more affluent areas. The violence only exhausted itself after three days of terror, and the atrocities that took place were often cited in future incidents as justification for clashes between the gangs of different neighbourhoods.

The epicentre, the very environs around the crash site, were spared. Perhaps because no one who walked amongst the survivors, who saw their faces and their tears, could possibly wish them further harm.

The worst afflicted were the injured. What little work was available in the slums was informal heavy labour.

There was nothing for those physically crippled besides begging on the streets, pleading for alms from those who had nothing to give.

After the crash, the closest charitable hospice had opened its doors to the injured and the dispossessed. It was quickly swamped, and the monks and their assistants made the decision to take possession of the unoccupied adjacent buildings in order to provide shelter for those who needed it. Casualties, typically those caught in the fire, trickled in, and then, once the Navy had landed, there were several waves of gunshot wounds for which the monks enlisted the help of a backstreet surgeon who had taken up residence there to avoid the authorities. The hospice actually started to empty in the early evening as many of the healthy went out to pick over what the Navy men had left behind or simply to be the first to move away. By nightfall, the monks closed the outlying buildings and concentrated everyone in the main ward. The occasional medical emergencies, and the outbursts of those recovering from shock kept them busy all the way through until the morning.

There was little respite. Everyone was busy, either with another's pain or their own. As a result, no one disturbed the quiet man huddled in one of the corners, who made no sound, but who breathed regularly enough. Those who glanced over at him saw that he was simply staring into space, and quickly forgot him as they attended far more critical patients.

The captain was sick, sick to his stomach. He was deeply sick to far lower, down through the floor, through the planet's crust and into its molten core. He had seen the crash site. He had seen Commander Ward. He had seen what they had done to Warrant. It had to be a mistake. It just had to be some kind of terrible, terrible mistake.

FIVE

COMMANDER WARD COULD not afford to relax and enjoy his triumph. Every individual screw in his little conspiracy needed tightening. He had landed back on the *Relentless* to be greeted by a flurry of intra-ship communiqués, each of which he obviously had to address in private and in person.

'Yes, lieutenant commander, all went accordingly. I will append my recommendation for your advancement to my report.'

'Yes, magos minoris, your adjustments to the shuttle were ideal. As we agreed, you have a free hand. Do what you will within your order.'

'Yes, chirurgeon, your evaluation was satisfactory. Do not forget what we discussed.'

'Yes, honoured astropath, I have another task, and further rewards.'

'Do not concern yourself about the commissar, I will take care of him.'

The funeral ceremonies would take place promptly, within a day, and Ward declared that the ship would be in a state of mourning until then. There were to be no non-vital duties, no communications except at the command-level, a day of prayer, fasting and reflection; it would allow him to catch up.

BECKET OPENED HIS eyes. He was not yet dead. His dream had been of Ward standing over him, a monstrous face, an expression of chill indifference, the cold touch of the muzzle of the pistol pressed against his temple.

His body felt cold, it felt dead. His mind still moved, though, and his eyes still saw the grey light of the early morning and the shapes of the huddled slummers around him. His arms and legs had cramped and seized up during the night, but he forced them loose. He tried stretching his face. One side of it moved, but the other, the burned side, was numb.

His feet felt frozen. Someone had stolen his boots. One of the monks had left a small bowl of soup by his feet. He reached down to pick up the dish, and then he saw his hand. The skin had turned a bloody red, stained with black dirt and scabs. Becket breathed through his initial surge of panic. He had had worse. His mind knew he had had much worse. It was just a matter of convincing his body. His body, though, had other concerns, and the clutch of his stomach reminded him of its more basic demands. He scooped up the bowl with his shaking, good hand and tried his best to pour the cold broth into the undamaged side of his mouth.

There was a murmur as one of the slummers shifted in his sleep, and Becket set the bowl down. He couldn't stay here. He had to keep on the move. He couldn't let them find him. He had to get out. Carefully, he pulled himself up the corner to his feet. It took him a moment to find his balance, and then he staggered out of the ward, out of the lobby and into the street. As he passed through the door someone behind him spoke, the accent melodious and husky, but Becket could not understand a word of it. He did not look back, and no one came after him.

The street was wreathed in mist. He must still be near the coast. The fog deadened the air, making it as quiet as the grave. Becket kept to the side, using the wall for balance. He tried to sort through his jumbled memories of the night before, tried to work out where he was. He was still in the slums, that much was certain.

Even as Becket concentrated on staggering along the roadside, the part of his brain that captained a ship of ten thousand men kept working, deducing, planning. Ward had not bothered to hide his killing of poor Warrant. It had been an execution. He had not cared who had seen him. That meant that he believed he had everyone in the landing party under his power. Everyone in the ship perhaps, Becket could not assume otherwise. Even if any of the crew from the *Relentless* were still on the planet, even if he could track them down, they would just turn him over to Ward.

Becket thought through his officers, to work out if there were any to whom he might entrust his life, but they had all been on that shuttle. Undoubtedly, he realised now, by design. At the time, he had been grateful to have been allowed a few hours with them all, but his peace had made them all one single, vulnerable target. All those guards, all that protection from a killer from outside, yet the bomb had been ticking beneath their feet the entire time.

The shame of it! He stumbled for a step as the emotion gripped him. There was shame enough in losing a ship in battle, facing front, going shot to shot with the foe. He had suffered that before and the loss was terrible, but he had given his orders with the Emperor in his heart. But to have a ship stolen from you? Snatched from your possession by one of your own? By a man whose grasp and ambition you had so critically underestimated. Yes, it was

Commander Ward who had struck at him and his, but that did not excuse Becket. A captain's power over his ship was absolute, but so was his responsibility. Any captain who allowed his ship to be commandeered by a traitor, worse, a mutineer, did not deserve his rank, and Warrant and the others had paid the price for his failure.

Ward had taken the *Relentless*, and Becket had allowed him to do so. He had watched as the first officer had stood over Warrant and stolen away his last connection with the *Granicus*. He could not reforge that link, and he could not restore the lives of the Emperor's officers taken, but there was no power in the galaxy that would prevent him from restoring to the Emperor what was His. The *Relentless* would be saved, even if nothing else could be.

Confessor Pulcher Purcellum rested his hand lightly upon Captain Becket's coffin and said a small prayer of speedy passage as it waited to be loaded into the firing tube. There was a body inside, the confessor had checked. The first officer had refused to allow anyone but the chirurgeon to see it, but the confessor's position did allow him some privileges. It was considered by all concerned that it was far better for a body to be recovered, so as to remove any shadow of doubt should battlefleet decide to investigate the matter. Departing from the system with the captain's body still lying on the planet wouldn't sit well with them at all.

One of his cherubs settled momentarily on the lid, but Pulcher shooed him away, as the master of ordnance directed his artificers to lift the casket. The confessor's vigil complete, he proceeded up to the viewing bay where the service would take place. Almost the entire officer corps was in attendance. The ship's guard of honour was there as well, though fewer in number than usual, the confessor noted. Of course, he recalled, they too had lost some of their own in the crash, though as non-commissioned men their remains would not be included in this service.

The ceremony proceeded very well, though the confessor truncated some of the achievements of the fallen in order to allow more time to impart the Emperor's wisdom and warnings of those who might fall from His faith. Pulcher could sense that this break from the traditional dull readings of honours awarded and actions fought would be more appreciated by the men.

One tradition that could not be ignored, assuredly, was the ship's salute. The caskets were set on their course by the Lord Principal Navigator, supposedly so that he could direct them back to the Emperor's shining Astronomican on Terra, and were then launched into the void. As each one departed, the *Relentless* fired a single cannon. Shot after shot, every one to herald to the Emperor that one of his loyal warriors was returning to face His judgement. Even Pulcher, who knew he had to be a pillar of strength for his assembly, felt a tugging at the heart and a scratching at the throat, especially as the final casket, the captain's went to the accompaniment of a full battery. Respect and power, it was everything that made the Navy great.

To close, Commander Ward led the company in a repetition of their battlefleet's oath and, with one last salute into the void, they all solemnly dispersed.

All in all, Pulcher considered it one of his most moving services to date and a great success. He would have appreciated, perhaps, a greater liberty to use such a unique forum to properly admonish the slide of godliness on the lower decks, but it would keep for another time.

He had a strong suspicion that the first officer would be far more open to his very reasonable requests in the future than he had been in the past.

'I HAVE SAID it to the Epitrapos and I shall say it to you, Dikaste Tabbuur. I am holding your government personally responsible for the deaths of my crewmen and the captain. It is quite clearly the case that some lapse in your security allowed these traitors the ability to strike at the Imperial Navy in such a heinous manner.'

'Commander,' the dikaste of the Epitrapos hurriedly interjected, 'please be assured that I have reviewed every single security arrangement, and they were all followed to the letter.'

'Then their design was flawed, dikaste, and that is your responsibility also.'

'We have investigated everyone who might have had access to that area, and there is nothing.'

'Just as you must have investigated the members of the Epitrapoi's personal guard? It was one of your men, *your* men, who managed to get within striking distance of Captain Becket. It was only the heroic self-sacrifice of one of my crew that saved his life. That crewman, I might add, is dead, struck down by a cowardly attack that you were unable to prevent.'

'You have my most sincere condolences on your great loss, commander.'

'I will be most sure to include them in my report to battlefleet,' Ward snapped back, 'along with the fact that Captain Becket's very last act was to reaffirm the sacred concordia, struck between your people and my Emperor, which you told us would lead to an expurgation of anti-Imperial sentiment amongst your people. Yet, here I read report after report of more demonstrations, and more rioting.'

'These things will take time–'

'The "sacred" concordia, may I remind you, also includes provisions for the seizure of your government and the enforcement of direct Imperial rule should you ever fail in upholding His laws. Incidentally, I was speaking a few moments ago to the provost-arbiter. Are you interested to hear his accounts of Thureoi attacks on his arbitrators? Are you interested to hear how your "reconciled" people are pounding at his gate?'

'The situation around the arbitrator precinct is most unfortunate. I am keeping fully on top of it. Matters will be settled as soon as they can be. Everything you speak of will be fully investigated, and the perpetrators punished. You have my word!'

'You have heard the stories, have you not, dikaste? About how the battlefleet responds to those who value its captains' lives so lightly?'

'Surely you cannot be suggesting–'

'Have you heard them, dikaste?' Ward asked, shouting the Pontic official down.

'Yes.'

'Have you ever heard of any officer being court-martialled for taking such just retribution?'

'No.'

'Neither have I, dikaste, neither have I,' Ward finished with the proper amount of menace in his voice, and then he cut the transmission. That would get their cooperation.

THE SUN SHONE brightly, brighter even than it had the day before. Becket did not have the energy to glance up at the vast, beautiful sky, though. His passion for revenge had ebbed as his fatigue increased. It was not gone, but had merely retreated into his bones, ready for when it would have its chance. He kept his head down. He did not look at the people he passed and they did not look at him. Their minds were too full of the news of the fighting not far away between the slum gangs, and the demonstrations further off in the city centre. They watched out for youths with weapons come to rob them, or government troopers looking for trouble to quell, not at a dishevelled traveller hunched with age or disease, who walked with purpose in his step.

After a kilometre or so, a group of street children had seen him, encircled him, and demanded money and food. Then they had caught a glimpse of his face, yelped and run off chanting, pointing and jeering. Becket had inspected the burns, now nearly a day old. They had swelled and started to blister. His face was still dark with grime and blackened blood. He fought the urge to wash it off, to wash himself clean of this foetid rat's nest and every experience he had had in it, but he resisted. The strategist in his mind knew that it was all the better to hide him.

He needed help. Stuck here without contacts or resources, there was nothing he could do. After the *Relentless* was resupplied, it would break orbit, and then it would take a fleet to bring her back. Whether the first officer acknowledged it or not, he had crossed a line, he was a mutineer. A mere order from battlefleet would not be enough to make him relinquish command. It would take ships and guns and blood to take the *Relentless* back. Becket wondered who could he turn to? He had not trusted the Epitrapos before, and he certainly did not now. He did not know how far into the Pontic government the commander's conspiracy stretched, but somehow Ward had got a message here ahead of the *Relentless*'s arrival, and someone had persuaded the Epitrapos to break from tradition and extend the invitation to him rather than the provost-arbiter.

Someone had made very sure that Becket would shuttle down to the surface, whether they knew what would happen later or otherwise. Whatever the case, if he revealed his identity to one of the government troopers, he would still be dicing on whether he reached an honest official before a dishonest one, and gambling that their superiors would be honest as well. Only the Epitrapoi's astropaths could send his message back to Emcor, whereas any official was more likely to contact the *Relentless* to confirm his identity, and then deliver him straight back into the hands of Ward and his conspiracy.

It had been a Thureos who had tried to kill him on the cathedral's postern. Had that also been part of the first officer's plans? Had he managed to reach out across the stars and convince one of this elite guard to make a futile stab in the name of Pontic independence? Surely, he could not credit even Commander Ward so highly. If Becket had been killed by a local assassin, Ward would have been forced to take the Navy's retribution out upon Sinope. It would have permanently tainted his precious relationships with the government. No, the two attempts on his life were unlikely to be connected. It had been simple coincidence, which just made his situation worse. There had been one local prepared to kill an Imperial captain regardless of the consequences. How many others would do the same?

He had only one option, one organisation that would stand by him, which even Ward's conspiracy could not have reached: the arbitrators. They had never wavered, never bent in their resolution to uphold the Emperor's Law across the galaxy. Imperial commanders, fleets, Guard regiments, even Chapters of the Astartes had at some time or another turned their back on Him, but never the arbitrators. So, as the fog had lifted and he had spied the city centre and its three towering constructs, the captain of the *Relentless* had set his course for the arbiter fortress.

'THERE IT IS, gentlemen,' Ward said catching the eye of each of the senior officers sitting around the table in turn, 'my full and final report on this tragic incident. I know you have all read it. Given the loss of Captain Becket, procedures require that each one of you either endorse or reject the narrative and my judgement. Therefore, I hereby request your endorsement at this time.'

'You have my endorsement, commander,' Lieutenant Commander Guir immediately stated. There was a chorus of assent from the other senior line officers.

'I endorse you also, commander, speaking as senior representative of the Ministorum assigned to this vessel.'

'Thank you, confessor. Chirurgeon, for the medicae?'

'I... I stand by my autopsy reports. I have no personal knowledge of the events that took place,' the chirurgeon commented, 'but I have full faith in the commander, and I give him my endorsement,' he finished quickly.

'Thank you, chirurgeon, I spoke personally to Lord Principal Menander, who expressed similar sentiments.' In fact, he had replied with a curt 'Your message has been received', but Ward knew that the Navis Nobilite would stay out of his business.

'I speak for the Mechanicus, commander,' Magos Minoris Valinarius said, 'and you have our full endorsement.'

'Thank you. Is there a reason that the magos majoris could not attend?'

'Alas, the majoris's health has declined rapidly since he heard news of the tragedy.'

'The Navy's best wishes go to him for a full recovery.'

'Thank you, commander.'

With the other endorsements given, all eyes turned to the last figure around the table, his steel mask impassive.

'Commissar Bedrossian?'

Unlike the rest, the commissar had a printed copy of the report in front of him. He flicked through a few pages, weighing it in his hand.

'Commi–' Ward began impatiently.

'I will have comments to append, as is my right, and as will be the expectation of my superiors.'

The silence stretched around the table as a few of the line officers shifted uneasily. The commissar could have them all shot where they sat, perhaps even just for the suspicion of what they had done. Finally, the cold, gleaming face rose from the report, the eyes behind the mask fixed upon Ward, who met his gaze unflinchingly.

'But… my comments will follow the line that the commander has already laid out.'

No one sighed with relief. No one sagged in their chair. One did not do those things around commissars if one did not want to receive their attention.

'Then we are all agreed. Thank you, gentlemen. I will have my report dispatched by one of our telepathica adepts as soon as I receive the commissar's additions. Let us hope it reaches battlefleet a mite quicker than last time,' Ward joked, knowing perfectly well that it would take even longer.

'A reminder, gentlemen, before you leave: I know it is all still fresh in your minds, but we are not going to let this tragedy be the reason that we fall behind schedule. We need to refresh our supplies, take on new men, and ensure that all data transfers are complete and as per schedule. It all needs to be done yesterday, so if we can please all get to it.'

The meeting broke up. The final pieces were falling into place. Ward allowed himself a moment of self-congratulation for a difficult job done well. Now, it was time to enjoy the spoils.

'WHAT?' WARD YELLED. 'What did he do with it?'

'He took it all, sir. He took it all off-ship,' the master chief stammered. When he had been released from the brig, he had been fully prepared to underline to the first officer exactly how much he was owed for the inconvenience of his incarceration. However, a few discreet words with his cargo chiefs had convinced him that Commander Ward was not in the most charitable of moods.

'Off-ship? When? Where?'

'It went to–'

'The *Tarai's Challenge*, of course. It was loaded in with the prize crew's transport?'

'Yes, sir. None of my lads knew about it, sir, until after it had all happened. There was this officer, he had these orders direct from the captain. He had proof and everything, apparently, some old mate of his.'

'Yes; Warrant.' Ward's mind flicked back to the crash on Sinopé, and the unconscious survivor Vickers had brought him. 'Becket had Warrant take… no, *steal* my collection, and then that scunner Aden raced it straight here to Pontus.'

'He had it declared as confiscated property, sir, for transport straight back to Emcor. It left before we arrived.'

'Can we catch it?'

'Sir?'

'You heard me, can we catch it?'

'Catch a despatch transport under Navy colours, carrying confiscated goods on a heading direct to Emcor?'

Ward considered it. 'No, probably not. Damn!' He banged his hand against the desk, and the master chief hurriedly made his exit. Becket, Warrant and Aden, if only one of those scunners was still alive so that he could damn well kill him again!

'THESE NUMBERS ARE completely unacceptable,' Lieutenant Commander Guir told the Pontic official. 'It is a very good thing for you that this came to me before it went to the commander, otherwise he would be having words with your superiors to get you shot for gross incompetence.'

'They're the best that I can provide, lieutenant commander, you don't understand how difficult things are down here. Three years now of famine, drought–'

'Do not tell me what I do not understand.' Guir replied. 'The battlefleet's tithe for men is very clear. If you have had three years of drought, you should have men fighting to sign up, get off-world and take what the Imperial Navy has to offer.'

'That's another thing, what with the demonstrations and what happened in the slums in south Sinope, no one will consider it.'

'You have nine continents on this planet, dozens of major cities, thousands, tens of thousands of towns, villages and whatever else there is, so do not insult my intelligence by claiming there aren't the men. There are the men, but you have just not bothered to find them. It does not look like you have left us any other choice than to be more compelling.'

'The press-gangs, they're very disruptive. They make things very difficult for us when you leave.'

'That will be your problem. The decision has already been made. Prepare whatever experienced men you have in holding, we will be finding the rest. None of the other ships will be breaking orbit until they have been inspected under pain of confiscation and impressment. Meanwhile, you will find the cattle. You have two days, and it has to be triple what you have at the moment.'

'Triple? That's absolutely impossible. You don't under-stand–'

'What? What do I not understand?' he roared.

'Nothing, lieutenant commander.'

'Good, have them ready in two days, and none of the half-starved weaklings you gave us last time. I want men that will survive a trip, maybe even two. I know all the tricks, remember?'

'Yes, lieutenant commander.'

With that, the press-gangs were unleashed.

SIX

IMPRESSMENT! THE WORD was a mortal curse amongst the men of the merchant fleet. To be taken from your ship, your comrades or your home to serve aboard the Emperor's warships for years, for decades on end, if you should be so lucky as to live that long. Many considered it as good as death. Even those few who were released from service might be stranded a sector away from their starting place, without the means to make the journey back. Such was the price the merchantmen paid for the dubious privilege of voyaging under the 'protection' of the battlefleet. Although, scant help they gave you, the merchantmen said, when you were struck by renegades or xenos two beacons shy of a system. As a result, merchant shipmasters were willing to pay well for warning of an Imperial warship at the outer limits. If they could finish their business and cut and run they would. Otherwise, they merely prayed that the mighty battlefleet had men enough today.

The reputation of the *Relentless* preceded it. All the shipmasters who had remained in orbit knew that their press-gangs would come searching. The Navy Articles prevented the press-gangs from taking so many from a single vessel that they would leave it unable to travel, so when the *Relentless* demanded crew lists from each of the vessels in orbit, the shipmasters sent them rosters cut to the bone, and hid the rest of their men on the surface, along with some of their more lucrative and less legitimate cargoes. They hoped that the Navy inspectors would consider them under the limit, although the Navy Articles were precious tight when they came up with their numbers for 'adequate' crew. Once the warship had left they could ferry their extra men back up from the surface and be away.

The *Relentless*'s inspectors were therefore met with countless tales of accident and woe on each ship they boarded: of sickness, of foul play, of desertion and of sheer mischance – anything to explain away the empty berths of the hidden men. The inspectors did not mind, and even expected as much. They played along with the fiction, dutifully noted down the shipmasters' tragic sagas, and checked that they had not had the gall to try to hide the men onboard ship. It was almost a ritual. Both sides knew that the real business was being done down on the surface.

Before the *Relentless* issued its first order of inspection, Senior Armsman Vickers and his men were ready on the planet. With the false crew lists provided by the merchant shipmasters, the *Relentless* had accounted for every single man officially attached to the merchant fleet. That meant that all the merchantmen below were without an official berth and were liable to impressment with no excuse or mitigation available. It was a simple game of hide and seek. The merchantmen hid and the armsmen sought, except that this game was being played for the highest stakes any of them could bid. The armsmen had little time and no taste for subtlety, so they stormed the flop-houses and hostels that were known for harbouring merchantmen all around Sinope. They seized whoever they found who looked like an off-worlder, locked them away, and then let them try to prove that they were not eligible to be pressed. The merchantmen, meanwhile, fought back with every means at their disposal, often enlisting the aid of the locals. The locals made a far tidier profit from the merchant fleet than they did from the battlefleet, and felt far less compunction about the use of lethal force, since they could hide in the areas of the city that even the merchantmen could not until the ship had left. The armsmen of the *Relentless* went in with their shotguns and batons, and, of course, Vickers was at their fore, smashing down barred doors, cracking heads and dragging out dazed merchantmen to be carried off to the holding pens.

Some merchantmen tried to outfox their seekers. They landed in remote areas and tried to hide, little realising that it was far harder to blend in outside the major cities. Often, the rural townspeople, alarmed by the invasion of these strangers, alerted the press-gangs, who found it simplicity itself to land nearby and pick the merchantmen up. Sometimes the merchantmen had already even been arrested for their troubles. So the game always returned to a brutal struggle in the cities, and in this way the *Relentless* replenished its own roster of experienced personnel.

The other human resource it required, the cattle, were obtained in a completely different manner.

BECKET CROUCHED IMPATIENTLY in the doorway as he watched the progress of the people's siege of the arbitrator fortress. It had taken him a day, as slow as he was, to walk here, and he had hoped, he had expected, to be able to walk through the door. Instead, he had been forced to wait the rest of that day and a night more, looking for his opportunity to slip inside. With the mob at their gates still strong and growing, the arbitrators had pulled back and shut themselves down, waiting for the crowds to finally disperse into smaller groups so that they could break out and strike back. He also noticed that the crowd had banners of purple and gold. The government's own troopers, overstretched as they might be, were obviously not minded to intervene for some reason. The few of them dotted around at the periphery stared on with bored expressions. They were there, it appeared, to keep the mob where they were. Even though this was a small precinct, Becket knew that the arbitrators must have fire-power enough to break through that crowd, though probably not without a significant number of fatalities amongst the protesters. Whatever the political game the Epitrapos was playing with the Provost behind the scenes, Becket had to get into that fortress.

'THANK YOU FOR your patience, provost-arbiter,' the Pontic official said over the viewscreen. 'You will be out of there soon.'

'We have never been kept here. We have only remained at your request.'

'Yes, provost, as I said, this was a direct request from the *Relentless*. Both they and I greatly appreciate your for-bearance.'

'It is only because of the request from the *Relentless* that I agreed to this for as long as I have. I know I took the decision to pull my arbitrators back in the first place, but we were ready to break out that night.'

'Apologies again, provost. It took us time to bring up the necessary ammunition and holding pens. I hope you will agree though that your efforts have been superb at allowing us to contain the outbreak.'

'When this is over we will be taking steps to ensure that there is no confusion over the sanctity of our presence here. This event must not be interpreted as a weakness of the Emperor's authority on Pontus.'

'I am sure it will not, and you have our support for any future actions you deem necessary. As for now, provost, we are in our positions and ready. If you would please begin?'

'Acknowledged.'

The screen flicked off and the provost's face disappeared.

'Well, at least this is going to be the last batch. He won't be able to say that any of them are weaklings, they've been shouting all day and night. If he can think of a better way to get triple numbers in two days then he can come down here and do it himself. Advance!'

BECKET LOOKED UP as he heard a murmur amongst the crowds. They'd seen movement up on the fortress walls. Arbitrators were deploying. They were finally coming out. The crowds roused themselves and stepped up to the ring of cover that they had established around the fortress. Those of them who had brought weapons began to draw and load them. Becket hurried forwards. If he could grab a vox-amplifier from one of the agitators he could call up to them. There were codes he knew, codes they would recognise and that he hoped would prevent them gunning him down as he ran towards their walls.

There. There was one that had been left lying on the ground. He hobbled over, but before he reached it there was a sudden roar from the crowd. The arbitrators had lit three floodlights within their compound, all pointed at the top of a flagstaff. There they were slowly raising a banner of the Imperial eagle. The mob started shouting and screaming their slogans again, every one of them clustered as close to the barricade as they could. It was deliberate provocation, designed to get a reaction. Designed to be a diversion, Becket realised as he heard the unmistakeable rumble of heavy motor engines underneath the chants. All around, behind the barricades, armoured land crawlers advanced against the mob. In the low buildings at the edges, windows were being knocked out by heavily armed government troopers. There was little time. Becket grabbed for the vox-amplifier, but the agitator had picked it up again to shout commands. Becket took hold of the amp and then kneed the agitator hard. A couple of others nearby saw it happen and tried to grab Becket, but he dodged away, and lost himself in the crowd. The land crawlers had all done a sharp turn and stopped, creating an impenetrable ring of steel around the protesters. More troopers poured out of them and started sighting their heavy weapons.

Emperor preserve me, Becket whispered as he fought his way through the panicking crowd to get to the barricade. He reached it and tried to clamber on top, slipping down as he was gripping the amp in his good hand. He felt hands upon his back and shoulders and he was heaved back up. The protesters nearby had seen him try to climb with the amp. They thought he was about to lead the rallying cry. So did the troopers, who picked him out as a priority target. At a single command, they fired: from the land crawlers, from the buildings, from all around. They were firing grenades, Becket realised, as he saw their trails arc towards the crowd. Gas grenades, he thought as they bounced spewing coloured smoke. He flicked the amp to maximum and pointed it at the arbitrators standing silently on their battlements. He inhaled deeply and tasted the sour bite of the tranq gas.

'Iudex...' he began, and then he fell. He was unconscious before he hit the ground.

Becket woke, drowning and spluttering. The water hit him again, the pressure pushing him to his side.

'Get up, filth!' The shout ricocheted off the high walls.

Blindly, dragged down by his sodden clothes, he clambered to his feet. He was instantly struck by another body flailing to his side. They both hit the ground, and were once more drenched by the torrent of freezing water.

'Up! Up! Up!'

He wiped his eyes and caught sight of the yellow cistern embedded in the wall. He hauled himself up on it and hugged the side before he was soaked again.

There were scores more like him: sixty, eighty, more, just like him. They were all being woken in this unceremonious manner and were splashing around, trying to find their footing in the shallow pool. They were in a pit nearly five metres deep and all around the edge were government troopers and crewmen of the *Relentless*.

Becket was struck, hard, in the shoulder from above.

'Off the side!' He looked up and saw the crewman above him with a long pole aiming another blow at him. Becket shrank away.

'Filth! Get those rags off and wash properly!'

They all stared dumbly up at the speaker, a brutish ogre of a man wearing the insignia of a petty officer. Then there was a second voice but speaking in a different tongue. It was a government trooper translating what the ogre had said. At that, the other conscripts jumped to obey.

'Ten seconds. Any man who takes longer will be shot!'

The ogre brought a rifle up to his shoulder to emphasise his point. The conscripts needed no translating for that. The petty officer counted down, and at three the last of the soaked rats, a beefy youth with a sullen expression, had struggled out of his clothes and stood with the dishevelled mob in the middle of the pit.

The officer lowered his rifle and passed it to the crewman beside him.

'Good. I am Crewboss Brand and you will still be cursing my name even when you are consigned to the Emperor's Peace. Now for your first lesson!'

The rifle cracked, and the sullen youth howled. He clutched his hand to the side of his head. Part of his ear came away where it had been shot through by the rifle bullet. He looked at his bloody hand in shock, and the watered reddened around his feet.

'You want to live? Don't be last.'

The petty officer waved his hand, and the jets of water sprayed the crowd again.

The officer and the other crewmen marched around the edge and off through a door. The government troopers kept a very close eye on their charges. They had been told the night before that any of them who lost one of the conscripts would be taking their place in the belly of the *Relentless*.

Two of them lifted a ladder up and dropped it down on the side of the pit. They shouted again in their own language, but it was clear, as the nearest conscript grabbed the ladder and started to climb, what they wanted. The rest of them pressed behind. Becket made sure he wasn't last.

As each man reached the top, he was seized by two of the troopers and taken into the room with the petty officer and the other crewmen, and did not emerge. Becket waited, naked, dripping wet on the ladder while the men in front of him each took their turn.

Then it was him. The troopers lifted him from the ladder and pushed him through the door.

'Well, well, what do we have here?'

Becket's arms were seized, and he felt the unmistakable pressure of a pistol against the back of his head.

'Well, Dzjeera?' Brand questioned the same government translator. A decrepit old man in a medicae uniform sat beside Brand. Becket did not recognise him, and he fervently hoped that the reverse would hold true. The translator cleared his throat and looked down at his notes.

'Protesters around the arbitrator fortress, it says, one of the agitators perhaps.'

'Oh, a rabble-rouser are you?' Brand looked straight at Becket. 'You're in my eye already, filth. You understand me? Bring him forward into the light. Let's get a look at him.'

Brand looked closer. His eyes flicked from the captain's face to his scarred hand.

'He's crippled, Dzjeera. He's no good to us. Throw him back, you can keep him. Bring us another one, or we'll have you instead,' Brand said, making a cursory notation on his checklist.

'Crippled, you say?' the government man replied indignantly. 'He's healthy, look at him. Those scars, they'll heal. He's tall, strong. Been raised well, you can tell; raised well, fell in with a bad company is all.'

Brand peered at the translator with suspicion, and then burst out in a nasty laugh.

'I'll get you conscripted into my crew one day, Dzjeera,' Brand chuckled, as he overwrote his mark, 'you just see if I don't. A few days up there, that'll sort your attitude.'

Brand glanced at the wrinkled medicae, who gave a weary nod, and turned back to Becket. Everyone waited, staring at him expectantly. The man with the gun to his head redoubled his grip and Becket could swear he felt the pistol shaking. Then he realised that there was someone else in the room, someone he couldn't see. Someone who was touching his mind, searching for a taint.

It was over as suddenly as it had started. His captors kept their grip on him as they pushed him past Brand and through the door behind into a room that stank of roasted flesh. There were two *Relentless* crew inside. They looked up with evil smiles, one brandishing a strange iron poker that glowed red-hot.

They plunged the heat-brand against the captain's bare chest. The metal was shaped exactly as the stylised 'R' of the *Relentless*, reversed. Becket could not hold back the scream, and the crewmen cackled.

'Welcome to the Navy!'

SEVEN

ONE THOUSAND, SEVEN hundred and eighty-two newly conscripted crew of the *Relentless* stood in ranks on the launching deck as they swore the battlefleet oath. Each had a freshly shaved head and wore rough, red overalls. Dark red, their guards had jibed, so the blood wouldn't show.

The crewbosses patrolled up and down the files, smacking the conscripts if they were out of line or slouching. A crewboss stomped past, and Becket's eyes flicked to his neighbour. It took him several moments before he realised that she was a woman. Even then, he could not tell where she might have come from. Without hair, in her formless uniform, the small holes in her ears and brow were the only mark left by jewellery she must have worn. There was nothing left of her old identity. She had become inhuman. Becket wondered if he appeared the same way to her. Where once the conscripts had been individuals, now they were just a mass, the human fuel that the *Relentless* consumed as readily as any other.

Six hundred and sixty-one of the conscripts had, the day before, been citizens of Sinope. Most had been marching in the streets against Imperial injustice, the rest had just been in the wrong place at the wrong time.

Eight hundred and twelve had, the day before, been inhabitants of the other cities, towns and villages of the nine continents of Pontus. Whether they had been running from famine, poverty or their enemies, each one had been desperate enough to volunteer for the life that the battlefleet offered. Few of the men spoke anything but their local dialect, and understood none of the words shouted at them or those that they were being made to say. They understood the crewbosses' blows perfectly clearly, however.

Two hundred and thirty-six had, the day before, been detained at the Epitrapoi's pleasure. The practice of worlds filling their quota with condemned men was forbidden by battlefleet. They wanted sheep, not wolves, but that did not stop it happening. Hard-pressed local recruiters found no shortage of convicts ready and eager to lie about their past to escape execution.

Seventy-two had, the day before, been crew on other vessels, discovered on the planet by the armsmen squads and pressed into service. They had fought bitterly to avoid capture, but once caught they had been equally fervent to demonstrate their space-faring skills to their captors. They would do anything to acquire the vital rank of trusted crew, which would provide them with a modicum of protection from the crewbosses' lash. Those who had qualified had been allowed to keep their clothes and their hair. They were marked out. They were not one of the herd.

The final man had, the day before, been a captain of the Imperial Navy, decorated, privileged, respected and obeyed. A fool.

Becket had not realised at first what was happening to him. The after-effects of the gas, the shock, the pain, had

all meant that he could not get his thoughts straight.
Then, as he stared into the eyes of the crewboss who had
assessed him, reality struck. He was being conscripted.
He was being delivered back into the hands of his enemies, his killers. He had panicked, had searched for any
escape, but they had simply taken it as his reaction to the
pain of the brand, and had kept him restrained as they
sheared his hair off.

When, strapped into a bulk lifter seat, he felt the familiar pressure of a shuttle launch against his body, a new
realisation dawned. He saw why the Emperor had placed
him back on the *Relentless*. He had been blind to it before,
he had failed and been cast down. Now, however, the
Emperor in His Mercy was granting him a second chance.
He had kept him from the arbitrators where Becket could
have done nothing but call for help and wait in shame to
be rescued. He had risen him up and placed him once
more amongst the stars, where he could rescue himself.

He had lost the *Granicus*, gone far beyond salvation,
but the *Relentless* could still be saved. Despite all the trials
that lay before him, at that moment Becket knew that he
was not being delivered to his enemies, his enemies were
being delivered unto him. He was a man without identity
amongst a multitude, and what he had thought to be his
penance was, in fact, his protection. The commissar, he
would find the commissar. Whatever influence, whatever
hold the first officer had over the other senior officers, he
could not touch one of the Emperor's commissars. With
Bedrossian's help, the *Relentless* would once more be his.

He stood in the cavernous launch deck, swearing the
oath along with the rest, as he had done for the first time
so many decades before. He swore his faith to the
Emperor, his service to battlefleet and his duty to the captain of the *Relentless*, whom he would not fail again.

THERE WAS NO standing on ceremony. As soon as the echo
of the last sacred words died down, the crewbosses'

shouting began. They were split off, a column at a time, and marched away. They were led to the stern, away from the command decks, away from the life he had known, towards the engines, down, into the lower decks. They passed through caverns with pools of strange bubbling liquids, past sealed vaults inscribed with terrible sigils. They clambered across gantries, clutching serrated banisters, across pits of monstrous hammers swung back and forth by gangs of human figures chained, both together and to the hammer. They went through fields where eerie glowing arrays hung from the ceilings, and climbed a giant monolith lined by chattering servitors, who regurgitated a number at each conscript that passed. All the way to the top, the conscript had the same number repeated to him again and again, each conscript hearing a number one higher than the man before him. The servitors' voices were too crabbed and distorted for Becket to hear each digit, but the numbers were high, very, very high.

They crossed a trail lined with men strapped, spread-eagled, to metal plates beaten into the shape of the Imperial aquila. Some were alive, some were not. They were crewmen, conscripts like them, suffering the harsh end of shipboard justice, and had been left out as examples to others. At the end of the grisly trail a black, malevolent building rose from the deck like a skull, the place of punishment. A word was whispered back down the line, a cold word: 'Perga'.

Becket knew their route had been carefully chosen, designed to impress upon the dirtfoot conscripts their true insignificance in this new world, to cow them into the willing servitude of their new god. Faced with the enormity and power of the machine in all its dark glory, knowing that his despair was manipulated gave him no comfort.

Finally, they arrived at their destination. As they passed through the portal and stepped onto the deck, Becket heard each man before him gasp in astonishment. A dozen vast towers rose up before them, soaring thirty metres into the air. The ceiling loomed far above their heads, almost lost to view in haze and smoke. Giant mechanical arms and cranes moved constantly across the ceiling and walls, tending to the towers, sliding from top to base. The towers were cloaked in deep shadow, dormant, restrained, but still with an aura of staggering power, should they be stirred to thunder. Their surfaces crawled and shifted as Becket stared at them, as though they were alive. Then, through the darkness, he realised that each one was covered in a labouring mass of men.

Brand and his crewbosses chivvied Becket's party on, leading them to the foot of the nearest tower. The base was encircled by long cogwheel rollers, and the crewbosses forced the conscripts onto them. They squashed eleven of them side-by-side onto each, and then chained their hands to posts at the top. At a command from Brand, the crewbosses drew their whips and landed a searing lash on the back of every single conscript, bawling at them to move. Instinctively, Becket and the others stepped up to the next tooth of the cog. The cogwheel rotated around, the lower step dropping away. As they were chained to the top, each man had no choice but to step up, and up again, to keep his balance.

A man slipped somewhere to Becket's right and fell, body stretched across the cogwheel, hanging from his chains. He screamed as the teeth of the cogs began to rip down his torso. His neighbours tried to slow their pace, but the crewboss behind them lashed them all the harder, and then tore into the fallen man, screaming at him to get up.

Becket's legs already ached from their walk down through the ship, and it was not long before his muscles began to burn. The rigours of the last few days, the crash, his injuries, little food or water, had sapped his reserves. With an effort, he double-stepped quickly and grabbed a firm hold on the post to which he was chained, which helped to steady him a little. The conscripts nearby saw him and quickly followed suit. After that, there was nothing more he could do, but keep moving and fight the exhaustion that was creeping up his body.

Twice, he slipped during the twelve hours that they were kept on the cogwheel. On both occasions he managed to catch himself in time, banging his knee and his head hard, and earning three more stripes from the crewboss keeping watch behind him. Countless more times, he heard first screams and later, as the tiredness gripped them all, dull plaintive cries from either side of him, as his fellows suffered a similar fate. He tried to will his mind away, to think of happier places, happier times, but his body refused to let him loose. He tried to clutch onto his rage at those who had betrayed him, had murdered his friend, but even that fled and hid somewhere deep inside.

There was nothing but the shortness of his breath, the aching of his muscles and the step, step, step driving the cogwheels ever onwards. What were they even doing? What did the power they were generating go towards? Was it stored in the tower? Did it go to the cranes that swept over his head? Was it for any purpose at all, but to drain their bodies and crush their spirits? He could not think. He did not know. He was the right and true captain of this ship, and yet this land below decks was more alien to him than the planet that wheeled so many kilometres beneath.

A prayer from long ago appeared, unbidden, in his mind. 'Imperator, partis meus patientia. Be here with me, be here with me.' He had learnt it as a young cadet to help him endure the regular punishment details. Through the hours, his lips twitched as he repeated the words from a different time, from a different life.

At last, the crewbosses locked the cogwheels and released him back onto the solid floor. He had begun the

shift resolute, determined to take back what the Emperor
had entrusted to him, determined to take revenge upon
those who had wronged him. He ended it feeling like a
shell of what he had been, nothing in his head but the
step ahead of him, pathetically grateful to be allowed a
square of deck and a few hours of rest before it all began
again.

COMMANDER WARD SETTLED comfortably once more into
the captain's chair. For the first time since the accident,
no, for the first time since Captain Becket had come on
board, he was safe. All around him, the bridge crew were
deeply engaged in the preparations to leave the planet's
orbit. Each morning for the last week he had fought the
urge to call up to the command deck and have them
crash-start departure procedures, to run from the scene
and put this entire unfortunate incident behind him. He
had, however, caught himself each time, and reminded
himself: protocol at all times. He had adhered entirely to
the dock schedule, supplies had been gathered and
hauled up from the surface, and he had paid the normal
respects to both the Epitrapos and to those continental
sub-governors who had presented themselves.

The press-gangs had gone out, conscripts had come in,
and the logisticians still chattered in a frenzy, trading and
matching communiqués, and would continue to do so
even as they headed out of the system. He had, of course,
personally arranged the Navy report around the incident,
and had been careful to show enough, but not too much,
interest in both the official Pontic report and the provost-
arbiter's report. He knew there would be nothing in the
Pontic report that would worry him, and by the time the
arbitrators reached the crash site, after their siege, after
the riots, there would be precious little left for them to
examine.

Ward felt the chain of affirmations through the sensors
of the captain's chair. The cartastra had calculated that the

manoeuvring rockets had left them in the correct orien-
tation. Auspex detailed the obstacles within the area and
declared that their path was clear. As usual, there was no
representative of the Mechanicus on the command deck.
However, a vox query confirmed that they were standing
by. The last checks were done and the parting communiqués were exchanged with the planet-side control
towers, although the *Relentless* would continue transmitting and receiving data until it reached the fringes of the
system. Every section was ready and waiting for his command.

'Fire main engines,' he ordered, with no small sense of
satisfaction.

The instruction was relayed and, decks beneath him,
the priests of the Mechanicus uttered a last benediction as
they stirred the awesome plasma engines to life. Every
man on board felt the slight tug against his body as the
Relentless broke orbit and began its journey out of the
Pontus system. Everything, the first officer considered,
was as it should be.

His contentment was interrupted by a buzz of activity
down in the curatium pit. One of the decks was reporting
damage. There had been a small drop in pressure in one
of the fuel intakes. The logisticians whirred as the data
started to feed into the captain's chair. One of the hundreds of intake cylinders for that engine had ruptured
and had flooded into the surrounding chamber. The
cylinder was immediately shut down, and further analysis was performed to ensure that the bulkheads in the
affected chamber had held, which they had. It was not a
critical problem as the other cylinders simply increased
their flow to compensate. However, to have an accident
on the first firing of the engines out of port was believed
to be an ill omen by the superstitious Navy men.

An investigative team of artificers and Mechanicus
priests was eventually sent to reclaim the area, and discovered that the misfire was the result of a line of

microfractures running along the side of the cylinder. It was most likely a problem that had slowly been worsening for years. It had been a matter of chance that the cylinder had failed when it did.

They also discovered that, in the press for space, one of the crewbosses had housed a hundred of the new conscripts in the chamber, who had then been sealed in as part of the routine engine activation sequence. They had all been incinerated within a few seconds of the rupture, although, given the current glut of unskilled workers, the loss was marked down as of secondary importance compared to the loss of engine performance.

The delay in the reclamation of the chamber was caused by a far more serious event that had occurred at the same time, but which, unlike the deaths of the conscripts, received far speedier reporting.

THE PRIVATE AREA of the Adeptus Mechanicus was not much changed since the last time Commander Ward had been there. The priests still walked past him with benign indifference, their focus devoted to other, higher matters. The testing areas he glimpsed in the rooms off the main corridors seemed as busy as ever. There was no outward show to signify their proclaimed state of public mourning.

There was no one at the entrance to the altar forge to challenge him, and so he stepped inside. The scene was just as it had been before: the magos majoris settled upon the altar, the denunctator standing rigid to the side, and all his other attendants arranged much as they always were. The only addition was a spindly creature, busying itself applying some substance to the face of the denunctator. Its heavy robes could not conceal the multiple limbs moving and working beneath.

'He could almost still be alive, couldn't he?'

Ward turned sharply to a voice in the darkness.

'Valinarius?'

'Of course, commander,' said the magos minoris, emerging from the shadows.

Ward nodded at him, and then turned back to the body of the majoris, ensconced within his frame.

'It was quick then?'

'Hard to say, commander. It was always due to happen some day. To commune with the spirit is a singular blessing, but the toll it can take upon the body can be fearful. Alas, much as I believed his soul was still strong, we think that when the intake cylinder weakened, he must have felt it within the machine, and then strained to try to prevent the accident. While there could be no doubt that his fortitude was ready to meet the challenge, the strain such exertions placed upon the body were too great.'

'A tragic loss, minoris... or should I address you as majoris now?'

'Not at this time,' Valinarius replied with a sly smile. 'The consideration of the appointment will come soon. Though I am the obvious candidate, we must allow the proper interval, both out of respect for the departed and also, of course, for the kerhex to do his work.' Valinarius nodded towards the creature painting the face of the denunctator, who still stood immobile.

'The officers and crew of the *Relentless* offer their deepest sympathies, and we will fully respect the priesthood's autonomy in its internal–'

'Workings?'

'Just so.'

'Thank you, commander. Or should I address you as captain now?'

'Not at this time, minoris, not at this time.'

They exchanged short bows of respect and complicity. Then, the first officer turned and left the silent tableau behind.

NOT FAR DISTANT, another regarded the *Relentless* with keen interest. Upon the bridge of his own sleek vessel,

Archon Ai'zhraphim's alien eyes glittered as he watched the Imperial ship make its ponderous progression out of the system. The archon knew that its belly must be bulging with all its new crew, and he felt the familiar stirring of the hunter within him. He and his warriors had been lurking in their orbit around this world for several weeks before the arrival of the human warship had forced them to curtail their slaving expeditions down the surface, but as long as he maintained the shadowfields, the humans' primitive technology could never detect him at such a distance. The landing parties, however, could not be so well concealed as they burned their way down through the atmosphere and back up again.

His followers were untroubled by the delay as they had already taken a multitude of these Pontics. Ai'zhraphim could barely believe the naivety of this world's petty ruler. Through his agents, he actually thought to try to bargain with them, to buy them off with slaves he could deliver from amongst those who would not be missed, disguised as an Imperial tithe. Ai'zhraphim had taken the slaves, naturally, but no pledge to one of the lesser races would prevent him from doing exactly as he desired.

His followers had fallen upon the Epitrapoi's tribute with gusto. The archon, however, found such fare dull, staple. The slaves were nothing more than cattle. Their lives had been bland, and their minds half-broken when they arrived. They were enough, perhaps, to sustain his less discerning warriors, but he had long ago developed more sophisticated tastes. For all that such tribute ensured the success of his raid and the ease and clinical efficiency by which it was collected, it was not the true pleasure for which he had ventured forth.

He had had ample opportunity to slip away when the warship arrived, if he had so chosen, but a sense had compelled him to stay. Every knife has two edges, he reminded himself, and his warriors had entertainment enough to keep them occupied. He had had his vessel retreat to a more distant station, to lay concealed and listen, his slave translators steadily distilling the sense from the brutish, guttural noises of the Imperial tongue.

The evident machinations at work on board the warship gave him a moment's amusement, as one might have at children pretending to be their elders, but it was the true size of their ship's complement that interested him the most. Added to which, these were not plain beasts, but seasoned men, men of experience and fortitude, soldiers trained to withstand and resist all but the most inventive methods. In short, they were his favoured delicacies.

Pontus could wait and, with ironic delight, Ai'zhraphim realised that the Epitrapos would believe that he had been true to his word, and would be willing to hand over more of his subjects when he returned. The archon issued the order to pursue the human warship as it left the system. The hunt began. He felt his own excitement, but he would resist it. He would be cautious. He would be playful. He would take his time, draw out every ounce of terror the beast possessed, and then he would slice it deep and drink his fill.

BECKET KNEW THAT the food they were given had an official name. Throughout his career, he had seen countless reports about its manufacture, distribution or shortage. To the indentured conscripts of the *Relentless*, though, it was only ever 'the slop'.

The conscript crews got the slop twice a day, once at shakeout and once more after duties. At shakeout, it was handed to them as they walked, smeared on hard-bread. After the duties were over, the shift had half an hour mess time to eat as much as they could, hot. There, the conscripts ate the grey, dour substance with their fingers. Everything they were given could be eaten, from the slop to the black-baked, hard-bread bowls, given enough effort. They were issued nothing to keep and nothing that could possibly be used as a weapon.

The recipe may have been designed, or it may have just evolved over the millennia that men had lived in space. Its great benefit, to the chief gastromo at least, was its versatility. No matter what foodstuff he had left it could always be rendered down to make slop, and the slop was important, for it provided every protein and nutrient needed to keep the body alive and working, with just enough intoxicant to keep the mind sedated and the man subdued.

The food, just as everything else in their lives, was all about control.

Their schedule was arranged to keep each conscript shift isolated and separate from the others and from what was happening on the ship. No one, not even the shift bosses, knew that they were even departing from Pontus until they heard the great roar of the engines as they broke free of the planet's pull. Each conscript worked, ate and slept only with his shift.

They were under the constant supervision of the crewbosses and it was impossible for Becket to slip away. Wherever they were marched, they were chained together. At their duty, the crewbosses guarded every exit. To sleep, they were herded into sealed chambers and left there for a few hours respite, but even then a crewboss was never far away. Becket once spent an hour holed up, crouched into a tiny service hatch, waiting for a crewboss to move away. He never did, and when they were rousted for shakeout Becket could only scramble back as the other conscripts rose before he was missed.

The crewbosses were all former conscripts and they knew every trick in the book. When one exhausted conscript summoned the energy to attack another they simply stood back, uncaring. In the case of accident or illness, they were equally unconcerned. If a conscript could not walk then he was dragged by his fellows. If he could not work then out came the batons and whips, which would strike and cut until he moved or he died. It was only once dead that the punishment finally relented. The bodies were left where they were for the rest of the day, until they could be collected for reclamation.

Even if he could slip out while the others were sleeping, Becket knew that he would be lost. The only route he knew back to the upper decks was the winding trail of misery that they had been marched along on their first day. He would never make the journey back without being stopped. The torn, filthy, red overalls marked him out for what he was. He could not afford to be caught. At best, he would land back in Ward's hands. At worst, he would be strapped to an aquila down the path to the Perga and left there to rot. Down here Commissar Bedrossian was a distant menace, simply a name, nothing more. Down here it was the Perga that filled men with dread. Lethargy, disobedience and failure were met with the quick retribution of the crewbosses' whips. Do more, however: strike back at a crewboss, try to escape, or speak of heresy, and you were dispatched to the Perga. Once you were sent there you did not return. Not long after they had come aboard, Becket's shift had witnessed their first example.

There were only a few others who disrupted their day-to-day lives. There was the occasional runner, one of the trusted crew, carrying messages between shifts. They would appear suddenly and deliver their messages in quiet tones to Brand, who would send them back, sometimes with a response, sometimes not.

The runners never even glanced at the conscripts. After the initial curiosity had faded and the duties ground on, the shift paid no attention to them in return. They became just another process, just another of the thousands of functions servicing the beast.

A dozen shifts after they had left Pontus, one of the runners came with a different kind of message. The shift was working amongst the battery towers, sanding away the oxidation, and risking instant electrocution with every stroke. The runner entered, saw Brand and went over, stealing glances all around him. He was young, this one.

Becket watched out of the corner of his eye, as the runner whispered to Brand and pointed towards one of the work crews. Brand nodded and beckoned over the crewboss. The crewboss came over, and Brand muttered quietly to him, nodding back towards the work crew. The crewboss went back and pulled out one of the conscripts. Becket did not know the man's name then. The crewboss spoke quickly to him, and then led him back to Brand. Two other crewbosses had gathered there, and they, the conscript and the boy runner walked out together. Becket's crewboss bellowed at them, and the duty continued.

The crewbosses who had left returned before mess. The boy runner appeared a few weeks later, never looking around, just like all the others. The conscript did not return, and the shift never saw him again.

That night, the nervous amongst the shift whispered to each other, the smart stayed silent, and the grisly commented that the slop had been meatier than usual.

Becket heard the man's name for the first time amongst the whispers: Asheel. The shift did not ignore the runners after that.

No ONE MOVED quickly at shakeout the next morning. The crewbosses shouted and screamed even louder to get the shift moving, and they were shoved through the slop line and out towards one of the lowest levels, near the hull. The atmosphere was chill and thin. Nothing went fast enough for Brand that day. He bellowed and ranted at the crewbosses whose whips cracked all the quicker to drive the work crews to get the duty done. Still, it wasn't quick enough for Brand, who frothed at the mouth until he finally grabbed his own whip and flayed the back off one of the conscripts to calm himself down.

Even the crewbosses didn't dare go near him, and gave their full attention to the conscripts, instead. One of them struck out at Becket, missed, and caught the man behind a glancing blow to the head. The man went down, and the crewboss started to beat him for his 'laziness'. Becket had not even seen the blow coming. His mind was dulled, his senses closed to the brutality around him. A second crewboss stepped forward, baton raised. Panicked, Becket stumbled forwards with his load, and then ran all the way down to the exit hatch. The second crewboss, denied, joined in with the first and laid into the unresisting conscript.

With the shift's attention turned towards the beating, Becket dumped his load with the rest and collapsed down to the deck for a moment. He started to shake with the sudden rush of adrenaline. He breathed deeply in the thin air to try to calm himself. The blood stopped pounding in his ears and he heard a muttering behind him. There was a strange figure standing in the entryway, chanting solemnly from a book.

His robes were made of fine cloth, adorned with holy scripts and purity seals. It was a lector, a junior preacher from the Ecclesiarchy cloisters onboard ship. He paused for a moment, glanced over at Becket, and then turned the page and took up the chant again. It was a blessing; he was reading a blessing over them.

An angry bellow broke the moment of divinity. Brand was advancing towards them, his face red, his words colouring the air. Becket shrank away, but Brand's anger was not directed at him. He roared at the lector, shouting that they were early, that he still had time. The lector, unperturbed, closed his book and stepped back outside the chamber. Unseen hands beside him wheeled the hatch closed and sealed it shut. Brand, incoherent with rage, hammered at the hatch with a spar of plascrete. He struck once, twice, and then the spar shattered in his hands. Spent, Brand turned on the shift and demanded that they sing.

The conscripts looked around at each other in confusion, but the crewbosses struck up a faltering tune. Brand started pulling out individual conscripts and quickly joined in. After a minute it became a cacophony as everyone made noise, any kind of noise, in order to ward off Brand's wrath. Through the clamour, the tune re-emerged, as the crewbosses sang all the harder and fell into time, 'Imperator, patronus, tectum.' It was a litany of protection. Becket had chanted it many times before, but only ever before they...

The ship screamed. The air was ripped apart. Becket fell to the ground. Men were falling all around him, clutching their hands to their heads, the conscripts shrieking in fear, the crewbosses forcing the words out as hard as they could: 'Imperator, patronus, tectum'. Nothing could be heard over the piercing roar as, just outside the hull, space was torn apart.

Brand was the first to his feet, dragging those nearest to him up as well. The conscripts needed no prompting to join in with the litany of sacred words, driven by panic as waves of energy crashed against the hull and the walls seemed to ripple. Becket shouted until his throat was raw: 'Imperator, patronus, tectum.' The words had never meant so much to him. He clutched at each one as though it was his only anchor to this world. The shift came together in fear and in faith, each voice part of a chorus of ten thousand voices that rang in unison throughout the ship. They bound themselves together to hold at bay the terrors that clawed and scrabbled at the energy fields that kept one reality separate from another until, finally, the sounds of the maelstrom receded. Crewboss and conscript alike fell silent.

It had been a successful warp jump.

BECKET HAD EXPERIENCED warp jumps countless times before, but always from a command deck, heavily shielded from the powerful energies at work. He had never before felt the full power of the warp engines' discharge, nor had he heard the noise of atoms splitting apart mere metres away. The danger was not over yet. The unity that had emerged between crewboss and conscript lasted as long as it took for Brand to draw his baton and smack it deep into a conscript's ribs for being too slow to get back to his feet. Worse was to follow. When the shift was over and the hatch unsealed, they were met by a squad of armsmen in full battle gear. The conscripts and crewbosses stepped through the hatch one at a time. They each stood there for half a minute, a few centimetres away from the six armsmen's shotguns trained at their chests. Then each one was ordered to one side. At the start it was quick, but then, after perhaps a third of the shift had gone through, the progress started to slow. Each man had to stand for a full minute, sometimes two, before being moved aside. The wait did nothing to calm the rattled conscripts.

Becket knew what this was: it was an exsacriamentum, a trial of purity, or a rudimentary one at least. Somewhere, hidden from view, there was a sanctioned psyker touching the souls of each man as they stepped out, searching for any hint of taint or daemonic influence. A gesture, a word, even a sign of strain from the psyker would be enough for the armsmen to fire and obliterate the unfortunate, and sometimes the rest of the shift would suffer the same fate. No measure was too great, and no precaution too onerous to ensure the safety of the ship. A single tainted soul on board whilst traversing the warp was a beacon for the unholy nightmares that existed there. A beacon and a portal, for the taken mind became a psychic conduit, a portal through the hull, through the shields and directly into the maelstrom. Ships had been lost in such a way. Ten thousand men's lives were at stake. Worse, their immortal spirits were in peril and might never reach their rightful place in the Emperor's Grace, but instead become a feast for the denizens of the warp.

Becket's shift had been trapped close to the hull during the transition. They had all been potentially exposed and so no risks were being taken. If a soul was tainted then the host himself might not even know it. The truth only came through the exsacriamentum. So, each man of the shift stood silently in line waiting to hear if they carried a monster inside them. The small mercy was that the unfortunate would not bear that burden for long. The blessed shot of the Emperor's guns provided instant absolution. The line stepped forward, and the exsacriamentum bore on.

What of his other secrets? What else might the exsacriamentum reveal? Would he be saved from the armsmen's shot only to be exposed to his betrayers? He should mould his thoughts to that of his disguise, and think like the lowest crewman. He should fill his head with nothing but thoughts of fear, resentment, fornication and gluttony, but after all that had happened to him, he found that his will had deserted him. He had ceased to care. On these decks, in this life, the edge was so close. Torn apart by shot, broken by a baton, a misstep on a battery tower, taken by a messenger, lost in the void, it was all the same to him. Every minute of this existence was a mere step from the Emperor's judgement. He had no will to concoct false thoughts. He had no will to think of anything.

The conscript in front of him did not share Becket's peace. The man shook with fear. He clenched his hands, and he muttered to himself in native Pontic. Words of prayer, no doubt, although it was wiser to pray in Gothic or else ignite the suspicions of his examiners. The shaking and muttering increased as they stepped closer and closer. The last two in front of the fearful man passed through quickly. Everyone's focus was fixed upon him. Right behind, Becket saw plainly into the dark corridor: the armsmen alert with their guns ready; the lector mid-breath, hand clutching his blessed seal; and two more like him, tattooed with marks of faith and fire, one with an incense burner, the other holding a book open, ready to turn the page. He could see no psyker, but one would be there somewhere.

At a command from an armsman, the conscript quietened, but his lips still twitched as his nerves danced through his terrified frame. 'Don't move,' the armsman said, but the conscript could no more control his body than he could control the stars. He balled his fists, scrunched his face and twisted his frame. 'Don't move,' the armsman repeated, his finger tense upon the trigger. He would not give the warning again. Their fire would take the conscript to pieces and, behind him, Becket too. If that should be his fate, Becket did not care.

A word from the lector and the armsmen pulled away. An all too human cry of despair dragged itself through the conscript's clenched teeth, and then emerged as the softest sigh. His shame ran down his filthy leg and pooled on the deck around his foot. The lector gestured, and the armsman dragged him off.

Then they turned to Becket, and he stepped through. He stood for the briefest moment, and then there was the lector's word 'Dimit' and he stood aside. As he moved, he saw the psyker. She was hidden behind the lector's broad frame, her empty eye sockets the tell-tale mark of the soul-bound. Her hazel skin was wrinkled, and her black hair cracked and frail, but neither could conceal the youth of her features. The judgement of life and death was being passed by a mere girl, little more than a child.

It was perhaps her face that inspired Brand to do what he did. He had shown weakness. Before the warp jump, they had sealed him in, taken the control from him, and refused his demands in front of the entire shift. It had been a blow to his authority, which, to his mind, had to be rectified. So, during the next shift, he found the conscript that had despoiled himself, held him down, and took out his eye with a knife. With that as an example to the rest, Brand felt comfortable that his authority was restored and that the matter was settled.

EIGHT

FACTIONS, BECKET REFLECTED, there were always factions. From the admirals at battlefleet to his fellow conscripts down in the depths, it was the same. Men found others of like mind, formed alliances, garnered success, and were betrayed, cast down. The only differences were the stakes. The admirals wagered with planets, ships, careers and lives, while the conscripts squabbled over crumbs and scraps. They had nothing, and yet some fought tooth and nail to possess even that.

In Becket's shift, the normal order of society was turned upon its head. The Sinopean urbanites, many of whom had been taken when the government's troopers crushed the protests, still stared and gawped as though this was merely a horrible nightmare. They found themselves at the bottom of the food chain. The volunteers from across the planet, desperate men fleeing famine and poverty, were at least accustomed to backbreaking labour with little reward, and so they ranked higher.

It was the convicts though, the condemned men who had been flushed out from the Pontic penitentiaries, who floated to the top of this brine. They had done more than simply volunteer, they had struggled for the privilege to trade the certainty of judicial execution for the vagaries of life and death in the service of the battlefleet. They found their own kind quickly, through their manner. They came well equipped with the tools of intimidation and fear to use against those beneath them, and with a proper subservient demeanour for those above. The one salvation was that, true to their nature, none of the twenty-three condemned in the shift knew or trusted the others, and so each looked for promising subordinates of their own from the lower ranks.

In the first few days, a few of these factions showed an interest in Becket. He was strong and well nourished, someone they might use as an enforcer if nothing else, but Becket kept his distance. He could allow no one close enough for them to chance upon his secret. There was no one left on this entire ship that he could trust, Ward had seen to that, and he could certainly not trust these degenerates, who would sell him out to the crewbosses in the blink of an eye.

Without a faction, though, Becket sank even lower, below the level of the volunteers and the pathetic urbanite protesters, who begged the former prisoners for protection. He could not get to the commissar alone, and yet he knew no one that would not betray him. He hit bottom, the true bottom, the lowest even of this dank society.

He was not entirely alone there, however. There were others, too weak, too different or too independent to find a place within the shift's burgeoning little hierarchies. It was one of those, a young man, only just grown beyond boyhood, who chose to latch onto Becket. His name was Ronah.

'*Pssst*, Vaughn,' the whisper came in the darkness. For all the time the shift spent together, there were precious few moments when they were free to speak to one another. To speak without necessity during shift or meals was to invite savage retribution from the crewbosses. It was only possible when the lights were out, and many then found sleep a more pressing necessity.

'Vaughn, you awake?' Ronah said again. Becket opened his eyes. Vaughn was the name he had given to the other conscripts.

'What is it, Ronah?' Becket asked as he always did.

'Nuffin,' the familiar response came back. Happy that he was not unwelcome, Ronah settled next to Becket.

'Gotta question for yer,' the boy said.

'What's that?'

'Yer speak Imperial well, don't yer?'

'I get along.'

'Yer get along, yer say. Ha! Yer speak better than the crewboss sometime, Vaughn.' Ronah caught the look in Becket's eye and hushed again. 'I've been talking to Sundjata and some of his lot.'

'You were talking to them about me?' The anger rose in Becket's voice.

'No, no, nuffin like that. Just talking, that's all. Sundjata and some of them, they want to learn more Imperial.'

'Why would they be interested in that?'

'Why? Yer not been listening around yer, Vaughn? There are more and more of us speaking it. Sundjata won't stay top dog for long, if he don't know what people are saying.'

It was true. More and more of the conversations that Becket overheard between the other conscripts were in Low Gothic, and fewer were conducted in any Pontic tongue. Pontus had no less than thirty official dialects, some of which were near incomprehensible to others, and there was extensive regional and social slang. Becket's fellow conscripts had been brought together from all across the planet, and no one could survive associating only with those few of their own kind.

'Tis more than that, though. Sundjata wants to learn 'cos that's what Brand and his bosses speak. That's what the messengers speak, the other conscripts. He wants to know what's happening outside.'

'You speak it pretty well, why not listen for them?'

Ronah pulled a face. 'Brand and the others speak too quick, they got a code.'

'They're not speaking in code. That's just battlefleet slang.'

'See, see? Yer know it all already. Yer the best one to teach him. Or, teach me and I'll teach him. It'd be good for yer too. Do it, he'll keep yer safe. Yer gonna need friends, Vaughn, and sooner is better than later.'

So the lessons between Becket and Ronah began. They spoke in the dark-time, in the middle of the sleep hours when they had the least chance of being overheard. Ronah never seemed to need rest. Somehow, he had protected his youth and vitality, from everything around him that tried to drain it. Ronah brought Becket words, words that he and the others had heard and wanted to understand, and in return Becket learned what the whole shift was piecing together about the world of the lower decks beyond their enforced routine.

THE RELIGIOUS SERVICES had begun not long after they had left Pontus. Every tenth day, instead of being marched straight to their duty, they were led into a bay that had been converted into an impromptu chapel, a mission down amongst the base and lowly. They sat in rows and listened to the lector in the pulpit rebuke them in a sermon for their sinful ways, and pray over them in arcane High Gothic. Then they shuffled out, and another shift shuffled in. For the conscripts it was an hour's respite.

'No work, no whips, just sit and listen,' Ronah sighed.

'You actually understand what they say?'

'Some, some. The sermon, yes. The prayers, no. They make no sense to me, but maybe I'm the only one.'

'I don't think so, Ronah. I doubt many down here would understand High.'

'But yer know, don't yer?'

Becket nodded.

'What's that thing he says at the end each time? What does that mean?'

'In Ius Imperator. In the Emperor's Justice.'

'I like how it sounds.'

'They say it over the dead sometimes.'

Ronah gave a mock sound of dismay.

'Maybe I should learn it then. Maybe I'll get to say it over Brand sometime.'

'Hah. I don't think he would care.'

'He's not a man of faith. I watch him during it all, standing there, hating it. Papeway says that the only reason he stands for it at all is 'cos of orders straight from the top deck. An hour praying is an hour not working to him. Would have moved shake-out up, I hear, so we lose the sleep instead of the work if it didn't mean a longer shift for him.' Ronah grinned. 'He's not a man who believes.'

Down here, Becket was surprised that anyone did.

'THAT BRAND,' RONAH began another time, 'he thinks he's so big, but he's nuffin. Tis a big ship and we're just one shift. There's dozens more, maybe a hundred more. Eskyma, he says that if we are the lowest then the other crewbosses, the ones who run the other shifts, they must think Brand is the lowest too.' Ronah spoke with great satisfaction. 'Some of the other shifts, the important ones, they don't do this guan work. They do important work. They live well.'

'The trusted crew.'

'That's the word! You've heard it too? They work all over the ship, not just here at the bottom. One of these days, that's where I'll be, when I get out of this place. Yer come too, then we'll both be out. We'll both be rid of

Brand, and then we'll become better than him, and then he'll get what he deserves.'

'DON'T YOU EVER sleep, Ronah?'

'Not since Brand gave me these,' Ronah said, pulling the top of his coveralls off his shoulders and turning to show Becket his back. It was criss-crossed with whip scars. They were deep and they were frequent, given time to heal and then reopened time and time again with a fresh beating.

'I am sorry,' Becket said.

Ronah half-shrugged, half-nodded and pulled the over-all back up. 'It don't matter. We'll get away from him soon, eh?'

'WHY DO YER care about all this?' Ronah asked suddenly one night.

'Why shouldn't I? We're going to be down here for the rest of our lives. We have to learn if we are to survive.'

'I know, but yer don't care about what's going on in the shift. Yer don't care who of us is strongest, who is talking to who, who wants yer on their side, who talks to the bosses. Yer only care about the outside, that's all yer want to hear about. Says to me that yer don't think yer going to be here much longer. I think yer planning to escape, but then I think, "Ronah, yer mad, we're on a ship, a ship in space. Where's there to escape to?" But then I think to myself that maybe this man, he's been here before.'

Becket stiffened, his mouth was dry. What had the boy discovered?

'I'm right, ain't I?' Ronah continued. 'Yer've served the battlefleet before? On a ship? Yer've escaped before? Maybe yer know how to escape again?'

Becket quietly released the breath he had been holding. 'Maybe.'

'Maybe, he says. Well, maybe the way to escape for one is the same as the way to escape for two? Maybe that?'

'Maybe, Ronah,' Becket said cautiously, but it was enough for the boy.

'Me mother, she warned me that I'd end up no good. She said, you run around with the gangs, yer'll get in trouble, one day the Imperials will come and take yer away. I never listened to her, never listened. I said that I was too quick, too small. Like the gilly fish, you know? Even if they caught me, they'd throw me back, wait for me to fatten up, become a man. Guess I was wrong. Guess I shoulda listened to mother.' Ronah chortled.

'Thought I was safe though. Thought I was safe. Wasn't a month before they took me that they took my coz, Framir. So I thought them Imperials must have sated themselves. It must be safe for yer. Felt sorry for my coz o' course, but he had it coming. He was getting in trouble all the time. Me mother always said the Imperials would take him one day, and she was right.

'Of course they took me as well. 'Spose me mother was right about me too.'

'Pssst, BIG NEWS, Vaughn. I saw someone today.'

'Who was that?'

'Djol, I met him when I was taken. We were next to each other when we came here. I saw him when we ate, he's one of the ones who makes the food and he remembered me!'

'He works for the gastromo?'

'Yeah, yeah, he made it out of the shift! But there's more. I said to him that I want out of the shift too and he's going to try to get me switched to the gastromo as well! Start as a messenger maybe, then maybe trusted crew. I'm getting out!'

ONE NIGHT, RONAH came over to Becket almost as soon as the lights went out.

'Vaughn, yer have to hear this!' Ronah was practically dancing with glee. Becket could hear some of the conscripts nearby stop shifting and start to listen.

'What? What's the matter, Ronah?'

'Sundjata, he heard something so fun! Yer know the fighting between the trusted crews?'

'Of course.' The shift had been whispering about little else. The jockeying for position between the trusted crews was completely alien and fascinating to them, especially when it was punctuated by the rare flurry of violence that occurred when the hotheads from two competing deck-crews collided. Now that the officers were spending almost all of their time enjoying life on the top decks, physical intimidation was increasingly the best way to acquire the choicest duties on the roster.

'Sundjata overheard two of the crewbosses talking. They said that Brand had tried to get transferred to a deck crew, had been all arse-kissing to their boss to try to get in with them.'

'Keep your voice down,' Becket whispered, but Ronah could not contain himself.

'Yer know what, Vaughn? They said no! They said no to the big bad Brand. After all his boasts, all his bragging, he's stuck here with us! Oh, yeah, he's a big, important man down here, but that makes no difference to them.'

Ronah stuck his chest out and pretended to march up and down, waving and gesturing like the crewboss.

'I am Crewboss Brand, filth! You remember my name! I am Crewboss Brand. You remember my–' There was a loud *brraaapp* as Ronah broke wind, followed by a chorus of sniggers from the other conscripts.

'I am Crewboss *brraaapp*, filth! You remember my name so you can still be cursing it when you burning in *brraaapp*!' There was more laughter, and most of the shift was awake. Ronah turned to his newfound audience.

'You laughing at me, Faveel?' Ronah pointed at the conscript and strode across to him.

'You laugh at me and I'll have your eye!' Ronah lashed out with an imaginary knife. 'Bet you wish I'd taken your nose, eh? *Braapp, braapp, braapp.*' Out of gas, Ronah carried on making the noise with his lips, as though he were playing a trumpet.

'You! Eskyma! You cheeking me? How you like my cheeks! *Braapp, braapp, braapp.*'

'Ronah!' Becket rose.

'Oh!' Ronah's eyes lit up. 'It one of the big bosses! Please take me away, Mister Boss! Take me away from this filth! See how good a worker I am? See how good I whip the men? I whip them open every day! Whip! Whip! See how good I kissy your arse! Kissy, kissy! Whip, whip! Kissy, kissy! Whip, whip! Kissy–'

Ronah was no longer able to stop himself. The beatings, the duty, the despair had built and built within him until he had finally cracked and given the madness a release. Now it possessed him, and the hooting encouragement of the other conscripts fed it all the more.

'Stop it, Ronah.' Becket dragged him back and threw him against the wall. Ronah flicked from mania to anger, and tried to push Becket back. With Ronah's slight form, though, it was no contest. Becket pinned him quickly against the side and held him tight.

'You bloody idiot,' he whispered urgently into the boy's ear, even while the shift behind them still bawled with laughter. 'Don't you realise what you've done?'

Ronah's body relaxed, and Becket gently eased his grip. With a sudden burst of strength, though, Ronah wriggled free. Becket let him go. Ronah shot an uncaring look back at him and stalked away.

Those of the shift drunk on slop continued to laugh heartily. The ones who still had their wits about them turned away, knowing the danger in mocking those who controlled their lives. The ones who were informers smiled in order to play along, even as they mentally composed their reports back to Brand.

His response was not long in coming.

* * *

IT WAS THE sixth week since they had left Pontus, and the shift had been herded into the steam room, an inter-deck service level that gave access to the waste steam exhaust junction. Though deep and wide, it was only half the height of the regular decks, forcing everyone to stoop or crouch to get through the entrance portal and move around inside. The deck was a forest of thick industrial pipes, running from side to side or plunging vertically from the roof down through the floor. They were all insulated to carry the superheated waste steam around the filtration system, but the deck was still as hot as an oven. Becket broke out in a sweat as soon as he stepped inside, and the salty liquid clung to his clothes, promising to scratch his skin raw when it dried.

The oppressive heat kept everyone quiet. The crewbosses explained the duty, and then left the shift alone. There was no room in any case to swing a baton or crack a whip. The duty was to replace the internal 'ribs' of each pipe. They were made of a special metal that corroded more quickly, protecting the metal of the pipe walls. It meant the pipe could be used for far longer without needing complete replacement. The ribs were sacrifices, and it was their duty to throw out the old and install the new.

It was difficult, painful work. Men clambered inside pipes barely able to fit them. The steam flow had been redirected, but their walls were still scalding hot. The conscripts swaddled their feet and hands in rags so as not to burn their skin. The heavy rib of each section had to be unbolted, manhandled down the length of the pipe and hauled out through the small access hatch. Its replacement was then passed back through, and bolted in place by the conscripts' bandaged hands. It was hard and heavy enough in the pipes that ran horizontally across the deck, but the pipes that plunged vertically from the ceiling through the floor were a far greater challenge. The conscript inside could not crawl, but had to work, dangling precariously on a rope held by his crewmates.

Becket's work crew formed up, the access hatch was opened, and he glanced into one of the shafts. It was thirty metres straight down to the closed valve below. There was another valve above their heads, but that was the only protection they had to keep the blistering steam from this section. Two men were picked out and the rest of the crew was split into halves. The chosen men were tied into a harness, and then they clambered down the shaft, whilst one half of the crew acted as their belay and anchor. The other half dragged the ribs up, once the climbers had unbolted them, and lowered the new ones down.

They all took each role in turn. It did not matter who was in the shaft, none of them was heavy now, not after nearly a month of slop. As a belay, Becket shuffled back and forth and trying to keep the harness line taut. Countless times, he felt the line draw tight into his waist as the climber slipped on a rib and fell. Once, one climber grabbed onto another to keep his balance and both slipped. The belay team was dragged all the way to the hatch, scrabbling for a handhold, before they arrested the descent. When it was his turn down the shaft, his fingers were wrenched, undoing the bolts; and his torso was cut as the harness bit into him. His wider frame made it easier for him to keep his footing, but it made it all the harder for him to keep his body clear of the hot surfaces. Every one of the conscripts came out of the shaft with red welts and burns across his body. All except Ronah that was, who, it seemed, could climb like a snake, and had fingers made of thermoplas. He'd have been lucky to have work like this back in the slums of Sinope, he had said with his gap-toothed grin.

It was a twenty-hour shift, but with Brand and the crewbosses sweltering in the corner, leaving the conscripts in peace, the time did not drag. As each pipe was finished, one of the crewbosses arrived to seal the access hatch and open the valves to release the steam. The work crew then moved on to open the next. Ronah's antics the night before were still fresh in the minds of many of the shift. They had each taken a part of his spirit, and it sparkled in their eyes, even as they laboured in the heat. The curt talk required for the duty was peppered with quiet banter and hushed guffaws. Becket also felt the change in mood. They all hurriedly fell silent whenever a bored crewboss wandered nearby, but it took little encouragement for it to start up again. Even when Brand passed by, bent almost double between the ceiling and floor, he was unconcerned by the snatched glances that the conscripts made towards him and the crewbosses. The duty was being done, faster than he might have expected. Perhaps the heat was enough to make even him docile.

The twenty hours were almost over, and the day of toil and sweat had left the conscripts near desiccated. The work crews had stopped talking, their mouths too dry. Becket's head and back ached, and his skin felt stretched over his bones. Brand and his crewbosses congregated around the last few teams working to chivvy them along. Ronah was working down in the pipe, bolting in the final rib. He had volunteered to stay down there for the last few hours, after every other conscript had been thoroughly scorched. Brand saw him fix the rib in place, and then gave the work crew the signal to haul him up. Becket and the rest on the harness line heaved to pull him out as quickly as possible. At length, Ronah appeared over the lip of the access hatch, grinning with relief that the shift was at an end. Brand leaned down to grab his harness and lift him up full into the view of the rest of the work crew.

'Come here, funny man.'

Brand's knife flashed and a bright red line appeared across Ronah's throat. Another flash and Becket and the belay team collapsed to the deck as the taut harness line was cut. Ronah was still smiling as Brand let go of him and let him fall down the pipe.

There was a dull thud, and then another, and then another as Ronah's small form hit the rib on one side of the pipe then curved gracefully to hit the other side and bounce back again. Brand stepped away. Becket scrambled forwards to the lip of the access hatch and looked down. A hundred metres below, emblazoned on the seal at the bottom, was Ronah's crumpled body.

As Becket stared, a twisted arm shrugged, and a tiny hand crept across Ronah's chest to clutch the gash at his throat. By the Emperor's Grace, he was still alive! Thoughts flurried through Becket's mind: he needed a harness, a stretcher, and something he could use to pull Ronah up again, anything! He just needed to get down there before–

Insistent hands pulled him away from the edge a split-second before a crewboss slammed the access hatch shut. They held him still while Brand activated the seal release. Becket's thoughts of rescue were lost in the unrepentant roar of the superheated steam as it was released from its confinement. Brand and the crewbosses walked away. The example had been made and the matter had been settled.

The work team that had been holding Becket slowly released their grip. The roaring from the pipe filled his ears. It raged louder and louder, until it became a scream, a scream that no human throat could ever make. Brand heard it and turned back. The work crew heard it and started to back away. Something had gone wrong. The steam had shot through the first seal, but was trapped once more. The higher seal had not opened, and thousands of pounds of pressure were piling upon each other, building, compacting, testing every millimetre of the pipe, searching for a weakness. A crewboss, bent double, rushed back to the controls and pulled hard to force the lever back and close the lower seal. It was already too late. The steam had found what it wanted and leapt.

A shrill whistle heralded its release as it forced open a micro-fracture around the access hatch, and escaped. The shift panicked and the men scrabbled for the exit portal, their fatigue forgotten in the rush to stay alive. The hundred conscripts of the shift became a single pushing mass, sandwiched in the tiny space between floor and ceiling, crawling over the weak and the slow in the desperate attempt to squeeze through the exit portal. Brand and the crewbosses were already there, heaving aside the bodies blocking their way and starting to push the conscripts back to secure the exit portal.

Becket knew that it was standard practice. The steam whistle was only the start of it. The pressure would build until the entire access hatch blew, and then the deck would be lost. Standard procedure: secure the deck, protect the ship, and any poor bastards left behind would die.

Unlike the others, his work crew had not run for the exit. They were farthest away and could see that there was no chance of escape through the mob. Becket realised that their terrified faces were looking to him. They were looking to him to save them. He was a leader again, and while his crew was in danger any feeling was self-indulgent, the practical was all. He grabbed the crewboss still straining to close the seals and dragged him down to them.

'There is no other way out,' he addressed them all. The voice of command came back to him easily, even shouting above the piercing whistle. 'We would have seen it if there was, so stop thinking about it. We won't make it out of here when that pipe blows. We need to protect ourselves. We need somewhere safe.'

With those words, he saw it. Across the other side of the deck one of the pipe access hatches was still open. Most of the work crew had deserted it when they heard the whistle and saw the stampede for the exit, but some were still on the harness line pulling hard to drag their fellows out of the shaft. Becket led his crew over to them, crab crawling to cover the ground as quickly as they could. As they approached, the anchor man on the harness line turned to face them.

'What's happening here?' Becket pre-empted him.

'It's Fidler,' the anchor man shouted back, trying to address both Becket and the crewboss behind him at the same time, 'The others dropped the rib on him. We can't hear him anymore!'

'Doesn't matter,' Becket replied, moving forwards, 'we're getting in there with him.'

A second whistle blew out behind them, brooking no opposition, and Becket set the crew to work. He had them lower the unfortunate Fidler to the bottom of the shaft and then tied the harness line at the top. The crew clambered inside and down, hanging onto the harness line for balance as they lowered themselves from rib to rib. A third and a fourth whistle had joined the first two, and as the last of the work crew disappeared down the shaft the captain knew that they had run out of time. Only he and the crewboss remained outside.

'I'll stay behind,' the crewboss shouted.

'What?'

'The hatch, it can't be closed from the inside. Someone needs to stay behind to close it!'

'Unnecessary!' Becket held up the second harness rope. He had tied it to the access hatch so as to pull it shut.

The crewboss shook his head. 'Nothing personal, scum, but I just don't rate my chances in there with twenty of you! It's better if it's quick!'

Becket pulled the rope tight and stared the crewboss straight in the eyes.

'Understand this, crewman! If I say you're safe, you're safe! Now move it!'

Once inside, both Becket and the crewboss started to pull the heavy access hatch slowly down on top of them. The damaged pipe finally burst completely and the jet of steam that charged out onto the deck blew the closing hatch shut with a sudden force that nearly knocked the two men off their feet and down onto the men desperately clinging to the inside of the shaft below.

The insulated walls of the pipe did their job and protected them as the temperature on the deck outside flashed from unpleasantly hot to fatal. All they could hear was the initial *whoompf* of the wave of steam flooding the deck. After that, there was little except the sound of their own breathing. They could hear nothing of the scores of conscripts who had still been fighting each other to get near the exit portal that Brand and the other crewbosses had already sealed.

It took fully half an hour for all twenty-three men inside the shaft to climb down as far as they could. The diameter, which had been barely big enough for a single man to work, could take no more than two men pressed side by side. Each man and his partner had to brace themselves on a single rib and against each other. No one could relax, or they would risk crushing the men beneath them. At the start they had all banged on the walls of the pipe to try to bring help, but the effort had tired them quickly. Only Becket carried on, knocking directly on the access hatch in an old Naval code for distress. Once settled, there was nothing to do but wait, and hope that rescue would come before their air ran out or, worse, the seal beneath them opened and the steam would boil them alive.

An hour in, Fidler at the bottom of the shaft regained consciousness and started screaming. His crewmates nearby quieted him and, at length, calmed him down. Not long after that, Becket could hear a soft sobbing coming up from below. He forced down the lump that came to his own dry throat. He was still their leader. This was no time for self-indulgence. He knocked all the harder to drown out his thoughts.

Two hours in, the complaints began. Men's muscles had cramped, their injuries had begun to fester, and they had gone nearly a full day without food or water in baking conditions. Becket remarked that there was plenty of water outside. The crewboss whom he was braced against had voiced no complaint. His every attitude was directed to match Becket's endurance, measure for measure. He even took over the distress message, beating it out in exact time. Becket didn't care about his power games. He was just so desperately tired.

Three hours in, the air in the shaft grew noticeably warmer. No one spoke any more. No one complained about pain or discomfort. Their bodies merely endured.

Four hours in, the access panel finally swung open and light flooded the top of the shaft. A figure in a full insulation suit peered in. There was a shout and gloved hands reached in and pulled out the crewboss. Almost as an afterthought, they reached in again for Becket, and began to rescue the rest of the men.

LATER, BECKET LEARNED what had jammed the second seal and caused the explosion that had boiled nearly eighty men alive. The report stated that it had been caused by a foreign object within the pipe that had clogged the upper seal. That foreign object was Ronah. Even in the dry, dispassionate tone that the report was written in, it still made him lose what little food was in his belly.

THE WHOLE DECK was awash with the condensed steam from the explosion. The reclamation team had not expected to find survivors. The crewboss, his name was Zwebba, Becket discovered, was whisked away for examination as soon as they were brought out. Two medicae orderlies, who had been there to supervise the disposal of the corpses, gave the conscripts a cursory once over. While they checked them out, Becket and the other conscripts knelt unspeaking in the water, staring at the piled, red-raw bodies of their former shift mates.

They were left staring at them for some time, while the reclamation team called around to discover where the survivors should be taken. Despite the conscripts' thirst, none of them was inclined to take a gulp of the water on the deck. At length, one of the crewbosses arrived with bread and water, and led them to a holding cell where they were reunited with the remnants of their shift, the ones who had escaped before Brand had closed the door.

It was this reunion that finally broke the silence between the survivors from the pipe. Those who had escaped had assumed that they were the only ones left, and there was a burst of relieved chatter as the two sides exchanged stories. There were no factions now, Sundjata the condemned man talked easily with the activist Kimeal as if they were the closest friends and not the bitter opposing faction leaders they had been the day before. Becket spoke little and let others like Papeway and Fidler repeat the tale, until those who had escaped had extracted every detail they could from it.

Inevitably, after the relief at seeing each other had faded, talk turned to their future, and to what would happen to Brand. Becket's work crew had recounted Brand's murder of Ronah and the resulting consequences in meticulous detail to the other survivors, leaving them in little doubt as to who should be held responsible for it all. Their ideas for the punishments that his seniors might have in store for him became increasingly lurid as their conversation progressed. Becket said nothing, for he knew exactly what would happen to Brand.

Becket's suspicions were confirmed a few hours later. The crewboss, Zwebba, reappeared. He had them file out for their end of shift slop, and then brought them back for their sleep hours. Zwebba did not volunteer any information, and no one was prepared to ask until Sundjata, who was afraid of nothing, spoke up as they were delivered back to the holding room.

'Brand? Nothing's happened to Brand. He'll be back for shakeout if you're missing him, filth.'

Then Zwebba sealed them in.

IT WAS DEEP into the sleep hours. The rest had finally exhausted their outrage and bitterness and were asleep. Of course nothing had happened to Brand. He had made the decision that had contained the damage to the ship. His seniors did not know what he had done to Ronah and, to be frank, Becket did not think that they would much care. Nearly eighty men had died, all told, had been extinguished in a moment, but they were conscripts, the human fuel brought onboard to be consumed. What was important was that the ship continued, scratched, but otherwise unharmed. As a captain, he understood, as the others did not, the true priorities of the Navy.

As a man, however, Becket felt the heat of the steam, the heat of his revenge. The dullness in his mind was gone, and he could focus clearly once more. Brand was a murderer, a coward and a betrayer, and his dead body would soon be laid out before the conscripts' feet.

'GET UP, FILTH!'

The familiar sound of Brand's voice filled the space and bounced off the walls.

'Up! Up! Up! Shake it out! Get moving or you go hungry!'

Becket opened his eyes. He had not been asleep; he had been waiting. Around him the decimated shift grudgingly started to clamber to its feet. Brand did not miss the looks they stole at him.

'Lost some of your mates, did ya? Lost some of your pals? You scunning dirt-feet! You stupid whoresons! Didn't you realise that you're all dead already? Your filthy mates, they got off easy! Easy, you hear me? By the end of today you'll wish you were flash-boiled with the rest of 'em!'

The crewbosses were taking no chances. There were only half the number that there were in the steam room, the rest had been reassigned. There simply weren't enough conscripts left on the shift to make their presence worthwhile. Becket stepped out of the holding cell and was instantly chained up to the conscript line. Only then was he handed his hard bread and smear of slop.

With so few of them, the shift moved out far quicker than usual. However, that did not stop Brand bawling each one of them out. They were marched off, and the chain headed down, straight down, to the arse of the ship, to the refuse reclamators.

The shift knew this duty well. It was where they were sent every time they had done something wrong. Every time they showed a little too much spirit, they were sent down here to have it broken anew. Each reclamator was little more than a giant vat buried down into the deck. Refuse from the entire ship flowed in. The conscripts sorted through it and picked out anything and everything that could be sterilised, reforged or reused that had been missed by the automatic filters. The ship could not afford to waste a scrap of it. When they were done, the conscripts climbed out. The load was drained down to be burned and compressed, and the final useless debris ejected into space. Then the gates above opened, another load dropped, and the conscripts climbed back in to start the process again.

Rancid waste from the gastromo's dens, material from the medicae decks too soiled for cleaning, the less toxic by-products of the experiments of the Mechanicus, all of it drenched in human effluence, were carried from every deck of the ship. The stench for the crewbosses standing on the edge of the vat was appalling; for the conscripts digging through the sludge with their bare hands it was indescribable. It was not long before the food they had just consumed added to the sewage they waded through. They worked though, damn, they worked. For those long hours, the only thing to live for was the few minutes out of the vat you got as one load went and another load came in.

There was little for the crewbosses to do. The conscripts were all down in the vat, with only a small ladder for them to use to climb out, which the crewbosses could lower in. Some of them sloped away, ostensibly taking messages, checking on other shifts; any reason they could find. Brand stayed though, immoveable, glaring down at the shift with as much hate as they felt towards him. Zwebba stayed as well, matching Becket, step for step.

Another load was finished, but the ladder did not come down. Brand ran his hand over the levers that controlled the top gates. If he opened the top gates and dropped another load in, it would bury the shift entirely. The lucky would die quickly. The rest would suffocate, trapped underneath the waste. The conscripts began to murmur and move towards the edges. Pull the lever, Brand, the thoughts echoed in Becket's mind. Pull the lever, you speck, you gnat, you insignificant bug, buried in the arse of this proud ship. You're nothing. You'll always be nothing. This moment is your chance, your last chance, to make a difference, to kill me. Pull the lever, Brand. Make a difference. Kill the captain of the ship. Bad luck that no one will ever know you did it.

The ladder came down, and the conscripts reached eagerly for it. Your mistake, Brand, your last.

The conscripts went up the ladder, one at a time. As they neared the top, each one had his hands shackled by Brand and Zwebba, and then were linked into the conscript chain. Becket waited his turn, near the back. He climbed the ladder calmly, and held his hands out as Brand and Zwebba reached out with the shackles. They locked around one wrist, and then Becket struck. His other hand shot out and seized the shackle from Zwebba's hands. He locked it clean around Brand's wrist, and then threw himself back into empty space. Becket's weight pulled Brand off balance, over the edge and down into the pit. Their bodies splashed down together into the foetid lake below.

Becket, who had been ready for it, came up first, dragging Brand with him, their wrists still locked together. Becket hit hard, once, twice, three times, flecks of the sewage flying from his body as the blows landed. He could not for a second relent, could not for a second allow Brand to rally or the crewboss's weight, his muscle, would prevail. Brand came up, roaring, the cudgel in his hand, swinging. It hammered into Becket's side, and he felt the explosion of pain as ribs broke. He reeled back, his free hand falling into the sludge to keep his footing, and Brand stepped forwards, maintaining the advantage. The cudgel slammed down onto Becket's shoulder, and he locked his shackled hand back to try to pin the cudgel down. Brand slid it out from the pin, and Becket's open hand, full of the excrement of the *Relentless*, plunged straight into Brand's face. Becket shoved hard, pushing the filth into Brand's eyes and down his throat.

Brand doubled up, gagging and heaving, but the cudgel was no longer in his hand. It was in his opponent's. One blow, two, and Brand fell back, a dead weight on the end of the shackle.

Becket gasped the noxious air in and out, and then looked up to the lip of the vat. Zwebba stood there, looking down, a chain drawn tight beneath his chin, held in the grasp of the smiling Sundjata.

'Get down here, all of you,' Becket ordered. 'Bring him as well.'

'WHAT DO YOU think you're going to do, Vaughn?' Zwebba spat as he was pushed in front of Brand's body. 'You gonna kill me after all. Then what? You gonna run? Nowhere to run. We're on a ship, you dirtfoot scunner!'

'You're forgetting, bossman,' Kimeal hissed in his ear, 'we're dead already. That's what Brand said. Now he's the one who got off easy. Maybe you won't.'

The other conscripts were not so bold. They formed a loose circle around Brand, still intimidated by his aura. Becket caught the eyes of each one in turn. They looked back, and they believed in him.

He held up Brand's cudgel, slowly, so they all saw it. He handed it to Sundjata.

'One strike to the head.'

'What?'

'One strike to the head,' Becket said again, and held his hand open towards Brand, lying prone in the filth.

'I get it,' Sundjata replied and did as he was told. When he raised his hand for a second strike, Becket stopped him.

'One strike only.' Sundjata nodded and relinquished the cudgel. Becket moved on to Kimeal.

'One strike to the head,' he said again. Kimeal took the weapon with relish, landed a smart blow straight to the back of Brand's head, and then gave the cudgel back. Then it was Fidler, then reluctant Papeway, then Ah Dut, then Efrem, then Mouzafpha, then Zercahyyab, and all the survivors of the shift, each one in turn. Some were eager, some were cold, some were scared, but none refused. The last conscript took his turn, but for Becket there was still one more man to strike.

'Zwebba,' Becket said.

'You're for the Perga, you know that, Vaughn? You and all the rest.'

Becket held out the cudgel to the crewboss. 'One strike to the head.'

'You're a crazy fragging scunner, you know that? You know that?'

Becket said nothing, he held the cudgel steady.

'Just bloody kill me, all right? Just get it done,' the crewboss ranted.

'Zwebba!' Becket cut in. 'You and I, we know each other. You know what he did. Now, take it. One strike to the head.'

'You don't know crap, Vaughn,' Zwebba muttered, and snatched the cudgel from Becket's hand. He stormed into the middle of the circle and pounded it down onto Brand's head, again and again until the skull was shattered. Brand was clearly dead, but no one knew when he had died, or who had killed him. Zwebba tossed the cudgel away.

'Now we're all dead men. You happy now?' Becket did not answer. He had no time to waste on the crewboss.

'Everybody out!' he called to the shift. 'We need to drop this load, and then open the gates and get working on another. Quickly! Quickly!'

The conscripts scrambled without a look back.

'Everybody, means you too, Zwebba,' Becket called.

'What are you doing?'

'The duty we were set. We're going to finish it. Then we're going to be hosed down, and marched back. We're going to eat our slop and get our sleep.'

'You can't just... What about Brand?'

'Someone came, a runner. Brand went away with him. The filth were all down in the vat, so there was no reason to worry. Haven't seen him since.'

Becket could see a thought spring up behind the crewboss's eyes. I will not die today. 'You gonna dump the body?'

'It's going to be dumped. It's going to be burned, and then it's for the void, with all the rest of the filth.'

NINE

In the chapel of the lower decks, the lector drew his sermon to a close and beckoned his congregation to rise and repeat with him those mysterious High Gothic words of prayer.

'Vaughn doesn't have a clue what to do,' Efrem muttered to his neighbour in their native tongue. 'Trust me, Kimeal, I can tell. Doing you know what, he's done for us all. They're just waiting now, waiting for one of us to slip, watching us.'

Efrem nodded at the strange faces in the assembly. Since there were so few of them left, another work crew was sharing services with them. However, this wasn't another convict work crew, these were trusted crew, proper ratings, and they had been sneaking glances at the conscripts for the entire service. They hadn't been the only ones over the last few days.

'You worry too much, Efrem.'

'Yeah? What happened to Zwebba then? Where's he been since it happened?'

'I don't know.'

'Maybe he's there, now, speaking out against all of us. What about the other bosses? They've all been changed.'

'Zwebba's not going to talk. It would be the end of him, and the others can't admit they weren't there. They're going to have to agree with whatever he says.'

'Why're you even taking orders from him, Kimeal? Before the pipe room you were one of the top men on the shift, and what was Vaughn? He was nothing, just that kid Ronah's weird translator. I don't understand why you put up with it.'

'That's right. You don't understand. I get it, Efrem. Believe me, I get it. I feel the weight of it, the fear, the guilt. If you think you can bargain for mercy in the Perga then you're a fool.'

'It's not mercy, it's justice.'

'They're not interested in justice, only order. What happened, it was practicality, Brand or us, nothing more, and he got enough of us before we finally wised up.'

'Whatever you say,' Efrem snorted. 'Don't know why I expected more from a white-livered urbo like you. We'll see if Sundjata thinks the same.'

'He does,' Kimeal said, sitting down as the last complex words of the prayer echoed away. 'He's the one who convinced me.'

It had been three shifts since they'd killed Brand, and five days since the shift in the piperoom. Seventy-eight men had died in a flash, but the authorities had not even blinked. They had simply repaired the damage and moved on. The same could not be said, however, of what had happened to Brand. For a conscript to strike a crewboss was to forfeit his life. The crewboss was immaterial on a ship of ten thousand, but the strike at the system truly mattered. The system gave them shelter. It kept them fed. The system kept the ship whole and safe as it traversed the void. If a conscript could strike a crewboss without swift punishment then the system would fall apart, and yet it had been three shifts since they'd killed Brand, and still nothing had happened.

Three nights had passed for the conscripts to relive those events and feed their anxiety about the consequences, what could happen to them, and the severity of the punishment that they could face. One word hung in the air in every conversation, left understood, implicit, and never spoken: mutiny.

They had had no indication that the story of Brand's disappearance had not been accepted. The shift had been put to work, fed and rested to the same schedule. The system was not concerned if a Brand disappeared into the ghost-decks or was taken by the inhabitants of the Perga. The system had plenty more Brands.

Do not bother with the lie that needs to be believed, Becket knew. Give them the lie that is easy to accept. The acceptable lie of the shuttle accident was how the officers had murdered him, after all, and the acceptable lie that he must have burned in the fire was how he had survived.

That was the way it went. The system, unharmed, prepared to move on. That was, until someone took a personal interest.

THE MESSENGER CAME for Becket on the fourth day. It was the same boy that had come for Asheel all those weeks ago. Fifteen new crewbosses had appeared at shakeout, each one suited, armoured, and armed with a baton and shield. The shift tensed, both terrified and relieved that the end had finally come. Becket paused for a moment in consideration, and then calmly stood them down with a gesture.

The messenger led him away with two of the trusted crew falling in behind. They marched him away from the conscript areas, prow-ward, heading towards the front of the ship, but they had not travelled far when they halted and ushered him through a side-hatch marked with the insignia of a security station.

The air carried the lingering, bitter odour of the common scrap the crewmen chewed, mixed with stale sweat. A man was inside, he wore a black coat, but it was not the commissar. He was sitting on one side of a thin fold-down table, and raised a hand to indicate the opposite chair.

'Sit down, captain.'

Becket did not move. The black-coat, with leisurely care, repeated his command.

'Why do you call me that?' Becket asked.

'That is what they call you, isn't it? Your shift? They call you their captain, don't they.'

'No, they don't.'

The black-coat didn't blink.

'In that case, sit down, scum.'

Becket sat. His two escorts bent his hands around the back of the chair and tied them tight.

'Names are important, don't you think?' The black-coat continued, 'You call a man a captain and you will see one side of him. You call a man scum and you see another. You call a man a victim, then that is what he is. You call a man a killer, then that is what he has become.'

'What do I call you?' Becket interrupted.

If he was thrown off his stride, the black-coat did not show it.

'Names are important. For example, the name for what we're having now is a conversation, but that could change very quickly if it does not proceed to my satisfaction.'

Becket was securely fastened, and he felt a sharp pain in his shoulder as one of the escorts plunged a needle in and injected a drug.

'Just something to help keep the conversation going, nothing to concern yourself about.'

Becket grimaced as the chemical made its way through his body. He felt his thoughts closing in. It felt like a sedative, but who knew what else was in there? The black-coat dismissed the escorts with a nod, and then drew a knife.

It could not possibly be Brand's knife; that must have been floating light-years distant in the void somewhere. It looked damned similar though. He laid the knife down on the table between them.

'Now, let us talk about Crewboss Brand.'

Becket knew better than to offer information without being asked. Tough it out. If he could get through this subordinate then he could get to see the commissar, the man who could save him. No doubt the black-coat would want to spin it out and try to trap him by tricking him into contradicting himself.

'You killed Crewboss Brand, you and your shift-mates, and then you threw the body out with the trash.'

Or perhaps not.

'Nothing to say?' The black-coat peered, unimpressed, at him.

'You didn't ask me a question.'

'You don't care to deny it?'

'We didn't do it.'

The black-coat laughed. 'Careful, scum. That's the second time you've lied to me.'

'I didn't ask you a question,' he continued, 'because I don't need to. The junior crewboss, Zwebba, he's told us everything.'

'If that's what he told you then he was lying.'

'You think we believe that Brand just wandered away? Ran off to the ghost-decks? Brand had been onboard this ship for fifteen years. He started off as a conscript, just like you. He worked his way up, fought his way up. He never backed down from a fight, not in all those years, and this is what he gets.'

What was the black-coat talking about? He did not sound as if he was conducting a cold, impersonal investigation on behalf of the commissar. This was personal. Emperor's breath! Becket realised that the black-coat wasn't from the Perga. He wasn't a route to the commissar. He was one of the work crews, one of Brand's allies getting even, and that meant that Becket was in serious trouble.

'I didn't do anything to Brand,' he muttered, beginning to tug at the ropes that bound his hands.

'Of course you did. We've been watching. It's obvious, the way your shift look at you that you're their leader, their captain. I tell you what though, give me a name. Give me the name of one of the men that you want to save. The others, they're on their way already, but if you're quick maybe they can leave one of them spare.'

The black-coat paused for a moment to let his captive absorb the news. They did not want just him; they wanted the entire shift.

'No? No one? Don't leave it too long. It won't be long before they've finished with them and then they'll be here. It takes a little time to get everyone together so the officers don't notice. That's why I had to keep you safe here, so that nothing happens to you, until everyone can enjoy it.' The knife was in his hand again. 'That being said, I'm sure they wouldn't mind if I took a little... something.'

He broke off in the middle of his sentence, Becket heard the muffled thump of meat hitting meat from outside in the corridor. The door-seal suddenly started to spin, and then flew open. A man stood, silhouetted in the dark room by the bright corridor lights behind. At his feet lay the slumped unconscious forms of the guards.

'You bloody blasted, Jakobus. What d'you think you're doing in here?'

'Ferrol!' the black-coat exclaimed, 'this is none of your concern. I have authority here–'

He squeaked as Ferrol crossed the room in a step, seized Jakobus by the front of his shirt and heaved him out of his chair.

'I'm making it my concern. As for your authority, you can shove it up your arse!' Ferrol replied, shoving him up against the wall. 'It's just like a little rat like you to try to go around everyone else and get to him first. What was in it for you, eh? Going to sell him on, were you?'

'You can't touch me, Ferrol!' Jakobus tried to break free of the tight grip, 'You know what will happen if you touch me–'

Ferrol punched the struggling man smartly in the gut. Jakobus's eyes bulged, and then he groaned gently as he doubled over and slid to the floor. Ferrol looked down at him.

"Spose I do now.'

He turned to Becket for the first time.

'Are you coming or what?'

FERROL LED THE way as they stepped quickly out into the corridor and away from the security station. Becket heard Ferrol talking, talking to him, but he couldn't clear his head. Ferrol grabbed him and shook him back to his senses.

'You're Vaughn, right?'

'Right,' replied Becket.

'You're right in it, you know? In it up to your neck.' Ferrol grabbed Becket by his shoulder and pushed him on.

'Wait! My men... My shift, they–'

'Yeah, they're in it too. That's why we've got to get back there quickly before–'

A shout from back down the corridor cut through the sentence, and Ferrol ran without looking round, hauling Becket with him.

'Blasted men've got thicker skulls than I thought,' Ferrol muttered as they shot around the corner, grabbed a deck ladder and slid down. 'You! Vaughn! Lot of people looking for you.'

'I know. Some of them already found me.'

'Hah! Jakobus, he's the least of your troubles. We're running from the floggers he's calling.'

'Who are they then?'

'If you don't shut it and run then you'll find out.'

Ferrol reached another deck ladder and started to climb. Becket reached forward, caught him in an iron grip, dragged him down and fixed his eyes with his own.

'And who exactly are you?'

Ferrol grabbed Becket back with equal force.

'I'm the best friend you'll ever have,' he said, and knocked Becket's hands away. 'Now, are we going to save your men or are you going to keep on black-capping me?'

Becket held his gaze and then let him go.

'Lead on.'

BECKET HAD CAREFULLY memorised the route his escorts had taken, but Ferrol ran the corridors with the confidence of easy familiarity, taking back-routes to keep them out of sight, and slipping into empty cabins or maintenance hatches whenever they heard the sounds of someone approaching. Each stop they had to make increased Becket's frustration. There had been a shout as they ran. They knew he had escaped, and his men were helplessly at their mercy. A single vox and the armsmen who held his men could shoot them down.

'Ever since we broke orbit from Pontus,' Ferrol said as they went, 'the deck-crews have been at each other's throats. Once the officers stopped coming down here, the old order tried to put themselves back in charge. 'Course, there were others who thought that it was time for a change, thought they deserved the top jobs more. They've been sniping at each other for weeks. They may not have wanted Brand in their crews, but the scunner was a good excuse. Couple of the crews think that if they can make an example of the one that did him in, that's you by the way, then they jump a few levels in the pecking order, if you get my meaning.'

'I understand, Ferrol, but we're already too late. Those men who took me to Jakobus, there were more left guarding my men. I thought they were just there to make sure they didn't come after me, but–'

'I sent a few of my lads ahead. They'll have sorted them out, don't you worry.'

They could hear the noise corridors away, the noise of dozens of men, angry men. Ferrol brought Becket to a halt.

'See, what did I tell you? The door's sealed. Your crew is okay for now.'

There was a giant crack from down the hall, the sound of a door being forced, a cheer from the work crews baying for blood, and then a loud scream from the first of them, as he found the defenders far better prepared than he had anticipated.

Ferrol caught Becket before he could run forwards. 'Wait a moment.'

Ferrol pressed a small button on his collar, and a few moments later more men started to appear from behind him. More trusted crewmen, but these were wearing the same colours as Ferrol, and each one carried a heavy tool, primarily designed for intra-ship maintenance, but equally effective at causing a hefty amount of damage to any person on the wrong end of it.

'This is my crew,' Ferrol said, with not a little pride in his voice. Becket recognised them. They were the same crew who had shared service with them the day before.

'You've been watching us.'

'We've been watching those watching you,' Ferrol replied. 'Now lads, not got long. Let's get stuck in.'

Becket picked up the buzz amongst Ferrol's men. The imminence of combat made the blood thunder in his head. He was once more the young lieutenant, leading the men of his boarding party into the teeth of the enemy's guns. He was the veteran commander, urging troops into the breach of the heretic's fortress. He was the captain, driving his ship into the heart of the enemy fleet, every cannon firing until the hands of the gunners blistered at the heat of the barrels.

'Forward!' he cried, instinctively stepping to the fore and advancing towards the sounds of the enemy. 'At them! At them!'

'You heard what the man said!' Ferrol shouted, falling in with Becket's pace.

'*Relentless!*' Becket cried.

'*Relentless!*' the crew roared.

Becket turned the corner and caught sight of the foe for the first time. They packed the corridor outside the holding chamber where his crew was barricaded. They were crowded around the fallen door, pushing their way in. They were Navy men, trusted crew. Men who weeks before would have greeted Becket with a smart salute and eyes fixed front, now met him with faces twisted in anger and eyes shot red with rage.

Becket charged forwards, his body flowing with the fighting instincts of his youth. His surprised opponents were only just turning to meet this new force. They were strong and well prepared, but they were concentrated around the door, not expecting to be attacked from behind. They were vulnerable. In his last few steps before the two lines made contact, Becket dropped his shoulder into a charge. It caught the man in the front rank full in the chest, battering past his guard and launching him into the row behind. Becket powered up and forward, driving both men back until the first tripped and fell upon the other. Becket pushed into the third row, and came face to face with a pug-like bruiser, who was already raising a hook claw to bring it crashing down on the captain's head. Becket was helpless for a moment, his momentum gone. Then he felt an almighty shove in the back, which drove him forward, head down. His temple smashed straight into the bridge of the bruiser's nose, and blood splattered Becket's face. It wasn't his own.

The bruiser disappeared, falling from view, as one after another of Ferrol's men piled in behind. Head up, Becket's instincts screamed at him, find your footing, fall and you'll be crushed by them too. He slammed his foot down against whatever was beneath him. It met something soft, but Becket forced it further, until it met resistance, and then he launched off.

There was no room for weapons since every man was jammed tight. Becket swung his elbows wildly to keep his arms free and punched hard at the faces before him. When his arms were pinned by his side, he struck out with his legs, kicking at ankles and knees, anything to get his foe to the ground. A falling man held tight to him and threatened to drag him down, but there was Ferrol, catching his arm and steadying him before delivering a sucker punch to a rating swinging a sledgehammer at Becket's head.

Pushed back and back, one of the foe turned to run, and then another, and then more. It became a rout. One of them, with the swagger and bark of a crewboss, tried to rally them, crying, 'Morley's Men! Morley's Men to me!' But the few who turned did not stand for long before they too scurried back to the bowels of the ship.

ONCE THE FIGHTING was over, Becket was first into the holding chamber. Half a dozen strangers instantly brought their weapons up and held them in his face. They only relaxed when they saw Ferrol come in behind.

'Keep 'em down, lads,' Ferrol ordered as he pushed through. A small dark-skinned woman at the front, hefting a heavy-duty nail gun against her hip, stood ready to report.

'Master.'

'Shroot, how did it go?'

'Well enough, sir, well enough. Turns out that Jakobus's men didn't want any trouble, which was fine by us as trouble was what we had come for.'

The strange men around her laughed, each one of them casually holding an improvised, but no less deadly, weapon. As they laughed, Becket looked past them. Someone was down on the deck. It looked like Sundjata, and Kimeal was kneeling down beside him, pressing a piece of cloth to his head. All the rest of his shift-mates were around them, safe and whole.

'Vaughn, get your crew over here. We've got to push off while we've still got a chance.'

His crew came to meet him, shaking his hand and clasping his arm as though they half believed he wasn't real.

'What happened here?' Becket asked, looking down at Sundjata.

Papeway stepped in, 'Caught him awkward. Went down hard. Still breathing, though. We'll just have to see when he wakes up.'

'We take him with us, as best we can,' Becket ordered, and the shift set to work improvising a stretcher. Fidler came over.

'You should have seen them in action, boss,' Fidler grinned, nodding over to the woman Shroot and the rest of Ferrol's crew. 'That one, the girl, she walked in, bold as anything. First one of them floggers who challenged her, she put two nails through his foot. Phut! Phut! Got their attention right off, she did! Should have seen them, boss.'

'Don't call me that.'

'Oh, 'course, yeah, Vaughn.'

ONCE THEY WERE safely away, nothing could prevent the two groups from celebrating their victory. Ferrol's crew generously shared what they had with Becket's men, who could not praise their saviours enough. The rations were basic, but it had been nearly two months since any of the conscripts had had anything other than slop and hard bread. It was only when the celebrations quietened that Becket had a chance to sit down and talk with Ferrol privately.

'Who's this Morley?' Becket asked.

'Who's Morley?' Ferrol laughed. 'You don't know who Morley is?'

'Is there something funny about that?'

'Not at all, Vaughn, not at all. Don't take it personal. They keep you conscripts sealed up tight. Morley's a lowborn scunner. He hasn't got much, but he's an aggressive blasted, I'll give him that. The deck-crew he heads up want to make a bit of a name for themselves. Ever since we left Pontus, they've been looking to expand, get better assignments, move up the ship. Morley's been pushing around some of the smaller crews like us, having a few scraps, trying to get them to sign up with him. The more trusted crewmen you've got signed up, the more you can draw in rations and pay, and the more duties you can take. Of course, with you he thought he'd hit the jackpot.'

'Because they think I was the one who made Brand disappear.'

'If he could be the one to take you down, then he'd be in business. Everyone would be talking about him. He could double his complement of trusted crew if he wanted.'

'And you don't?' Becket asked, realising that they were at the crux of it. Ferrol had done him and his men a great service, but that did not mean he could trust him.

Ferrol heard the suspicion in Becket's voice. 'That's not our way, Vaughn. We didn't go up against Morley to turn you in ourselves. We just needed to clip his wings a bit, get him off our backs for a while. My men and I, we're not like the others. We're not a deck-crew, not like the others at least. We're a real crew.'

'Of a ship?' Becket asked, a piece of the puzzle that was Ferrol fell into place. 'That's why some of your men call you master. You're a shipmaster?'

'Used to be. Used to be. The *Moreno*. She was as ugly as a scow's backside, but I thought she was beautiful. High-grade goods transport. Never much room on her. She weren't big, but she was home.'

'What happened to her?'

Ferrol's faced darkened. 'She was taken.'

'Raiders?'

Ferrol let out a hollow laugh. 'Raiders? I never let no bloody raiders take my *Moreno*. No, it was the floggin'

battlefleet that took her. She got commandeered in port.
Fleet said they needed her for a war. I said that there
weren't no war around here. They wouldn't need the
Moreno for a war anyway. Couldn't carry a regiment,
couldn't carry supplies enough to make her worth the
while. No armour, guns or shields. No, they were blowing plasma dust, probably a Fleet bigwig who couldn't get
a ride any other way.

'Oh, I got their compensation, right. Not much use to
me without a ship, and there were no ships to buy. I need
a ship to work. Without work, half the crew left, took
their share. Those who stayed with me, we had to sign on
with a mass cargo hauler bound for Pontus. We got here,
came down to the surface to see what could be bought,
got pressed and that was that.'

Ferrol fell silent. Becket did not know what to say. He
knew such things happened, and by the Emperor, they
could be far worse. When the great threats rose, when the
sector was endangered, worlds were devastated and entire
battlefleets were mobilised to the fight. At those times,
each ship, every ship would be pressed to its defence.
Those that could be would be converted into warships,
their engines pushed to their brink to power weapons
and shields. Their power systems were so overloaded that
they as often destroyed themselves as their enemy, and
they took their crews with them. Those that couldn't be
converted were made to run the supply routes, and left
vulnerable to the raiding parties of the foe as well as the
normal xenos pirates that swarm to battlefronts looking
for booty.

There was a role as system defence for even the most
decrepit, or in the last resort as fireships, filled to the
brim with explosives, and for those their only hope was
that with their deaths they might scratch their enemy.

When the Emperor called, men were expected to sacrifice both their ships and their lives in humanity's defence,
just as He had done. Becket had never seen so great a

threat that it would cause a battlefleet to fully mobilise for war, and by the Imperial Will he never would.

'So, master, yes,' Ferrol started up again. 'Some of them, the ones who like to remember the good days, call me Master Ferrol.'

Becket found himself watching the door again.

'You don't need to worry, Vaughn. You'll be safe enough here, for tonight at least. Morley and the others'll be too busy licking their wounds and trying to keep their own in line.'

'They'll be back, though, Morley's lot, or someone else.'

Ferrol took another swig. 'You're the catch of the day, my friend. Give it a few months to calm down. Head down to the ghost-decks, that's what I say.'

Becket shook his head. 'I can't. I need to get up to the top decks.'

'The top decks? You won't get anywhere near them.'

'I know, I know, but if I can make it past the Perga, then at least I'll have a chance.'

'The Perga? There are ways around that, but unless you're one of the deck-crews you'll never make it. Take my advice, there's nothing up there. Whatever you think is up there for you, leave it be.'

'A deck-crew? You're a deck-crew.'

'Oh no, Vaughn, oh no. You're a marked man, didn't you hear me say so? I only pulled your fat from the fire once so as to stop Morley and his lot getting above themselves.'

'You think they won't find us on the ghost-decks? Why did you bother if it was just to delay the inevitable for a few days? Why did you bother?' Becket demanded, exasperated.

'Why did I bother? Because Brand shouldn't have been allowed to get away with what he did!' Ferrol snapped back. 'And you shouldn't be strung up for taking him down. There's a lot of bad in this galaxy, but some things are just plain wrong.'

Both men paused for a moment after the outburst.

'Listen, Ferrol,' Becket began, 'you help me with this and I'll help you and your crew.'

'How are you going to do that?'

'I'll help you with your escape.'

'Our what? Escape?'

'This is not your first time serving onboard a battlefleet warship, is it Ferrol? You've been onboard the *Relentless* for a few weeks, and you're already climbing the ladder as though you were born to it. You've served before, and that means you must have escaped before. That means you're looking to escape now, or am I wrong about you?' Becket knew he wasn't wrong, it was exactly what Ronah had seen in him.

Ferrol stared at Becket hard. 'No,' he said at length, 'you're not wrong, but what can you do?'

'Access codes to the launch bays.'

'You know them?'

'I can get them, and more. In return, you get me to the top decks, and you make me and my shift part of the deck-crew.'

'Your shift as well? Forget it. I get rations and pay for trusted crew, not conscripts. You, all right, but not the rest. Do you even know who you have there? Who they are? What they did to be onboard this ship?'

'It doesn't matter. They're my men. It's my condition.'

Ferrol leaned back and ran a hand through his short hair. 'I suppose, if it comes to another fight then we could use the extra hands.' He pursed his lips with a look of thoughtful deliberation.

'Vaughn, you have a deal, but I've got a condition of my own.'

'What's that?'

'No one, absolutely no one, joins my crew without swearing themselves to me, no exceptions and no allowances. I cannot be the master of a crew whose loyalties are divided. For your men, that means I cannot have them looking to you every time I give them an order. For you, that means you don't go up there until I say we're ready. I don't know what you're planning to do, but I'll bet it has the potential to bring the Emperor's own shit storm down on our heads, so only when we're ready. That's the only way this is going to work.'

'An oath of honour? Down here?' Becket almost scoffed.

'You think it's funny? So do a lot of others, but I think, for you, it'll actually mean something. Do you agree to it?'

Becket hesitated. He had never wanted his command of conscripts, but now he found it was harder than he thought to give it up. But Ferrol could put him on the road to reclaim what was his. Which was the greater priority?

'Agreed.'

BECKET LAY AWAKE in the unfamiliar bunk. His body had grown so accustomed to sleeping only after collapsing in exhaustion that, now, he found his mind would not settle.

He knew so little of his men, and yet he had been so quick to take command, and so fierce in their defence. They were his, and if they were his they must be worthy. The *Relentless* had been taken from him so violently and since then he had been allowed nothing to call his own: not a space, not the smallest object, not even the few clothes he stood in. The Emperor in His Grace had offered him command again, be it ever so meagre, and he had seized it with both hands.

It was a command that he should have baulked at. Conscripts were tithe-recruits, men 'granted' to the Fleet by the planetary governor to fulfil his Imperial obligations. To avoid the worst excesses, battlefleet had strict criteria on the calibre of man that they required, but it made little difference. It was a golden opportunity for the governors who could fill the ships to the brim with the detritus of their societies, and battlefleet would kindly take it all away. Criminals, subversives, agitators and those unfortunate enough to incur the governor's displeasure, but who were not worth the time and trouble of execution, all flowed out from the prisons and the madhouses and were never heard of again. The recruits were often eager for it, as they were told that it was a second chance, a fresh beginning, a parole from their internment. They played along with those who came to teach them how to pass the Fleet's screening process, enjoyed the extra rations offered to build up their weight, and repeated the lies that they had been instructed to tell. By the end of it, some of them even believed that battlefleet would give them a better life and for a very few, by the Emperor, it was even true.

A soft footfall drew his attention to the far end of the barracks. It was that woman, Shroot was her name, stepping quietly into Ferrol's quarters. Predictable enough, Becket assumed, for the two of them to have such a relationship. Women on ship almost invariably had a patron, even on the lower decks it seemed. Shroot, however, was nothing like the officers' toys or the molls of the shiftbosses. Becket had watched how Ferrol had spoken with her earlier in the evening. He did not talk to her as though she were part of his entourage, he spoke to her as a commander does to a second. So, perhaps there was more to this clandestine visit than met the eye.

'This wasn't part of the deal.'

'I know, Shroot.'

'Twenty-four new crew... this might work with just him, but not with all of them.' The woman shook her head. 'One we could learn, one we might be able to trust, but not all of them.'

'You sure about that? Do you think any of them want to be here?'

'You sure that not one of them wouldn't sell us at the first opportunity for a safe berth from the Perga? And what about the shiftbosses?'

'They don't want the men. They don't want the mouths. We're still bursting full of the dirtfoots netted from Pontus.'

'They'll want their cut, though? About Brand?'

'He's not guilty.'

'Hah, how do you figure that?'

'Trial by combat, Shroot. He won, and Morley ran. That makes him not guilty in my book.'

'If you want people to care what's in your book then start your own religion. If a shiftboss thinks he's got something coming to him then someone's gonna pay. We've made a lot of fast friends on this ship, we've risen quick, too quick for some, and we've got the man. They're gonna expect from us.'

'They're bloody hypocrites. They didn't want Brand when he was alive. The conscript chains was the only work he could get.'

'That's why they'll settle for payment, and not blood.'

'If payment's what they want, then I'll pay it, Shroot. It's worth it to get him.'

Shroot paused for a moment, choosing her words with care. There were some things that Ferrol had to understand.

'These men are gonna cost you. Now, the crew has stayed tight and true with you, through a lot of foul skies and worse, but don't go getting these dirtfoots confused with us.'

Ferrol took a moment. Shroot was never less than frank with him, he relied on it as much as he respected it, but she always maintained an attitude that was as hard as the bolts in the nail gun she wore on her belt. It was rare for her to group herself with the rest of the crew when she spoke of their spirits.

'Is that your mind or the rest of them as well?'

'Doesn't matter, it's going to be their mind when you tell them tomorrow that we're bunking up with the dirt-foots for the duration.'

'Ah,' Ferrol paused. Shroot had already guessed what he had decided, 'I see you know my thoughts before I do.'

'Like that's such a challenge,' she muttered, breaking the gaze and looking down, adjusting her holster. 'Just don't forget us, is all. It's gonna be tough on us too.'

'Trust me, Shroot, it's not going to be a patch on what the dirtfoots are going to face,' Ferrol replied. 'Did you stop in on Jakobus, by the way?'

'I did. He sends his regards, and a promise to pay you back for that gut-punch you gave him the next time you two cross paths on a dark deck.' Ferrol laughed, even as she continued. 'He wants to know when he'll get paid.'

'He did well. Take it round to him tomorrow, early, before the shifts change.'

'He might ask for more… for the gut-shot.'

'Then offer him another one,' Ferrol replied breezily. He dismissed her with a nod of the head. 'Fair skies, Shroot.'

'Fair skies, master,' she said as she walked out of the cabin.

TEN

ACTING SUB-LIEUTENANT Baisan looked at the chronometer on the wall and sighed. This would take a while. He had had plans to stop off at the Junior Officers' Mess that evening after his shift. Gawdon had just last night revealed that he still had a batch of ashrajeed left over from his man on Sinope, and that he was in a gambling mood. Yes, yes, it had been something that Baisan had been greatly anticipating, but now Lieutenant Aryll had pushed this dratted incident his way.

He flicked through the reports on the desk that Aryll had given him. It was all tediously familiar reading: some sort of fight had broken out between two rating crews. On the top there was Aryll's initial assessment, and he had marked the incident as worth 'further investigation', a further reminder that 'regulations must be upheld at all times' and that, especially having so recently taken on new labourers, 'examples must be made'. Beneath that was the meat of it: a rather colourful account of the incident from a rating whom Baisan presumed was one of the lieutenant's paid informants looking to engender some goodwill. There were no names, of course, nothing as useful as that amongst the ill-constructed prose. Finally, there was the medicae report that was there to add some legitimacy to the entire affair. The medicae said that several men had been brought to him at the time, all suffering from injuries caused by blunt instruments. None of the men said anything about a fight, of course. The lower orders were notoriously tight-lipped unless money, women or liquor were involved. The medicae had dutifully appended their explanation of a 'serious tumble' from a maintenance rig, and had gone on to emphasise his own opinion of the likely cause.

Normally, Baisan would not have bothered with the whole affair, passing it down to his shiftbosses to present him with the culprits. However, Aryll held the keys to his promotion to full sub-lieutenant. Baisan knew that he had to impress with something before the next round of advancements because Acting Sub-Lieutenant Ortus had been buttering Aryll up for months, trying to edge him out of the running.

In any case, this kind of behaviour was all too much. The common crew should be saving their energies for their duties, not getting into rucks with one another. The Emperor knew they were slothful enough when he gave them orders to carry out. No, his duty was clear. He would have to postpone the appointment with Gawdon for another time. This investigation would have to be thorough and exacting, and he would tackle it personally. He would present Aryll with the culprits and let it be known, plain and simple, that on his shifts the regulations would be upheld on all occasions.

He knew that he had a special talent for extracting the truth, especially from the lower orders, who could hardly be expected to match his intellect and ability. If the Emperor had determined that his path should be a little different, Baisan knew without a doubt, that he would be wearing the black coat and cap of the Emperor's honoured commissars by now.

A face appeared at his door. It was the first interviewee, and by the Golden Throne he was a ragged one. He looked at Baisan in dumb askance and the acting sub-lieutenant ordered him in with a curt gesture. This was the one that all the scuttlebutt had been about. Baisan would not normally have listened to it, after all, the power of his insight and observation would be more than sufficient. He was, however, a firm believer that there was no smoke without fire, and the proverbial smoke was simply pouring off this one.

'What's your name?'

'Ferrol, sir. Trusted crewman, sir.'

'Yes, yes, I see that, Crewman Ferrol.'

'Sir.'

'I've been ordered to investigate reports we've received of an altercation.'

Baisan let the words hang in the air, giving the crewman a chance to confess his guilt or, more likely, construct some ludicrous lie in a pathetic attempt to exonerate himself. The crewman kept silent though, body, face, eyes, all unmoving. Perhaps, the officer considered, he was too ignorant to understand the word.

'A brawl, that is, involving some of your men.'

'A brawl, sir?'

'Yes, yes, a brawl, Crewman Ferrol, which–'

'I find that very concerning, sir,' Ferrol interrupted.

'Concerning?' Baisan repeated, taken off guard, 'Yes, yes, indeed, very concerning, and obviously–'

'Strictly against regulation, sir. Very serious matter, sir.'

'Yes, yes, it is–'

'It should be investigated at once.'

'Well, that's what I–'

'If some of my lads were set upon by assailants and then were forced to defend themselves, steps must be taken. I mean, sir, if I may, sir, it's all very well that they feel the bonds of shipboard loyalty prevent them from reporting their attackers to the proper authorities. It's commendable in its way, but the regulations must be respected, and it's a point of their duty to the Emperor, sir, to identify these transgressors and allow them to be punished.'

Baisan sat there, his mouth slightly open as he tried to catch up with the conversation.

'I'm very glad that you brought this to my attention, sir.' Ferrol dropped his gaze from eyes forward and took a step towards the desk.

'What? Oh, good, good–'

'Are these the reports, sir?' Ferrol snagged them from the desk and started examining them closely with a serious frown upon his face.

'Actually, I don't think that–'

Ferrol's eyes flashed up again.

'I presume that you'll want a report of my findings within twenty-four hours, sir.'

'What? Oh? Oh!' In his mind, the conversation suddenly clicked back onto its tracks. 'Yes, yes, twenty-four hours, crewman, without fail.'

'Yes, sir.'

'This is a very serious matter, crewman. Regulations must be respected.'

'Yes, sir.'

'This is your responsibility, crewman. You must find out what happened. It must be investigated at once.'

'Yes, sir.'

'I shall expect your report within twenty– No, I shall expect it within twelve hours.'

'Twelve hours, sir?'

'Yes, yes, twelve hours, crewman. Are you deaf? At once means at once.'

'Twelve hours. Yes, sir. Very good, sir.'

'Good. Good.' Baisan stared at Ferrol as he stood in front of him, unmoving. 'Well? Dismissed!'

'Yes, sir.' Ferrol pulled a snappy salute, turned on his heel and marched out.

Baisan shook his head. The cheek of the man, questioning his orders, trying to lollygag and waste time. Did this scum take him for a fool? He checked the chronometer on the wall. Why, he had dealt with it all far quicker than he had thought. He would have time to stop in at the mess after all.

'STEADY AS SHE GOES, Mister Crichell,' Commander Ward directed. 'Keep her straight and level.'

'Aye, commander.'

'Mister Kirick, how long until we are within range?'

'Longest effective range in fifty-five seconds, sir.'

'Good,' Ward replied. It had been nearly a week since the last promising contact and he had become increasingly impatient. He had no doubts as to the loyalty of his bridge officers, but he also knew that every Navy man, no matter how sober and rational, had a streak of superstition. It couldn't be helped, part and parcel of staring into the infinite each day. Even those who had not been involved in the conspiracy felt the tinge of ill-fate around this voyage, with the loss of the captain, the others in the shuttle and then the magos majoris in such quick succession. Ward knew that it was vital to present them with the rewards of victory as soon as possible. However, it was beyond even his power to conjure luxury laden cargo vessels to inspect and tithe out of thin air.

'Any ident information on the target, Mister Aster?'

'Not yet, sir.'

'I want it within thirty seconds, understand me? Ah, Guir,' he said as the lieutenant commander settled into the seat beside him, 'our quarry for the day is being coy with us.'

Guir grunted in acknowledgement and kept his attention on the forward view-portal. Lieutenant Commander Guir, Ward decided, was becoming entirely too inflated

with his own self-importance. He had been acting sec-
ond-in-command ever since the old captain had so sadly
passed on, and now he was so again. What more had he
expected from his complicity? Beyond his endorsement,
Ward had no more control over his promotion than he
had over the comings and goings of the merchant fleet.

Guir caught Ward's irked look from the corner of his
eye. The commander had become increasingly short-
tempered and irrational since they had left Pontus. Guir
had hoped that once they had returned to their familiar
routine, Ward would calm down a little, but if anything
the reverse had been true. The dark thought lurked at the
back of Guir's mind: if Ward was capable of killing a
captain then removing any of the rest of them would
present him with no difficulty whatsoever.

'I have ident confirmations, sir,' Aster reported. 'It is the
Arc of Elona. Cogitators confirm that she is in our records.'

Ward looked down as the data scrolled across his
screen and his eyes lit up. A choice target, it was about
time.

'Mister Keister.' The newly promoted bridge officer
looked up. 'Full scans of the target, confirm against our
records. Complete threat assessment.'

'Yes, sir.' There was a touch of hesitancy in the reply as
Keister grappled with his console.

'Guir,' Ward muttered to his second, and nodded in the
direction of the struggling auspex officer. Guir went to
stand over his shoulder.

'Entering longest effective range, sir,' Kirick reported.

'Mister Aster, begin communication,' the first officer
ordered. 'Mister Keister, any movement yet?'

'Nothing yet,' Guir replied.

'Risk assessment, sir,' Keister piped up, 'minimal
armour and shields. No significant weaponry. Vital systems operational, engines online, but unengaged.'

Ward could imagine the chaos on the target's command deck with an Imperial warship bearing down upon

them, and orders and counter-orders being thrown around. They could not run, and they could not fight. Surrender was their only option.

'Mister Aster, any response?'

'No, sir.'

'Entering maximum effective range, commander.'

'No activity? Nothing at all?'

'No, sir.'

'Mister Keister, confirm their operational systems and active scans. Do they even know we're here?'

'Yes, sir. We are receiving hits from active scans. Our auspex shows all systems operational, vox array online, hull at full... Wait, there's something.' New lines ran across his screen. 'That can't be right.'

'What, Mister Keister? Mister Guir?'

Guir pulled the console away from Keister.

'Auspex shows a single hull breach. Zero systems operational. Zero active auspex hits. Zero engine signals,' Guir replied quickly.

'What?' Ward was out of the captain's chair.

'It's drifting, sir.'

'The cargo?' In a flash, Ward saw his chance to start rebuilding his collection vanish.

'Cargo bays appear... intact.'

There were no sweeter words to Ward's ears.

'Ready the launch bays. Senior Armsman Vickers, prepare your squad to board the derelict. We cannot allow whoever perpetrated this atrocity to escape. The glorious traditions of the *Relentless* forbid it.'

SENIOR ARMSMAN VICKERS floated gently down a deserted corridor aboard the *Arc of Elona*. It was dark, only his suit lights illuminating the path ahead, and it was quiet. It wasn't just quiet, it was absolutely silent. All Vickers could hear were the sounds of his breath and his heart. The omnipresent hum of the engines was gone. They were dead, and the auxiliary generators were drained so there was no power. No power meant no lights and no gravity. It meant that his squads were having to laboriously open every door and hatch by hand, a process made even more difficult by the bulky spacesuits they had to wear as the ship had lost its atmosphere. They had not even been able to find a cargo manifest, so every bay and every container had to be checked individually. As a result, their progress was interminably slow.

The first officer, however, did not appear to mind. In fact, as Vickers reported their findings back to him through their private channel, Ward grew increasingly pleased. The information Ward had intercepted about the rich cargo the *Arc of Elona* carried had been borne out, and, as the ship had been declared a derelict, he could claim all of it. It had taken Ward years to build up what he called his 'collection', and while Vickers was never sure of its true extent, a haul of this size would surely go a long way to rebuild it. More than that, the bounty he would be able to dole out to the officers would ensure their loyalty for the rest of the patrol. Vickers, as usual, would receive nothing, except perhaps a single item he might specifically request. That was the price he paid for the first officer's silence and protection from those who would otherwise destroy him.

He reached a junction, and pushed off down one of the branches. The cargo in the main holds was plentiful enough, but there would be more hidden somewhere. There always was.

He was eager to find it quickly and get off the derelict. It was not just that the crew was missing, no survivors, not even any bodies, it also troubled Vickers to see a ship, any ship, in such a condition. His faith did not lie with the Emperor. The Emperor was not a god of his kind. Those local gods he had been taught as a child had been weak, distant, a story, and they did not deserve his faith. When he had first seen the *Relentless*, however, through a transport's porthole, *there* was a creature that was worthy:

a god that had rained fire down upon those who defied it, yet cradled its followers inside itself and kept them from harm; a god that was real; that did not demand your belief, but merely allowed it. Glorious *Relentless*, he mouthed, Dei Veritas. He ached to return there. Here, these dead halls, were too close to his nightmare, the nightmare that one day his god might die.

Ah, his unerring instinct told him, as his eyes fell upon a bulkhead otherwise indistinguishable from any other, here we are.

'COMMANDER, SIR.' VICKERS'S strong voice was unusually quiet over the private vox.

'More good news, Mister Vickers?' Ward answered.

'Sir, I have found survivors.'

Ward's blood froze. 'Survivors?'

'They were hiding in a smuggler's berth, sir. Three in all,' Vickers said, a little strained. The rescued men were dancing around in front of him in the suits they had been living in since they had been attacked. One was smiling, another was shouting and the third was trying to embrace the senior armsman. They were all gesturing wildly. Vickers's vox was not tuned to the ship's frequency so he couldn't hear what they were trying to say. Their actions, however, spoke volumes.

'It was a raiding ship, sir, renegades, maybe xenos, I'm not sure. A big raider surprised them. They were hit and boarded, and so they hid. If we bring them back aboard, we will be able to question them fully.'

Ward said nothing. Vickers knew what he was thinking. With some of the crew alive, the *Arc of Elona* could no longer be considered a derelict. Its cargo remained theirs. Worse, under the Navy Articles, the *Relentless* was obliged to take the survivors and their cargo to their next destination. Doubtless, Ward would be able to appropriate some of it during the journey, but nowhere near as much as he had planned.

'Commander?'

'Report back to your squad, Mister Vickers. A transporter will be docking shortly, supervise the transfer of cargo.'

'And the survivors, sir?'

'There were no survivors, Mister Vickers.' There is no one to lay claim to my cargo, no inconvenient passengers aboard my ship, no one to complain if I seize it all.

'If we bring them aboard, sir, they may be able to tell us–'

'It is to be done here and now. There are to be no loose ends. Do not forget, senior armsman,' Ward said, emphasising his rank. 'Do not forget what you are and what you owe me. There were no survivors.'

'Yes, sir. I will call my men.'

'Do not involve your squad, Mister Vickers. Deal with it personally.'

'Yes, sir.'

Vickers had done much in Ward's service over the years, but never before had Ward's hold over him bitten so deeply. Hide your eyes, glorious *Relentless*, hide your eyes, Vickers prayed to the ship. This is not a day for you to remember.

ULTIMATELY, COMMANDER WARD considered the expedition entirely satisfactory. The *Arc*'s riches had been brought aboard and the containers instantly dispersed among the vast cargo holds. The crewmen he used would have to have their share, but it was still a staggering haul for his personal use. There was only the matter of the earlier misidentification to resolve. Keister, Guir and then Ward went through the earlier auspex logs and found no reason for the sudden reassessment. They had even recorded hits from the *Arc of Elona*'s scans. Such an explanation, however, would not satisfy the questions being asked by the command crew.

The official explanation of record was operator error. Keister took the blame and was removed from his command deck duties. He retained his lieutenancy in exchange for his silence. However, the bargain proved to be ineffective. Bitter, Keister informed several of his mates in the junior officers' mess, in strictest confidence of course. From the stewards who overheard them, it filtered down through the petty officers, and thereafter to the ratings. It was not long before it was being whispered on every single deck that this patrol was cursed.

The gossip-mongers did not know that part of the truth behind the curse was parcelled and dormant within the cargo containers, looted from the *Arc* and hidden within the ship's belly. If they had known, they would not have whispered, they would have screamed.

If Becket's men had thought that their lives outside the conscript shifts were going to be soft then they were cruelly disappointed. The deck crews were responsible for the maintenance of the ship's corridors, transit chambers and thoroughfares. On a ship over three kilometres long with over six hundred decks the deck-crews had to patrol hundreds of kilometres of corridors, everywhere from the titanic engines at the rear to the mighty ram at the prow. There were few places that were not catered for: the more sensitive areas of the ship such as the armoury and the launch bays – those 'independent' sections controlled by the Mechanicus, the Navis Nobilite and the Adeptus Astra Telepathica – and the ghost-decks.

As Becket learned, however, the deck-crews enforced the most stringent restrictions. The more prestigious deck crews guarded their privileges to maintain the upper decks jealously. There, the enterprising crewbosses believed, they could gain easy promotion by impressing the officers who walked past them without a second glance. Men from other deck-crews who were caught on another's turf without good reason would have a very bad time of it indeed.

Ferrol's crew, meanwhile, was far further down the ladder. In leaner times, when crew numbers dwindled, they would be left fighting a losing battle against the advancing decrepitude in the lowest reaches. In such circumstances the costs of keeping sections functional would outweigh their utility. The decision would be made to mothball some so that others could be kept in decent repair. Some decks had been left closed for years, decades even. The longer a deck was left closed, the harder it was to reclaim it when it was needed once more. A few, perhaps, had been used only rarely in the *Relentless*'s thousand year history, and thus this neglect the ghost-decks had grown.

With the current glut of men aboard, however, Ferrol's crew was working to expand the habitable decks. The sections that had been most recently closed down were being renovated and reopened. The work was hard. They were distant from the conveniences of the more established decks, it was heavy work with little recognition and, so near the ghost-decks, there were the stories. Some of Ferrol's men had tried to scare the newcomers with tales of the daemons that lurked in the darkness, but they had little effect. The conscripts had killed their monster already.

The work could still be dangerous: the electrical conduits needed to restore heat and light were very old, ceilings and floors could collapse, pipe-leaks could fill chambers with toxic gas or liquids, a few sealed areas near the hull had bled out some of their atmosphere, and the moment when the seal was cracked open would be accompanied by an eerie wind as the air blew back in.

Ferrol thrived on it all. The ponces could keep their brown-nose decks, he would say. Down in the depths they could operate with little supervision. Maybe once between services a very junior lieutenant might come to inspect what they had done. For the first few days, the crew had kept a wary eye out, waiting for any retribution that might come from Morley or any other of Brand's allies, but as another service came and went without incident, they began to turn their attention back to their more covert activities.

The deck-crews were not only responsible for the decks, but also for the areas in between. The steam room was not the only place that existed in the gap between one level and another. The ship was riddled with inter-deck service levels, crawl spaces, shafts and ducts. It was a labyrinth, accessible only by those with the necessary equipment, which of course Ferrol's deck-crew had. While the bulk of the crew were busy with section renovation, Ferrol sent teams into the interdecks to map their way through.

'There's your way past the Perga,' Ferrol had shown Becket. They had travelled deep into the interdecks. They were only a kilometre or so up-ship, but it had taken them several hours in the dark, cramped conditions.

Becket flashed his torch where Ferrol was pointing, and the light followed the floor before disappearing into a black rift where the shaft dropped away. The gap was about fifteen metres wide. Beyond it, Becket could see the other side where the tunnel continued on.

'Are you sure? I can't see far across,' he asked.

'As sure as we can be. Every other route we've tried has turned off, turned back on itself or just come to a dead-end. This is the only one we've found that goes past this point.'

'How deep does it go?'

'Thirty-five, forty metres in every direction, up and down, left and right. It used to have one of those giant fans in, we reckon, to keep the air flowing downship so the officers wouldn't have to endure the smells of the lower decks. Wouldn't be too bad if it weren't for the climb back up on the other side. The walls are smooth, no grips.'

'It's not particularly welcoming.'

'I don't think it's meant to be.'

'Have you tried bridging it?'

'We only found it two weeks ago. It's possible, I suppose, but manhandling spars long enough all the way up here would be a job and a half. We'll cross it, when the time comes.'

Watching Ferrol at work, amongst his men, Becket began to appreciate how the former shipmaster had managed to keep his crew together. He knew every man, not just a face, not just a name, he knew their tempers, he knew their goals. He knew what drove them and he knew what quelled them, and that knowledge allowed him to keep his command, despite all that had happened to them. Becket had issued an order on the *Relentless*'s bridge and it had been obeyed because of his rank. In the pipe-room and in the sewage pit the conscripts had thrown their lot in with Vaughn through sheer desperation. Ferrol's men followed his orders simply because they came from him.

If Ferrol had been in the same situation as he had, Becket had wondered in the sleep-hours, would he have done anything differently? Would he already be back in command of the ship? Would it have even happened to him in the first place? Would he have seen Ward for what he was at a glance?

Down here Ferrol could be the master once more, as he had been on the *Moreno*. His unfortunate tale, the loss of his ship, would have found resonance with any captain worth a damn. It was also, Becket had concluded, a lie.

The oath he had taken with Ferrol kept him bound, by his honour at least, to Ferrol's service, but Becket knew that Ferrol had not relied on his honour alone. He was constantly watched. When Ferrol was not with him, the woman Shroot was there, always accompanied by at least two or three of Ferrol's men. Becket might not be shackled to the conscript chain any more, but he still did not have his liberty, and who could say what his new captor's plans for him were? At least Brand had been straightforward. Ferrol was a mystery, and Becket needed an edge.

'Fidler,' Becket muttered in the young man's ear as they sat in service.

'Yes, Vaughn?'

'I need you to find someone for me.'

Magos Majoris Valinarius was at one with the *Relentless*.

It had taken time. For weeks, he had been getting closer and closer to the highest levels of communion with the machine-spirit. There had been false steps, there had been retreats, he had been tested, but it had finally accepted him. He inhabited every part of it. His skin was chilled by the void that touched the hull, and his heart beat in time with the thrumming of the titanic engines. Power flowed through his veins like blood, each chamber was a cell of his body, each corridor a capillary, and the great metal infrastructure formed his bones. Communion was not quite complete, however. There was a gap, a blemish within his perfect union. It was an absence, a blind-spot. Try to focus upon it and it would slide away.

He reassembled himself, disengaging from the spirit, pulling each part of his psyche back, and flowing towards the altar forge. The blemish was an itch inside the back of his skull. For a split-second, he saw his body as though he were another, and then he snapped inside.

Valinarius.

Valinarius opened his eyes, his real eyes, and saw the empty chamber before him. That voice, it had surfaced in his mind at the very moment of translation. It sounded old, creaking. Was it the ship? Was he close to the final communion? Had Nestratanus enjoyed such intimacy? If so, Valinarius could begin to understand the dedication his former master displayed. To be called by name, to be recognised by a holy creature of such power, such majesty, it was a thrill such as he had never before experienced. He was almost tempted to submerge himself once more, but no, he had to resist. He had come out for a reason. He gently removed the couplings that connected him to the altar he lay across, and shakily stepped down to stand by himself.

He was alone in the grand altar forge. Nestratanus had had his court, his attendants, because he was unable to function under his own power. Valinarius had no such problems. He was still fit, still relatively young. He had no need of such pandering, and, after his first disastrous attempt at communion, he had been glad that he had been able to conduct his experiments without witnesses. The old magos should have stood aside for him long before. Then, he could have started Valinarius's training, and he would not have had to make so many painful mistakes. If only he had stood aside, well, then he would not have needed to be pushed.

Valinarius realised that his attention had drifted back to the spirit, as it always did these days. There had been a reason why he had emerged, but what had it been? The first officer had wanted to speak to him and had set a time. Valinarius checked his internal chronometer. He was already late. It was strange, with the spirit he was aware of so much, and yet time always slipped past him. Time, he supposed, had little meaning to the immortal machine-spirit. He would have to find the commander. His words of his invitation had been routine enough, but there had been a touch of agitation in his tone. The magos nudged down his cowl, ready to walk amongst others. At the gate, however, he heard the commander's voice. He must have come looking for him. He was in conversation with one of the adepts, Tertionus was his name. Valinarius could have interrupted them, since the commander was surely here to talk to him, but his instincts made him hold back and watch them instead. They spoke for another minute, and then the commander left. Tertionus bowed, the expression on his face covered by his hood. The magos stepped out.

'What did the first officer want, adept?'

'Exalted magos,' Tertionus said, bowing deeply, 'the first officer conveyed a desire to speak with your august self.

He laboured under the belief that a meeting had been prearranged.'

'And how did you reply?'

'I informed the commander that you were in meditation, exalted one, and that you were not to be disturbed. Was I incorrect in that, holy magos?'

'No,' Valinarius said after a pause, 'you were quite correct. Did the commander impart to you his intended topic of discussion?'

'The commander did not entrust me with that data, exalted one.'

'And that was all?'

'Pardon me, exalted one, I do not understand you.'

'There was nothing else that you or the commander spoke of?'

'The commander did display great insistency, exalted one, however he did not indicate that the matter was of paramount urgency and could not be delayed, and so I maintained my position.'

Valinarius did not believe it. The conversation he had seen had not been a subordinate fending away a truculent superior, it had been altogether too amiable. Similar, Valinarius noted, to his own discussions with the commander, at least before his promotion.

'Very well, adept. I will travel to see him shortly. Make the necessary arrangements.'

'I will do so at once, exalted one.' Still bowed, Tertionus backed away, facing Valinarius until he was at a respectful distance.

That's the way, adept, Valinarius thought to himself. Don't turn your back to me. I certainly will not turn my back to you.

LIEUTENANT COMMANDER GUIR stepped onto the bridge of the command deck. He was half an hour early to begin his watch, but he had been unable to rest properly. The large view-portal was blank as they were currently traversing the warp along a trade conduit between two beacons. The first officer was in the captain's chair talking to someone beside him. Guir stepped up and saw the dark presence sitting there. It was Commissar Bedrossian. Guir was taken aback for a moment. Only the day before, he had addressed a most serious matter to Commander Ward about the commissar. Two of his chiefs had come to him with information that one of his petty officers had been passing information to the commissar in return for payment. The officer had run up various debts amongst his peers, which he suddenly had money to clear, claiming he had managed to do a little profitable trading on Pontus. He had been asking questions as well, nothing incriminating, but certainly out of character. Then he had been seen talking to one of the commissar's cadets and at that point the chiefs had come to Guir.

'How much does he know?' Ward had asked.

'About that business? Nothing. He was, and he will be, kept well clear of anything of a sensitive nature.'

'Then I do not see your problem, Mister Guir.'

'The commissar has a spy amongst my men, first officer. That's my problem.'

'A spy? What a dramatic word, Guir. You make it sound as though any moment now the storm troopers will arrive and haul you away. All you have is a little rotten apple, who splices a few yarns to the commissar to escape a whipping for being brought in disorderly. Drink, I hear it was.'

Guir had been speechless for a moment.

'Oh, did you think that none of your men talk to any of mine, Guir?' Ward had continued, 'and I am certain that a few of your own keep their ears close to the deck on your behalf.'

'That's entirely different.' It was. Maintaining an awareness of the undercurrents flowing on the ship was part of his duty.

'Of course it is, but, now that you know the man's name, perhaps you should look for the opportunities inherent in the situation.'

Guir had understood, but he had still not been happy. 'I thought that the commissar would be dealt with.'

'I am dealing with him, lieutenant commander. If you doubt it, perhaps you're not watching closely enough.'

Well, Guir was watching closely now, as Ward and the commissar exchanged quiet words before his very eyes. Seeing them there, the inadvertent thought slipped into his mind, what if Ward had been turned completely by the commissar? The plan for the shuttle crash had been his, but he had used others to carry it out. Could he possibly convince the commissar that another mind had been behind it all? If he did, he could sweep away all his fellow conspirators in a single stroke, and take the *Relentless*, owing nothing to anyone. Perhaps the storm troopers were coming for him after all.

'Ah, lieutenant commander, you're early,' Ward said, seeing his second hovering by the side of the dais.

'Yes, sir, if you would prefer I can return at–'

'No, not at all. As you can see there are no–'

A small alarm rang from the consoles at the front of the dais and, on the command deck, the chatter around the auspex array suddenly peaked. The new auspex officer reported:

'Vessel detected, commander, at extreme range, full astern.'

Astern? Guir was surprised. The only vessels they should encounter were merchantmen, and they should appear from the fore or abeam. Surely nothing along this route could outpace the *Relentless*?

'Do we have an ident?'

'Difficult, the warp currents are distorting... We have it. Coming through. It is the...' the operator faltered for a moment, and rechecked his screen.

Guir and Ward glanced at one another. This was the moment of uncertainty, the moment that would decide whether they were predator or prey.

'It's the *Arc of Elona*, sir.'

ELEVEN

'Kimeal, you're always full of the same crap.'

'You want me to show you what I'm full of, Sundjata?'

'You just can't shut your face about your stupid bloody marches. Wake up, no one here gives a frag.'

'We were marching for the people! How many of us must be crushed under the tanks of the Epitrapos? How many of our sons and daughters must be taken from us by the Carrion-Emperor. We were marching for you, you ungrateful–'

'You weren't marching for me, that's for sure. You weren't going to do nothing for me, sitting in that cell, were yer?'

'Well, that's where animals belong, in a zoo!'

'Least I'll get to meet yer mother–'

'That's it!'

Kimeal and Sundjata had been snapping at each other for days, and everyone knew it was just a matter of time before one or the other blew up. Kimeal, the former agitator, had thrown the first punch, but the condemned man was certainly determined to finish it. The other conscripts jumped in, trying to pull the two away from each other, but as the fighters' indiscriminate blows connected with them, they too laid into the pugilists and each other. Ferrol stepped out of his room. He had started to bellow an order to stop them all when Fidler and Zercahyyab, grappling together, barrelled into him.

By the time Ferrol had pushed them off him and got back to his feet, the brawl had spread to his own men, and it took nearly fifteen minutes, and no little bruising of his own knuckles, to get things back under control. It was only after another half an hour of demanding answers and tearing a strip off both crews that he and Shroot finally noticed: Vaughn was missing.

Ferrol swore profusely, and threatened to throw all of Vaughn's men to their enemies unless they talked. Most of them stared at him defiantly, but the older conscript, Ferrol recalled his name was Papeway, raised his hand.

'Master Ferrol? I will tell you where he went.'

BECKET SLID HURRIEDLY out of the crawl space and replaced the grille behind him. For all that this was his ship, he was in enemy territory. If he was spotted, he'd have to run back to Ferrol. If he was caught, then that would be it for him. Either way, he had to try.

He came to a halt outside a cabin marked just as Papeway had described. The old miner's directions had been dead-on. He opened the door and saw the black coat hanging, pristine, on a rail. There, sleeping, lay the man he had come to find. Becket knelt down next to him.

'Hello, Jakobus.'

SUB-LIEUTENANT HOFFORE could not bear it any longer. The auspex alarm would not stop ringing. He wanted to put his head in his hands, to jam his fingers in his ears, but the eyes of everyone on the bridge were upon him.

Every sensor, every piece of data he had before him told him that the *Arc of Elona* was behind them, matching their pace, and yet he knew it wasn't. When it had first appeared, they had tried everything they could. They had turned, they had slowed, and, despite the strenuous objections of the Navigators, they had come as close to a stop as they dared amongst the currents. Each time they did, the *Arc* would gain ground and then disappear. They would continue on, and then minutes, hours, a day later, there it would be again and the alarm would ring.

Hoffore was the third new auspex officer assigned to the bridge in as many weeks. The last one had dutifully reported the sighting, again and again, and Commander Ward had finally screamed at him to get out of his sight. So, Hoffore had had to take the console on the dais, and he had waited and waited. Then the alarm had rang. The first officer, his tone as cold as ice, asked him to report. He said it was a fault, and had managed to drag out his 'repair' for nearly an hour before the *Arc* vanished once more and he could settle back at his post. Then another hour passed in silence, two hours, three.

All the old stories came back to him, all the night terrors that his brothers had used to scare him as they lay in the dark: ships of the dead, phantoms in the warp, unholy heralds of disaster, and the unnatural monsters that lurked within the maelstrom and gleefully feasted upon the frail mortals that thought to pass through their domain. As he had grown though, he had left such things behind. He wasn't a child any more. He had fought in battle, soldiers had looked to him as a leader, he had taken a woman and had children of his own. There had, of course, always been the whispers, the truths behind the tales that you began to learn serving in the battlefleet, and the real stories of the death and madness of those who had dared the maelstrom.

Another hour, Hoffore sighed, and that would be it, his watch would be over. Then it would be another poor sod's problem.

The alarm continued to ring.

'THERE IS A perfectly rational explanation for it all, Pulcher,' Ward announced to his guest over dinner.

The confessor looked up from his dish, puzzled. He hadn't asked about anything.

'It may not be obvious to one who isn't a Navy man, such as yourself, but to me it is quite clear,' he continued. 'We are being followed by a ship that we identify as the *Arc of Elona*, and yet it cannot be. We passed the same vessel not a few days ago, and it was a gutted shell. What can it be? An auspex error? Our arrays have been checked, and checked again, and are working perfectly. Perhaps it is a strange kind of warp echo, but no, it has reappeared too regularly for that. Some of my crew would have it that it's some malignant presence, a mystical being hunting us down for our sins. What say you to that, confessor?'

Pulcher was caught mid-chew, hastily swallowed and coughed, 'Heresy! The Emperor alone is our judge. Tell me who these crewmen are, commander, and I will have them brought in.'

'Yes, Pulcher, but we must allow the men their simple superstitions sometimes. It keeps them occupied. They find it easier to believe that a dead ship might return to haunt them as a spectre than that there may simply be two ships.'

'Two ships?' the confessor echoed.

'One as bait and the other as a net. It is not a common practice amongst pirates and raiders, it's rather time consuming, but it's not unheard of. They take a vessel near a beacon, and then leave it and lie in wait. When other ships investigate, they spring the trap and attack. Except, with the *Relentless*, they caught a bigger fish than they could handle and so they let us leave. Now, they're simply following our trail. Maybe they're just trying to judge our destination, or maybe they're looking to pick up some of the crumbs we leave behind.'

'I see.' Pulcher was silent for a moment's contemplation. They must be strange raiders indeed to leave such considerable cargo behind, no matter how much Ward had tried to cover his loot as the collection of 'evidence'. 'And the auspex readings?'

'An illusion, Pulcher, nothing more. At extreme ranges, our auspex relies heavily on the signals the target sends out. If you can reproduce them, then, at the greatest distances, one ship can fly another flag, so to speak.' Ward smiled at his own turn of phrase. 'The only problem with it is that you have to conceal your ship's emitters, leaving you blind, deaf and helpless, with your engines fully shut down. On Emcor, we're taught the accounts of those few captains who've believed they could use such a manoeuvre for tactical advantage. Trust me, they did not last long.'

'Ah, well, that's all tremendously heartening, commander. How did you come to finally solve the puzzle?'

'Oh, I realised it at once, Pulcher,' Ward lied.

'Then why–'

'Why continue the charade? It has been a learning experience, confessor. You can tell so much more about a man's character when a little pressure is exerted: who will stand by you and who might betray you.'

Pulcher glanced down at the rich meal he had just consumed. Surely Ward wouldn't have, would he? The first officer continued talking, apparently oblivious to Pulcher's consternation.

'We share a common goal, Pulcher, you and I: the faith of this ship's crew. Faith in the Emperor, and faith in those He has chosen for command.'

'That is true, in its way.'

'The faith of this crew was struck a great blow when He took our captain from us, a blow from which, I fear, some amongst us remain shaken, even some who are closest to me.'

'I see.'

'I feel that it is my duty to help those under my command at this time of crisis. However, these are proud men, unwilling to show any sign of their inner turmoil except, perhaps, to you, *confessor*.'

'Some disclosures, commander, are sacred between the supplicant and the Emperor. I am a mere intermediary, bound by my immortal vows.'

Ward raised his eyebrows. 'I hope you do not think that I would ever suggest that you breach your covenant with Him, confessor.'

'Of course not.'

'WHAT DID YOU tell him, Jakobus?' Ferrol asked, shaking the beaten man thoroughly.

'I didn't tell him anything, I swear!'

'You told him something, otherwise he'd still be here!'

'He knew you hired me already. He never even asked me!'

'But you confirmed it, didn't you, you pathetic piece of–'

'All he wanted to know was why I called him captain, that's all!'

'And what did you say?'

'You never told me why! Just that I should, and that I should tell you how he reacted. It would throw him off balance you said.'

'Blasted!' Ferrol cursed as he dropped Jakobus to the floor. Captain Becket was further ahead than he'd thought.

FERROL AND HIS crew snaked through the familiar interdecks that led upship. As they approached the rift, Ferrol could see a light shining on the far side. He and Shroot shone their torches across, and there was Becket. He did not even look up. He just continued calmly wrapping up the two chains he had brought with him to swing across the rift into a neat pile.

'What happened to the men I sent ahead to catch you?' Ferrol called across.

'Look beneath you,' Becket replied. Ferrol did so, and saw the feet of his crewmen, who were hanging upside down over the rift, feet secured to the lip of the tunnel by shackles. 'You may wish to pull them up before they regain consciousness,' Becket called, 'or you may prefer to wait. I imagine that depends on what kind of person you are.'

Ferrol waved his crew forwards, and they began to haul their unfortunate colleagues up.

'You gave me your word of honour,' Ferrol said.

'And you lied to me,' Becket replied.

'You lied to me! You lied to me every time I said Vaughn and you said "yes"!'

'So you do know who I am.'

'Of course I know. You could be burned, your head could be shaved, you could be painted bloody blue, it wouldn't matter. You took my command, you took my ship, the *Tarai's Challenge*, it was nothing to you, was it? But it was everything to me.'

Becket stopped and regarded Ferrol anew. His mind went back to a conversation he had shared with Ward standing on the bridge of the *Tarai's Challenge*. He remembered the commotion out of his sight when he had ordered the ship to be confiscated, a commotion caused by the shipmaster. He had never learned anything of the master of the *Tarai's Challenge*, but then, he had not cared to.

'You took my bloody life. So no, I would never forget your face.' Ferrol gave a hollow laugh. 'I never would have known either if you hadn't done Brand in. Word got around pretty fast about this conscript who had got one back and might even get away with it. He sounded like a good man, maybe someone for my crew, someone I should check out. Can you think how I felt when I

clapped eyes on you, standing there, saying your prayers?
I might never have known. I might have just assumed
you'd have burned to a crisp back on Pontus.'

'And so you hired Jakobus to take me out of my crew,
so you could befriend me, and then lead me back so we
could save them all. Or was Morley in your pay as well?'

'Damn you, he was bloody gunning for you like a battle-
ship broadside. You've never done anything but cost me,
both as captain of this ship and as a member of my crew.'

'Saving me for yourself? I am surprised you were able to
restrain yourself so long.'

'Oh, you're just another lackey of the eagle, aren't yer?
It's all about you, and let your crew be damned. I saved
you because with your help I could get my crew out on
the next planet we hit. My crew is what matters to me. I
don't reckon you can say the same.'

'My crew is why I'm doing this, for all the thousands of
them that deserve better.'

'Sundjata, Kimeal, Fidler, Papeway, what about that lot?
You've forgotten them already. You've left them behind in
the hands of a man who hates you.'

'You have forgotten, Master Ferrol. They swore alle-
giance to you. They are your crew now, and your crew is
what matters to you.' Becket started to turn away. 'If you
should be tempted to have a lapse, then consider this: if
you know who I am and what I am about to do, then you
also know that His Holy Wrath will have nothing on the
fury I will mete out on you and yours if you touch a single hair on their heads. Consider that, Master Ferrol.'

'You listen to me,' Ferrol shouted as Becket stepped up
towards the top decks. 'I can tell you now, you're wasting
your time. They were all in on it, you hear me? They were
all in on it!' But Becket was out of sight.

'Shroot! Get me something, anything to get me across
there. I'm not going to bloody lose him now.'

* * *

THE TWO MIDSHIPMEN sauntered down the upper deck corridor engaged in friendly dispute.

'Admit it, you've never seen one,' the young midshipman said to his mate.

'I have, you just don't believe me 'cos one look at it and you'd leg it,' his mate replied.

'When then?'

'Back on Emcor, before we left. One of the old master chiefs from the *Ferocious* carried it round with him in a box.'

'Carried it round with him? Now I know you're a liar. You couldn't carry it around in a box.'

'Not the whole thing, you duster, just the head. Anyone knows that you don't carry around the whole body. It might come alive again!'

'It'd never.'

'It might. Ask anyone, they'll tell yer. He gave me a tooth.'

'He never! Show it me!'

'What's it worth?'

Before the midshipman could reply, they both jumped back as the squad of armsmen rounded the corner before them. The boys snapped a polished salute as the burly men strode past, surrounding the commissar as he strode from his quarters and down the hall. The silver face did not glance at them. Behind them clattered the commissar's cadets, trying to catch up to the lead party without sacrificing their dignity.

Becket watched them all from the crawl space beneath the floor and shook his head. What had happened whilst he had been below? Commissar Bedrossian had tripled his personal bodyguard and they followed him everywhere he went. There were more, constantly stationed at the door to his quarters and in the corridors nearby. It was hard to imagine an Imperial commissar being afraid, but Bedrossian obviously had grave concerns about something to be taking such precautions.

Becket was ragged, unkempt and utterly filthy from dragging himself through the interdecks. Any of the bodyguards were likely to shoot him on sight if he simply tried to approach the commissar. At the very least, the commotion it would cause would herald his return to every single officer on the deck. No, he could not risk it. The cabins that lined the corridor, however, were more promising. If he could clean himself off and steal a fresh officer's uniform, it would give him the seconds he needed for the commissar to recognise him.

Becket crawled back into the side-tunnel and pulled himself along until he reached the nearest cabin. There was a service access panel in the wall, near the floor. He unscrewed the bolts with his deck crew ratchet, and ever-so-gently eased the panel forwards a fraction. It was dark on the other side. Becket held his breath and listened, ears sharp for even the lightest snoring on the other side. He could hear nothing. Encouraged, he pushed the panel out further and looked inside with his torch. The room was empty. Becket sighed with relief, and eased himself through the hatch. There were no alarms and no traps. He was safe. He stood up and stretched out his body. It felt good after so long cramped and crawling. He saw one of the bunks, hard and small compared to his former chambers up here, but after his months down below a bed of clouds and silk could not have looked more tempting. There was little time to waste in such fantasies, however. He lay down the torch and switched on the light above the sink, divided off from the rest of the room in the corner. Becket suddenly felt the dirt ingrained in his skin and the filth that covered him. It itched. He could not wait to scour it off.

The main light flicked on. Someone had walked in.

Becket shot back and flattened himself against the partition that ran between him and the door. He couldn't breathe. He could hear the sounds of someone rummaging through a trunk: a young voice muttering in exasperation and then triumphantly seizing the forgotten object; then silence. Becket could almost see the person turning to leave, and then spotting the glow of the sink-light. Leave it be, Becket thought as hard as he could. Get off, you're running late. Leave it be.

Then there were steps, quick steps, getting closer. The cadet-commissar leaned in to hit the switch. For a split-second, the cadet saw his attacker: the wild, hunted man hiding right beside him. Then he was lifted bodily from his feet and slammed back into the wall. He tried to shout, but a grimy hand smothered his mouth. He tried to shake loose, but the grip held him tight. All he could see was a face tarred black, and the bloodshot, blue eyes.

'Listen to me,' Becket whispered. 'Don't struggle. Listen to my voice.' The cadet could only panic and stare.

'Close your eyes,' he whispered. Then he commanded in a familiar voice, 'That's an order, cadet.' Another hand covered his face.

'Listen to my voice.' The tones were strong now. 'You remember my voice. You know who I am. I am your captain. Nod your head, cadet. Show me that you understand.'

The cadet's nostrils flared as he tried to breathe, but he nodded his head.

'Listen to me, cadet. This is an order from your captain. In a moment, I will take my hands away. You will not scream, you will not strike out. We will talk. Nod your head if you understand.' The cadet nodded again.

The hands were removed, and he could breathe and see once more. He looked at the man before him. It was no longer the savage, it was his captain, bedraggled and unkempt.

'Now,' the captain said, 'what is your name?'

BECKET HAD NEVER paid attention to the cadet-commissars before. They were simply always there, in Bedrossian's shadow, and yet outside his responsibility. Meeting this eager yet serious-minded young man, seeing inside the small cabin he shared with his three colleagues, gave him a flash of insight into their lives. It was scrupulously neat and ordered, as would be expected, but here and there an item revealed a glimpse of their personalities: a well-worn catechism, an icon of the Emperor. This cadet, Micael, had a list of numbers beside his bunk, counting down. The first two-thirds of them had been neatly crossed through.

Becket had given him a highly abbreviated account of the crash, his survival and his way back aboard ship. The cadet did not question the gaps. He did not question what the captain had been doing down below since they had left Pontus. Life in battlefleet instilled obedience, and his training as a commissar had taught him to guard his thoughts carefully. He listened attentively, with a solemn expression, an inexperienced youth presented with circumstances far beyond what he had been trained to deal with. He offered to fetch the commissar.

'Where has he gone?' Becket asked.

'The command deck, sir. He said he had to talk to the commander.'

'Then no. We cannot call the commissar away under Ward's nose. We can do nothing that might raise the commander's suspicions.'

Becket had been planning his next steps for weeks. The commissar had the authority to remove the first officer at a stroke, but Ward's claws were sunk deep into the officers. Commissars were terrifying, awe-inspiring figures for many servants of the Imperium, but would a man who had tried to murder his captain really hesitate from taking the next step down his renegade path?

Becket knew he would have to be careful. The commissar would have to sound out those officers in critical positions and determine their true loyalties. Ward would have his die-hards, but how many had simply accepted what they had been told?

'Cadet, tell me, how was the crash explained?'

'The report, sir, that was sent to battlefleet, concluded that it had been a pilot error, but I remember thinking that was strange, sir, because there had been talk before-hand of a mechanical problem. Staj, that is Cadet Kosow, sir, said that the commissar and Commander Ward had spoken, and that the commander was bad-mouthing the Pontics, saying that there were holes in their security.'

Becket tried to recall the face of the pilot, but he couldn't, even though he had hauled his corpse away from the shuttle controls. So, all the blame was being laid upon him. If it had been a mechanical failure, either of instruments or the machine-spirit, then there would have been further investigation. Just the same as if it had been the responsibility of a Pontic, battlefleet would expect a culprit to be found. Blaming the pilot was the quickest and cleanest way.

'What else did the report say?'

'Oh, I have a copy of it, sir, if you prefer?'

'Yes, thank you.' Micael went to his bunk, reached underneath and pulled out a trunk.

'The commissar, sir, gives us a copy of his official com-muniqués to read. It's part of our training.' The cadet said, a touch ruefully, 'to prepare us for the day when we might have to write the same ourselves. Here it is.'

Micael handed it to Becket, who started to skim through it.

'I suppose it's a bit strange, sir, for you to have a chance to read it, I mean.'

'Yes,' Becket replied without looking up.

Cadet Micael decided to remain silent as the captain read. Summary, background, timeline, analysis, even the most extraordinary events were reported in the same unexceptional manner; such was the proper battlefleet way. Becket shook his head; the gall of his first officer, including the chirurgeon's fabricated autopsy report on the captain. Obviously, the chief medicae officer needed to be watched. At the bottom were the endorsements of the senior staff, including a slightly longer narrative from the commissar himself. These were followed by a few caveats and notes on minor lapses, and then:

'Having reviewed all information herein and ascertained its truth through personal interrogation of witnesses and examination of all remains and material returned to this vessel, it is my judgement that First Officer, Commander Tomias Illoni Certhunian Ward should exercise all powers and privileges of captain of this vessel, until such a time as it should be thought fit to make a formal appointment to this post. Signed, Bedrossian, commissar of the Emperor.'

Becket stopped reading. He could faintly hear marching outside in the corridor, and the cadet turned to the door.

'That might be the commissar now, sir, shall I look?'

Becket did not answer. He didn't move, but simply read the lines again. Bedrossian had lied. He had flat out lied. Why would he lie? Becket shook, suddenly chill.

'Shall I get him, sir?' the cadet asked again.

'No,' Becket whispered. 'No,' he said again more forcefully. The report fell from his hands and he turned to the cadet.

'What's the matter, sir?'

'He was in on it.'

'Sir?' Cadet Micael saw the look in Becket's eyes and backed away slightly.

'From the very start. He must have been.'

'I don't understand, sir. Should I get the commissar?' Micael edged towards the door.

'No!' Becket lunged at the cadet and dragged him back. 'You cannot tell him. Do you understand? You cannot tell him!'

Micael stared back. The savage had returned. He tried to pry himself free, but the captain's fingers clung to him like a vice. He shouldn't hurt the man, but the fear was rising within him. He pushed away hard and they both twisted and fell, the captain landing on top of the cadet.

Becket could not think, he could not think. Everyone had betrayed him, everyone. He had to stop the cadet from getting back to Bedrossian. Had to hold him still. He couldn't let him get up, couldn't let him talk. He had to have time, time to think. He lifted the cadet by his lapels, and then slammed him back against the deck. He was still for a moment, but then he started fighting, trying to squirm from the grip. He tried to shout, to call to those right outside the door. Becket smothered his mouth again and banged his head down, once, twice, and then again and again, until he finally realised that the youth had gone limp. The heat receded from Becket's head and he let his breath out shakily. He had to move quickly. He could be discovered any second. He dragged Micael over to the access panel, closed the trunk and shoved it back under the bed. He grabbed the torch, and only then noticed the report lying where he'd dropped it. He picked it up, looked back at the locked trunk under the bunk, and then shoved it under his shirt. He switched off the main light, and then the sink light, and finally dragged Micael out into the side-tunnel, replacing the panel behind him.

Emperor's breath, what in the stars was he supposed to do now?

FERROL FOUND THEM at a junction, where the shafts opened up, almost wide enough to stand or lie. Becket was so grey with dust and dirt that he was barely distinguishable from the walls. There was a lighter, pinker streak running down each cheek from his eye, but Ferrol did not mention them. Instead, he threw down the chain that he had brought with him.

'In case I needed to drag you back,' he said.

Becket nodded and tried to swallow.

'How did you know?' Becket asked.

'What?'

'That he was part of it as well?'

Ferrol thought for a moment.

'I didn't,' he said. 'I was just trying to stop you.'

Becket looked at him blankly, and then nodded his head.

'Who's this?' Ferrol went to Micael.

'One of his cadets. He came in on me. I thought he could… I told him everything. Then, when I realised, I had to knock him out. I don't know what I can do with him. I can't lock him away somewhere. I can't stop him talking.'

'I wouldn't worry about that,' Ferrol said from the cadet's side. 'He's dead.'

Becket continued staring off into the distance. He brought his hand to his mouth and started chewing on his knuckle. He kept nodding and staring. Ferrol stepped over to him and gently pulled his hand away.

'We'll take care of this. We'll take care of it.'

TWELVE

BECKET LAY IN the dark. His body ached, his throat was raw and his head was burning up. He had been lying, sweating, in his bunk for three full days, ever since he had returned from the upper decks. The cadet's body had disappeared, dealt with as promised by Ferrol and his crew. His own men, Sundjata, Fidler and the rest, were well. As Becket had predicted, Ferrol had not touched them, merely keeping them under close guard for their part in his escape. Partly to train them, partly to keep them under control, Ferrol had divided the conscripts amongst the work teams as much as possible, and there were few amongst his crew who had not worked alongside them, and heard their story of life in the conscript shifts. It was not his crew's sensibilities, however, that informed Ferrol's motive in treating Becket and the conscripts leniently.

'It's no surprise to me that you're sick,' Ferrol said, walking into the cabin and switching on a lamp. Becket shielded his eyes from the light.

'The others, the crew,' Ferrol continued, 'they think you've been hiding away. They think you're afraid to face them, afraid to face me, but I know better. Any man who takes a fall like you have doesn't fear much, and it isn't squeamishness about that boy either, not deep down.

'You've just given all you've got to give, that's all. All the strain and all the worry you've had, you've been holding off, and now it's taken its chance to come back and hit you all the harder. There's no problem with that. There's nothing you need to do anymore. I'll be decent to you. You'll come along with us when we make our break for it. Then, when we're safe, you can go your own way and get a message back to your battlefleet. I'll even give your men the choice of who they want to follow, although I don't see many of them being too keen to go back to the life of the conscript chain gang. Some of my crew won't like bringing you along, but I reckon you've still got some access rights, maybe even a top-level override that'll get us into the armoury.'

Becket tried to frame a thought, but Ferrol cut him off.

'You can argue if you like. I got no trouble leaving you on this scow to rot. I've already got a man finding a contact there. You see, unlike you, I can trust my crew.' Despite his words, there was no malice in Ferrol's voice. 'So you can lie there for as long as you like, mourning over how someone stole your life. Believe me, I know what it's like. We both lost a life. The difference is that I know how to take mine back.'

Ferrol closed the door and, in the darkness, the fever dragged Becket down once more.

BECKET HAD MANAGED to start eating again when the deputation of conscripts arrived. It was Kimeal and Sundjata.

He greeted them. 'Fidler not come with you? I would have expected him to want to be here.'

'Master Ferrol has him on an assignment,' Kimeal replied. It was Master Ferrol now, Becket noted. 'Master

Ferrol keeps him busy. He says he has a knack for finding things… and people.'

'Then Master Ferrol has a good eye for talent. How are you doing?'

'We want to understand,' Sundjata interjected.

'Very well,' Becket said. 'What?'

'Is it true? What we hear?'

'That depends on what you have heard,' Becket said remaining calm, 'but yes, most likely it is true.'

'You were the captain of this ship?'

'I still am.'

Both of them paused, thinking. Kimeal spoke first.

'Master Ferrol says that you are the reason he is here.'

'He is correct.'

'Are you the reason that I am here?'

Becket rolled the question over in his mind.

'No,' he said. 'You are here, Kimeal, because the Epitrapos wanted to silence his opponents, and the conscript-tithe to the battlefleet was his opportunity.'

'But if you had still been in command at that time… would it have made a difference?'

'Most likely not, no.'

'None of that matters to me,' Sundjata interrupted. 'I volunteered for this. I ain't got no one to blame for all this but myself. What matters to me is what happens now. Master Ferrol, he's got a plan. It sounds risky, but maybe it can work. What about you? You got anything left or was that it?'

'I don't know. I can't see how a dozen, two dozen men, could take back the ship.'

'Fair enough. You think of something, we'll listen to you, Vaughn.' Sundjata looked at Kimeal who gave a curt nod.

'My name is not Vaughn, you know?'

'You think mine's Sundjata? Course not. It's just who I am now,' Sundjata said as they left. 'Same for you.'

* * *

THE CONFESSOR DID not like this progression of events. He had expected the circumstances of Captain Becket's demise to give him considerable leverage over Commander Ward in order to aid the establishment of true faith amongst the crew. Ward had, however, made it quite clear at supper last evening that he considered any debt he may have owed the confessor to have been paid in full. Worse, he had dangled the confessor's new initiatives in front of him. He had said he had reports of the risk they posed in concentrating crew together, the time lost because of the services, and the danger to the *Relentless* as a result. Ward had acquired support enough to cancel them at a stroke, and what could the confessor do in reply? Report an offence in which he was implicated up to his neck? Worse, though Ward never so much as hinted at it, was the thought that the first officer might look to deal with him permanently. After all, could a man who would kill his own captain be trusted to hold fast against a servant of the Emperor?

'Does something displease you, eminent confessor?' the lector asked nervously. Pulcher had not deigned to inspect the below deck chapels since the consecration, and appeared unimpressed by their achievements.

'No, no. Do continue on,' Pulcher replied. The lector smiled in relief and carried on describing the works he had performed. He had, Pulcher realised, one of the most droning, irritating voices he had ever encountered. No wonder he had been consigned down here. Pulcher's cherubs had already taken flight at the sound of it, and he felt inclined to do the same. There were several more chapels down in this odious place, and he wanted to get around to them all and bolster their fortitude. If the commander wished to use them as a pawn then he would have to start paying considerably more interest in them.

At length, Pulcher was able to make his excuses to the interminable lector and move on. His cherubs had disappeared, no doubt on the hunt. They would find their way back to him, they always did.

IT WAS THE end of a work shift and Ferrol's men, amongst others, were trudging back in a long column from the renovation sections towards the barracks areas. There was a commotion ahead of them. Two blue, winged children fluttered and swooped down upon the men's heads. Some of the crewmen were trying to knock the cherubs down, but the more experienced hands shouted at them to leave them alone. They knew better than to interfere in anything of the confessor's. The life of the crewman who touched them would not be worth living and, given that it was the confessor, the fates of their souls might be in some doubt as well.

The cherubs suddenly stopped their carefree high-wheeling and dived down the column. They had sensed something familiar. The crew around Becket panicked a little as the cherubs fell towards them, but the creatures pulled up short. They hovered in front of Becket, their wings beating rapidly, screeching their dreadful chatter. Becket quickly pulled off his jacket and swept at them, warding them off. The others took up the idea and the cherubs, bleating and protesting, were driven off and flapped away.

The crew laughed and cheered, but Becket did not. The cherubs had recognised him.

THE FLURRY OF wings in the vestry caused Pulcher to put down his entertainment for the evening. Dressed for bed, he shuffled over to the door and looked out. He saw his cherubs flapping and pecking at the subdeacon on vigil, who was attempting to protect his face with little success. Pulcher clapped his hands sharply together to draw their attention. The cherubs shot away from the unfortunate subdeacon and landed on his shoulders. Each one immediately launched into a stream of screeching chatter, projecting bizarre, blurred images into his mind.

'Brother Tev,' he said, gently dislodging them, 'you know better than to play games with them this late.'

'Yes, your eminence,' the subdeacon said, scraping low.

'As now I have to calm them down, you shall have to chastise yourself. I will review the scars in the morning.'

'You are most wise, your eminence.'

'Yes, yes, yes.' Pulcher waved him away. He took the cherubs firmly in hand, and concentrated on the jumbled images they were putting into his head. 'Now, my darlings, what are you trying to tell me?'

LIEUTENANT COMMANDER GUIR was not sleeping well. His thoughts were fevered. The first officer's mania at this supposed pursuit by a dead ship had been wearing on them all. At its height, he had wanted for nothing more than that ship to disappear as soon as it could, but now it had gone for good and yet the atmosphere felt worse. He and Ward had not spoken of anything outside of formal reports for days, and he was sure that his men were hiding something from him. They were keeping a distance from him, and talking amongst themselves more, and Guir was sure that he had seen one of Ward's flunkies amongst them. How could the first officer be turning them so easily? Did loyalty count for nothing any more? He had to discover what was at the root of it. He would find out tomorrow. He would start applying a little pressure to the weaker links. Yes, that would be the way.

He blinked his eyes open. He had slept for only a few hours. What had woken him? A sound, the sound of someone testing his door. Was someone inside? He shifted, casually stretching his limbs as a sleeper might do. His hand slid to the side of the bed and touched the grip of his pistol. A cold claw seized his wrist. The lights flicked on. The commissar was there, and so were others.

'Lieutenant Commander Guir,' the commissar said. 'You have questions to answer.'

* * *

'BROTHER DAINAN?' PULCHER called the next morning.

Subdeacon Dainan entered the confessor's chambers, eyes lowered, and prostrated himself.

'Get up, get up.'

'Yes, your eminence.' Dainan got to his feet and quickly glanced around the room. The confessor was at his writing lectern, quill in hand, intent upon his scribing. As Dainan watched, the quill shot out and was refilled in the ink bowl, shaped as two hands held out in supplication. The candles had burned low and the bed had not been slept in.

'How is Brother Tev?' the confessor asked without looking up.

'He is… quite ill, your eminence. He was taken to the medicae deck.'

'Hmph, most inappropriate. Ensure he knows, Dainan, that if he does not present himself back here by the nocto then it will be the same again.'

'Yes, your eminence. Is that all, your eminence?'

'No. There are services today in the lower deck chapels, are there not?'

'I believe so, your eminence.'

The confessor put the quill back in its holder and held up the piece of parchment he had been writing on. The ink still shone and he waved it dry with a flick of his hand.

'Ensure that this is added to each service within the prayer-rite. Ensure that the men are watched carefully as it is said. Make a note of any reaction. I will need to be able to find those men afterwards. Here.'

Dainan's hands shook a little as he took the scroll. He knew that there were words of power, which could make the unholy squirm and tear at themselves just to hear them spoken. He had never heard them spoken, however.

'Are there dark powers at work, your eminence?' he asked with a fervent rush of courage.

The confessor pondered the question.

'It is too early to say, brother, too early to say.'

'DID YOU KNOW about the plot to kill Captain Becket?' the cadet asked.

Guir tried to shake his head. He couldn't. He couldn't move properly, couldn't think. There was light, but there was nothing to see, just a grey ceiling in front of him. He felt his eyes cross for a moment and then straighten. His tongue lolled out of his mouth.

'I repeat, did you know about the plot to kill Captain Becket?'

There was a ball in Guir's stomach, a choking heavy clench. It rose up his gullet, up his throat, and into his mouth.

'Yeuth,' the clench came out.

'Were you a part of that plot?'

'Yes.' It came out clearer this time.

'Were you the leader of that plot?'

'No.'

'Did you conceive the idea to kill Captain Becket?'

'No.'

'Was Commander Ward the person who first suggested the idea to you?'

Suggested the idea? They never spoke of anything directly, they had never needed to, but there had been innuendo, implication.

'Yes.'

'Were you directly involved in causing the crash of the shuttle that killed Captain Becket and forty-seven members of the crew of the Emperor's warship, *Relentless*?'

'No.'

'Did you conceal evidence of another's direct involvement in the aforementioned crash, and did you fail to report such evidence in your attestation appended to Commander Ward's report to battlefleet?'

There it was, the question, the answer to which could get him shot. Say no, or say nothing, he ordered himself. It was too late to escape his fate, but at least he could show them how a man could stand proud. Just say nothing.

'Yes.'

The cadet didn't pause. That wasn't enough. There was more.

'Have you ever heard the name Cadet-Commissar Micael?'

'No.'

'To the best of your knowledge, have you ever been involved in initiating, enacting, ordering or suggesting an attack on one of Commissar Bedrossian's cadets?'

'No.'

The strain that had been in the cadet's voice relented. He looked over at the commissar for approval to continue and Bedrossian gave a small nod.

'Do you trust Commander Ward?'

'No.'

'Do you believe he is fit to command the Emperor's warship, *Relentless*?'

'No.'

'Would you be prepared to remove him from command?'

Guir's head reeled. What was this?

'Yes.'

'Would you be prepared to kill him?'

'Yes.'

When he said it, he knew it was true.

The commissar had remained quiet and allowed his cadets to work. It was important that they took every opportunity to learn, but they had enough. He leaned across the slab that Guir lay unmoving upon and looked down into his confused eyes.

'Thank you for your patience, lieutenant commander. You will be glad to know that you are among friends.'

* * *

BECKET KNELT, HIS head bowed in prayer, as the familiar words of the lector's prayer-rite rolled over the assembly. His sickness had passed, but the fever-dreams he had had still plagued his sleep: Ward and the commissar standing over Warrant's body, which then became his own; being beaten and suffocated in the refuse tank by Brand, who became Ferrol; sitting alone in his chair on the bridge of first the *Relentless* and then the *Granicus;* and the shining Emperor appearing in space before him, and casting him down in disappointment, down and down.

Since the fever had broken, Becket had kept his mind filled with ideas, concepts, designs, exploring every last option he had. The more he thought, the more out-landish his ideas became. Killing Ward would not be enough. How many would there have been in the con-spiracy? They would have to die too. Could he trust their seconds or were they involved as well? Even if they weren't, he knew that Ward controlled the entire officer corps through his patronage. They would all have to go, every single officer.

There it was again, the impossibility of it all. If he went with Ferrol then he could probably satisfy the strict duty he owed battlefleet. He could find a way to send them a message. They would take the steps the Articles dictated, recall the *Relentless,* and if it refused to come, they would send a battle group out after it. It would all take years, decades, but once it was started it would not be stopped. Ward or, more likely his heirs, would resist, and the entire ship would suffer for his decision.

Alternatively, he could crawl away. The captain could stay dead, and Vaughn could go on and live a different life. How much longer would it take before Ward's depre-dations were noticed by Emcor? Or would they ever be? Was he the kind of captain that battlefleet wanted to suc-ceed? No, Becket could not accept that.

His duty to battlefleet, however, paled in comparison to his duty to the Emperor. He had sworn an oath to Him that the *Relentless* and its crew were under his care. That oath could be satisfied by neither of those choices. There had to be another way, and so he prayed fervently to His icon sited in pride of place above the lector. The icon was plain enough compared to the grandiose centrepiece of the main chapel above decks, and to the ornate, gilded pieces that he had seen on pilgrimage, but it was nonetheless well-sculpted. The Emperor's body rose from the frame, encased within the most holy Golden Throne that sustained his life.

What an existence, to be entombed alive. Did He mourn his loss, Becket wondered? The legends he had learned as a child were of a god who walked as a man, who brought salvation to all humankind in the time of darkness and strife, who led the blessed legions out to conquer the galaxy once more, and founded the Imperium of Man. Did He abhor what He had become? What He had to endure to cling to life and remain the shining light, the only hope for mankind. That was His gift: sacrifice.

'Hear me, captain.'

Becket opened his eyes. 'Hear me, captain.' He heard again. He had not dreamed the words. He looked up.

'Hear me, captain,' the lector said again. It was all in elaborate High Gothic, woven into the prayer-rite. Was it mere chance? Was it intended to expose him? He couldn't be sure. He ducked his head down again.

The subdeacon, who was observing them, saw the small movement and made a notation. He did not know why the confessor wanted such things to be recorded, but his report, as ever, would be as exemplary as it could be.

GUIR LOOKED OUT through the slit at the long row of bodies emblazoned upon aquila. This was the first time he had been inside the Perga, the dividing line between above and below. It was not spoken of often in the upper decks, as the rich inhabitants of a fine city might not speak of those who kept their sewers working. The commissar had said that it was the safest place from the first officer's agents. No one looked too closely at the Perga, lest they attract the attention of those who dwelt within.

'So you were part of the plot to kill the captain as well, commissar?' he asked.

'I was not a part of it, but I knew.'

'What did you know?'

'I knew not to inquire too closely.'

Guir nodded. He had been with the commissar on the bridge when it had happened.

'What was your price?'

The commissar paused. 'What do you mean?'

'The price Commander Ward bought you for! We know about me already: advancement, promotion. That was the way the old captain ran it: you stayed close, and you did whatever he asked. Ward operates the same way, but none of that applies to one of the Emperor's commissars.'

'That is not a topic we will discuss.'

'But there was one? You were bought and paid for?'

'Yes.'

'But now you've turned.'

'As have you.'

'But I am his subordinate. I am not one of the Emperor's most righteous commissars. You have the authority to remove him at a stroke, to march onto the bridge and execute him right there–'

'And I will use my authority, but little good will be done if the shot that kills him is succeeded by the one that kills me. He is being drawn to the life of the renegade, and he is taking those who follow him along.'

'Forgive me, commissar, if my questions are invasive,' Guir said, his voice heavy with sarcasm, 'but you had your chance to satisfy yourself as to my intentions and so I merely–'

'You want a similar opportunity?' the commissar cut in. He swept his coat off and made to lie down on the interrogator slab. 'Proceed if you wish.'

'No, that will not be necessary.' A cynical thought had struck him. 'No doubt even such a persuasive method can be fooled.'

'As you wish, and yes it can be done. It is a rare mind that can do it, however.'

Guir stared at the commissar. 'There is one thing that you can do, a show of good faith.'

'Name it.'

'Show me your face.'

Bedrossian's hand instinctively went to his mask. 'It is not... pleasant.'

'You are able to take the mask off, though?'

'There is no power in the mask. It is, as it appears, simple steel, nothing unique. On rare occasions, I even allow one of my cadets to wear it, so that the crewmen will think he is me, and so that they can taste what it will be like for them when they are commissars.'

For a moment, Guir thought that he would refuse, but the commissar reached up and undid indiscernible clasps. He took the mask off and laid it to one side.

Guir looked upon Bedrossian's damaged face. The mouth and nose were indistinguishable as features. The skin was red and black, burned deep by something fiercer than fire, more biting than acid. Above it all, though, his blue eyes shone clear. The wounds were the rewards of his service in a war still raging far, far away.

'Does it hurt?' Guir asked.

'Yes,' Bedrossian replied. The answer came from a slit where the mouth should have been.

'Thank you,' Guir said. 'Please put it back on.' He turned away to allow the commissar his privacy. How hard it seemed now, to trust another.

'So,' Guir continued, 'we have reached an understanding.'

'We have reached an understanding. It is time to agree the way forward. I have the authority, and you have the men to ensure that it can be used. If we can secure the

most vital locations, and strike directly at him with over-
whelming force then we will be victorious. The
Mechanicus will not get involved, nor will the Navis
Nobilite, but the main armoury, the launch bays and the
bridge must all be in the hands of your men.'

'My men?'

'Yes?'

'I have had… doubts over some of them. Ward's agents,
I believe–'

'There I may help you. Commander Ward removed a
sizeable quantity of cargo from the *Arc of Elona,* and his
agents have been making liberal offerings to members of
your staff to undermine your authority. Each believes he
is one of only a few who have been approached. If they
learned of the extent to which such offers have been
made, they might rightly become concerned about the
sincerity of the commander's offers. I also have extensive
files on many of them, which you may find will add
weight to your persuasive power.'

'Keep your files, commissar. I did not obtain the rank
of second officer of this ship by being an innocent babe.
You would do well to remember that,' Guir replied, 'but
thank you for your information. That will be enough.'

'By the way,' Guir added, 'there was a name you asked
about: Micael? Who is that?'

'He is a cadet of mine. He has disappeared.'

'You have no idea where he might be? Why he went?'

'He is not one of your common crewmen that might
run and hide or be swayed by money or women. As to his
whereabouts, my suspicions are that he is with the
Emperor. As for why… that is a question I believe only
Commander Ward can answer.'

THIRTEEN

THE GLOWING IMAGE of the *Relentless* flickered and disappeared from the archon's display. Once again, they had lost track of the Imperial ship within the channels of the warp. He waited a moment for it to reappear, his gaze gliding along the lights depicting the tides and flow of the maelstrom. Somewhere in his mind he could hear the baying of the creatures out there that spoke to him, that called his name in his father's voice to come and join them. Ai'zhraphim's victims thought they knew fear, at his hands they believed they understood the true nature of terror. They knew nothing. Even upon his greatest works, he had not elicited an atom of the horror that swirled around them. Yet it was his destiny, it was for his people. They had killed their gods, and this had replaced them. Ai'zhraphim knew that he was a thing of nightmare, and what plagued the dreams of one such as him? It was this.

As it was with him, so too he knew it was with his followers. The *Relentless* refused to reappear upon his display, and Ai'zhraphim knew that action had to be taken. To be weak, to be indecisive in his world was to invite death. To do the same in this godless place was to invite far worse. With a gesture of his control sceptre, the dark sphere that enclosed him became transparent and then faded from view, revealing him in all his magnificent glory to his subserviants toiling beyond. To command, there were times when one should watch, and times when one had to be seen.

He cast his gaze imperiously down the length of the long, thin bridge at his dracon and sybarite subordinates. They did not see him immediately as all their posts looked forward and his throne was behind them. The stern was the position of honour, for treachery and betrayal were the bread and meat of his kind. To have your back to another was to lay yourself at his mercy. His followers had to labour before him, never knowing whether his eyes were upon them, whether he would strike them down unawares.

Though he appeared without fanfare, it took only moments for his minions to notice him and turn and bow. They had not survived and ascended to their privileged positions for nothing. Once they had all adopted the subservient pose, Ai'zhraphim made a minute gesture with his sceptre. His throne began to hum gently, raised from its rostrum, and then swept up into the air to a commanding height.

He bade his minions rise, and he glided steadily over the barriers that separated each section. The bridge had been carefully designed so that the archon could see all, but no section could see into another. Ai'zhraphim found it useful to keep his minions divided in this way, and encouraged a healthy competition for his favour between them. He knew that they were mundane precautions, and that no one was fooled as to their intent. Nevertheless, such was the way of his kin. As much as they knew that such infighting was part of the archon's control, they

were unable to resist plotting and scheming the downfall
of their rivals. Ai'zhraphim did not question their nature,
but he took comfort that it ensured he was troubled only
by the ablest of conspirators. It was by such methods, he
mused, that egotistical individualists, driven only by their
own amoral self-interest, could function as a society.
Alliances had to be formed, the weak must serve the
strong, control must be maintained and, from time to
time, examples must be made. Now was that time.

He had been failed. The Imperials' trail had been lost
and not recovered. Such failure, however insignificant in
the grander scheme, could not be allowed to pass without
consequence. With a stroke of his sceptre, Ai'zhraphim
dissolved the walls around the kunegex position. These
were the trackers responsible for maintaining the trail
and, as they were revealed to the rest of the bridge, the
unfortunates inside fell to their knees in supplication.

Ai'zhraphim guided his throne closer, looming over
them. The position's sybarite nodded unnecessarily in the
direction of the warrior at fault, unnecessarily because, even
now, his cowering fellows were hastily edging away from
him. Ai'zhraphim paused for a second, enjoying the mixture
of apprehension and expectation that hung in the air. He
grazed at a control on the armrest and the gargoyle muzzle
within spat a vicious, serrated harpoon, its white cord
snaking out behind it. The point caught the guilty warrior in
the shoulder, went clean through, and then pulled back to
dig deep within his flesh. The warrior screamed from the
impact and from the pain enhancers that coated the point.
He was flipped into the air, and, with an intricate control of
the psycho-plastic cord, Ai'zhraphim spun the figure until
the cord wrapped around his victim in a tight shroud, stifling his cries. The struggling package was snapped back and
stored neatly in a cavity beneath the throne, to await the
archon's pleasure.

Ai'zhraphim glanced at the remainder of the kunegex,
who were wisely standing as still as statues. He

considered whether a further example needed to be made, but decided not. It had only been a trifling inconvenience after all.

Gliding back, he raised the walls between the sections and gave the new course to the navarcos. The *Relentless*'s course was patently clear, and the hook was already lodged within its belly.

THE AUDITOR AWOKE. His first sensation was cold. His body was cold, his limbs were cold, his brain was cold. His thoughts were trapped, locked deep within the permafrost. There was nothing there any more but desolation: no memory, no identity. Why was he even awake? What had awoken him? He felt no movement and there was no light. There was something though, something at the limit of his senses: a heat. He wanted that heat. The heat would make the cold go away. He had to be near it.

He could feel his body now. It felt dead, leaden, but his commands were obeyed. He was in a casket. He pushed against one side and, with some effort, swung it open. He had been lying down. He had not realised. He pushed himself out and found his feet. It was still dark, but his eyes were beginning to discern the lines and edges of his surroundings. He was still closed in. The room was small, It was full of things and the ceiling was low. The heat was still far away, but there was no door out.

He clambered onto the things and scraped himself along the ceiling, looking for an opening. He found a bump, a tiny device that hummed as he touched it. It hummed, and then the ceiling moved, rising above his head. He was free, and the heat beckoned him on.

'IT DOESN'T SOUND right,' Guir said. 'How many of the armoury crew must Ward control? Yet he sends one crewman from below decks to try to bribe a single one of them? It doesn't–'

'Only the master of arms and his second have the necessary access,' the commissar replied. 'Both of them underwent individual review and screening by my–'

'So you think that makes them incorruptible?' Guir shot back. 'As incorruptible as a commissar perhaps?'

For once, Bedrossian did not cut him off. Instead, the words hung in the air between them.

'Before he may draw arms, he must provide a rationale. Every senior officer must, including Commander Ward,' the commissar said, breaking the silence. 'If he does not, or if his rationale is inadequate, I will hear of it immediately. Unless, that is, he has turned the master of arms or his second.'

'So bring them in as you brought me–'

'It will tip our hand before we are ready. No, it is better to follow the source.'

'You really believe that Ward would try something like this from below decks?'

'What better way to disguise that he is behind it?'

'I'm not certain.'

'Then consider, lieutenant commander, the opportunity that it presents.'

'What opportunity?'

'Legitimate concern. A threat to the ship. To find this man we could send a few agents, who might root him out within a week, or we could take dozens, fully armed, hit the lower decks, take him and extract his confession. Then we would have both the proof and the means to strike.'

THE CONFESSOR SAT back at the news he had received. The lector was still prostrate on the floor.

'That was the full extent of his confession?' Pulcher asked.

'Every word, your eminence.'

'And they are after one man, specifically, with orders to take him alive.'

'Yes, your eminence.'

'Hmmm… could it possibly be a coincidence?' Pulcher muttered to himself. 'Though our fates are His, and the trials and tests before us of His design.'

He heaved himself out of his cathedra and moved over to the lectern.

'Guide me, Imperator, guide me,' he prayed, and then wrote out a note. He sent it out with the lector to be delivered immediately and sat down once more.

After a little thought, the confessor stood up, crossed to the lectern, scribbled a second note and sent that off too. The Emperor may know which of the two sides would be ultimately triumphant, but if He did, He was keeping his opinions to Himself.

WARD QUICKLY READ the note that had been handed to him by the solemn subdeacon. It said nothing of which he was not already aware. His plans were already in place.

THE MESSAGE CAME through to the captain loud and clear. The lector had appeared at the hatch of the work area and declaimed it loudly in High Gothic. The others had thought it was a blessing before a warp jump, and when that did not occur, had dismissed it as yet another fathomless ritual of the Ecclesiarchy. Becket understood though, and, as the lector went off to the next work area, he had gone straight to Ferrol, who was less than convinced.

'"The one garbed in black and silver, he comes for you"? That was it?'

'I do not know how, but someone within the priesthood knows or suspects who I am. It's a warning that the commissar is coming.'

'It's a warning, it's a trap, or it's just a blasted prayer. Go if you want, go down to the ghost-decks. We'll come for you when it's time.'

'The commissar will not just be after me.'

'If it is the commissar, if it even was a message. If we run now, we look guilty. Do you think I can pull this off, hiding and scavenging what I can? No. I have to stay here, and do right by my men, all of them. So, go, Vaughn, get out of here.'

BECKET LEFT THEM, but not to hide in the ghost-decks. He had prayed for the Emperor's guidance and it had been delivered. A third avenue opened up before him. He could think of no means by which he could both remove Ward and save the ship, but then, staring at the Emperor's image within the Golden Throne, Becket had realised that he had unconsciously been including a third criteria within his considerations: personal survival. Now, he could see that any two of three could be met. That was the Emperor's lesson for them all: sacrifice.

LESS THAN AN hour later, Lieutenant Aryll marched into the renovation section with two bodyguards. The crewmen working there scrambled to their feet.

'Surprise inspection,' he snapped, and the crewmen stood to attention. 'Who's your team leader?'

'I am,' Ferrol said.

Aryll pretended to consult a data-slate in his hand: 'You are Crewman Ferrol?'

'Trusted Crewman Ferrol, yes, sir.'

'Good, I need a word with you outside, regarding one of your work crew. Follow me.' Aryll waved for him to join him, and marched out, leaving his bodyguards behind. Ferrol shot a warning glance at Shroot, and walked out after him.

Aryll was waiting for him at the end of the corridor, his face impassive. Ferrol stepped over the lip into the corridor. There was a swish right beside him, followed by an explosion to the left side of his skull. The blow had been meant to knock him cold, but it merely staggered him. He stumbled to his right, clutching his head. Strong hands took hold of his arms, bending them back, and something was forced into his mouth. A hood was dropped over his face and everything went black.

As SOON AS Ferrol was out of sight, Aryll's bodyguards had pulled their shotguns and levelled them at the work team. The team edged back, but the guard held fast. There was a heavy thump from outside, and Shroot saw what was about to happen. The guards fired.

SHROOT RAN FOR her life. The first shots had blown her crewmates at the front back upon their fellows. The next shots had caught the second row as they turned to run. The third and fourth volleys took those who had dived for the cover of the walls. She had dived, she had rolled, and shot had bitten into her side. She should not have survived, but she had, and she had run.

She could hear the sounds of the guards in pursuit, and, for a split second, she risked a glance behind her. Nothing. She turned back and an arm appeared before her, stretching out from the wall. It grabbed her tight and pulled her in. She struggled and scratched to get free, but hands seized her wrists tight and drew her deeper in and away.

'Get off me!' Shroot shrieked, trying to squirm away. 'Let me go! You won't take me! You won't!'

'Quiet, Shroot. Sound travels in here.' Shroot looked up and saw the captain's face.

'How did–'

'I heard the shots. I came back.'

'This is your fault,' she hissed. 'This is all your fault.'

'Silence, Shroot,' he said. She was silent, and they waited, hiding in the walls.

FERROL COULD FEEL no pain. He could feel nothing at all. The last thing he had felt was the block going into his neck, resting against his spine and shutting down his nervous system. After that there was nothing. They had even unshackled his hands and his feet as there was no need to restrain them anymore. They had left him the use of his mouth, as they would need that, and his eyes, as they wanted him to see. His body was laid out, reflected in the parabolic mirror above him. He could not turn his head, and so whichever way he looked there he was.

A man blocked the light for a moment. He was wearing a dark red coverall, 'so as not to show the blood,' the line the crewbosses had used to scare them ran through his thoughts.

'Crewman Ferrol?' It was a clipped voice. He couldn't see the speaker.

Ferrol gurgled. His brain felt as though it was spread across the hull.

'Have you ever heard the name Commander Ward?'

His reply came before he could even understand the question.

'Yes.'

THE SURVIVORS OF Ferrol's crew had gathered together.

'We have to go after him.'

'He's probably dead already.'

'No one comes out of the Perga. The only way we see him again, is strung up outside.'

'You'd just cut and run would you? What if that's what he'd done when you–'

'Listen to me, all of you. Maybe he was the only one they were after. We don't know why–'

'They didn't just take him.'

'Maybe that was a mistake.'

'You're both being idiots. There's only one thing we can do.'

'All I'm saying is–'

Becket heard them go on and on. For all their urgency, they talked around the same issues again and again, trying to find a consensus that simply did not exist. Each one of them felt that he had a voice, a say. In a flash, Becket's envy of Ferrol's easy command style disappeared. Ferrol showed attention to each of them individually and they loved him in a way that no crew of Becket's ever had. Ferrol had placed himself at the heart of how his crew ran, and now he had been snatched away, they all expected the same consideration from each other as they had received from him.

Shroot was the only one who could break the deadlock. The crew looked to her as his anointed heir, but she was merely trying to manage the opinions flying back and forth, and was not imposing her own. Becket studied her carefully. She simply did not know what the right decision was, and her fierce loyalty to Ferrol was suddenly tempered by the weight of command. They had lost men before, left them behind, even, when events demanded. The men understood that it was part of their life. The first decision should have been easy. She should walk away now, take the crew down into the ghost-decks, and ensure their safety. But what then? What about the second decision, and the third, and all the ones after that? She could not imagine what they would do without Ferrol.

The conscripts had stayed quiet; Becket too. These arguing crewmen did not look to him for leadership. He could not simply command them, but then, had he not simply commanded the conscripts all those weeks ago? No, he had not sent them into the pipe, he had led them.

Becket caught Sundjata's eye and then stood. Sundjata, and then the rest of the conscripts, followed. The argument stopped, and Ferrol's crewmen looked at them. The captain spoke to them all.

'Master Ferrol came for me once. Now I will go for him. That is all.'

He led the conscripts away.

'I AM GLAD you are coming,' Becket said to the small woman who appeared at his side.

'You really thought we weren't?' Shroot replied.

'I know Ferrol would never doubt you.'

Shroot bridled slightly. 'It's no easy sell taking the Perga, you know? That place, no passages, no pipes, no vents that lead there, none we can use at least. There's a reason it was designed that way, to make sure that no one could do the thing that we're about to do.'

'I would never have proposed such an action if I did not have a way to accomplish our goals.'

'Oh, you got a plan? Oh, praise the Emperor,' Shroot sneered. 'Even if your plan works, have you thought about what happens then?'

'Of course.'

'Then what?'

'You can take Ferrol, run to the ghost-decks and do what you can to survive.'

'And what about you?'

'I am going to the upper decks, and I am going to do my duty. I am going to kill Commander Ward.'

Shroot laughed. 'You're crazy. Even if you drop him, you'll never make it out alive.'

Becket paused and looked at Shroot with his measured gaze. 'Sacrifice,' he said. 'That is His lesson.'

'So you admit that you instructed your crewman to approach Artifex Roto?'

'Yes.'

'And your purpose in doing so was to gain access to weapons contained within the armoury?'

'Yes.'

'Were you acting on the orders of Commander Ward?'

'No.'

'Were you acting on the orders, instructions or suggestion of any other party?'

'No.'

The cadet looked up at the commissar. It was the third time they had been through the questions, and the subject

had never varied in his answers. Guir took Bedrossian out of
the interrogation chamber.

'How long is this going to carry on, commissar?'

'For as long as it takes.'

'I'm no chirurgeon, but even I can tell that his body
cannot be left in this state for much longer. What more–?'

'This is the connection to Ward. This is the proof we
need to convince his pet officer corps that he was infil-
trating the armoury so that he could move against them.'

'He has denied it every time we have asked.'

'The subject is lying! Or had that fact eluded you? We
asked him if he had had any contact with any of the command staff and he said, "yes." Filth like that! What other
contact would he have had?'

'We went through them one by one and he denied each
one.'

'Exactly! He's holding out on the name. He's blocked
it! We are wearing him down. We will extract that name
from him if he speaks it with his last breath. Then we will
have all we need.'

'Listen to me! It doesn't matter. We seize the bridge. We
execute Ward. You have the authority for that! The officers will fall in line when they see which way the current
flows, but we must move now.'

'One more time then, Guir. One more time. If he
denies it again, we'll have no further use for him. If he
admits it... then he'll be our prize exhibit.'

The two of them stepped back inside. The commissar
stood the cadet down. From here, he would complete the
questioning himself. Ferrol had heard the commissar's
final words before he entered. He had been meant to hear
them, to know that this was it. These men wanted him to
admit that he was the agent of the first officer, and Ferrol
would have been more than happy to spin lies and tales
to suit whatever they required, but the block in his neck
and the wires in his head were a hard bypass, dragging
the answers direct from his mind to his mouth without

his control. He could not lie, and yet they kept asking and asking.

Then, the thought emerged. If they were posing the questions time and again they must expect different answers. If they thought he had been lying then it meant it must be possible to lie, and if it could be done then he, Master Ferrol, would do it!

VALINARIUS SOARED ONCE more within the heart of the machine. It should have been ecstasy, but there was always that gap, that part of the communion that he could not obtain. He had tried to ignore it, had tried to enjoy the spirit in every way he could, but he was frustrated. His communion had to be total and complete.

He felt a tugging sensation. He was being called back. Someone needed him. He had wanted to be left undisturbed, but he could not afford to allow his self-serving underlings free rein. No, they could not use that excuse again.

As usual, his body appeared, installed across the altar, and he snapped back in. Again, there was the last echo of the machine-spirit that lingered.

Murder.

'I DIDN'T!'

The magos's cry cut through the chatter of the command deck. Though it came through the vox, no one on the dais could have failed to hear it.

'Magos?' the first officer asked cautiously. In warp space, you could be certain of nothing. 'This is Commander Ward.'

There was dead static at the other end. Then there were the words.

'I am the magos majoris.'

'Good,' Ward said with more confidence than he felt. 'We are reading a distress signal, and will be jumping back to real space to investigate. Please attend, or send a representative,' he added.

The vox-line cut off.

Shortly thereafter, Tertionus appeared and supervised the firing of the warp engines. He did not offer any other information, but simply asserted that the condition of the magos majoris was strictly an internal matter.

THE COMMAND DECK burst into action as the screeching sound of the warp engines diminished. The cartastra whirred as it mapped the visible stars and calculated their galactic position. The auspex arrays and the associated banks of logisticians hummed into activity, searching the local area. The perennial image of dark sky and bright stars appeared once more on the main view-portal.

'Minor displacement from intended exit locus, within acceptable limits,' Sub-Lieutenant Hoffore reported.

'Distress signal relocated, commander,' Lieutenant Aster said. 'Target is beyond extreme range.'

'No other auspex hits received, sir.'

'Any identification on the target?'

'Signal contains ident information, sir,' said Aster, 'merchant ensign. It's in our registry. The *Piadore*, sir, a Mule-class frigate. No information on previous or current destinations.'

'No signs of any other vessels in the area? Absolutely none?'

'Absolutely none, sir,' Hoffore replied.

'Very well. Mister Hoffore, set for continual auspex scans. Mister Aster, call the lieutenant commander and the commissar to the command deck immediately. Keep it slow, Mister Crichell, the *Piadore* will have to wait. We have business to take care of first.'

As his bridge officers set about their tasks, Ward noticed the senior armsman standing silently beside him.

'Is there a problem, Mister Vickers?'

'No, sir.'

'Good,' Ward replied. 'I have not forgotten your concerns, Mister Vickers, but this is the best way: draw the mutineers out into the open, and make a clean sweep of it. A final showdown between the loyal and the renegade, in the finest traditions of the *Relentless*.'

'Aye, sir,' Vickers replied, and moved off to his position.

'Lieutenant Commander Guir, please report to the command deck. We are approaching a ship in distress.'

'Commissar Bedrossian, your presence is requested on the command deck. We are approaching a ship in distress.'

The messages came through one after the other to their vox-receivers.

Guir looked up from Ferrol to the commissar, who crossed to the intra-ship array.

'It's true,' the commissar reported.

'Do we have what we need?'

The commissar nodded. 'Your men know their targets?'

'Yes.'

'Then let us go.'

When Becket arrived at the gathering point outside the Perga, one of the scouts that had gone ahead reported that an armed party had already left, with the commissar and Lieutenant Commander Guir at their head. Ferrol was not among them. Was he already dead? They would find out soon enough.

Becket tugged at the collar of the unfamiliar uniform that he wore. He was only glad that Ferrol disposed of nothing that might be of future use. There was no way to sneak into the Perga. Its sides, back, roof and floor were sealed off by reinforced bulkheads. It was a fortress, and there was no way to attack except head on.

The auditor stumbled on. The heat was still distant, but he could sense its thrumming as he drew closer.

There were others around him, heading in the same direction. The auditor felt them by his side, but they were cold as well. He had seen them as they joined. Their faces were twisted. Their jaws were distended and bulging, their throats puffed and swollen. The flesh of their faces hung off their bones, and a few wispy hairs adorned their scalps. Their bellies and thighs hung loose, some torn open and crudely stitched, some pinned and braced, the skin pockmarked or folded across itself. They were misshapen. They were deformed, not by birth but by choice, and he was one of them.

The auditor paid them no mind. They ignored him. Though he knew, he did not feel. The heat beckoned him on.

BECKET MARCHED DOWN the road to the Perga. He refused to look at the bodies strung up and hanging on either side. His focus was fixed on the gatehouse at the end. He walked brazenly, as did his men behind him, as there was no way to conceal their approach. Becket was shaved, his hair close-cropped for the first time since his savage conscription. The worst of the burn-scabs had fallen from his face. He had seen his reflection and could see his old face there for the first time. There was one difference, however: the clothes he wore were not his impressive Navy uniform, but the plainer black garb of the cadet he had murdered.

Becket had not wavered when they had found it for him, had not baulked when he had pulled it on. The young man's clothes had been cut tight, but they fit over his bony frame. He could feel the blood soaked into the fabric as he walked, but he did not stop. He would not allow that blood to be for nothing.

The inhabitants of the Perga, the creatures that lived there and earned their daily meal from the terror they extracted from the crewmen they were brought, saw the group approach. They were wary. The commissar had warned them that this was a time of crisis, that there may be those who would look to take advantage of it, to seize a vital place such as the Perga. But was this not one of the commissar's emissaries leading the group? He had said to trust his cadets as they trusted him, but they were wary. They knew they had enemies, and could only trust themselves. They could not even trust the commissar. He and they had an understanding, but he was not one of them. They would wait. They would not allow this cadet entry, but they would hear what he had to say and judge for themselves.

The cadet would reach their gate, and there he would halt to give his explanation. Instead, he spoke words that they did not understand, and their locked gate slid open. They panicked. Their fortress had been breached. They went to call for help, but the ship-wide alarms were already ringing.

ARTIFEX DOSTOYAKEV SWEATED in front of the generators. Each one was supposed to be heavily encased to ensure that none of the heat escaped and, by and large, the strategy had proved to be almost entirely effective. That minute fraction that did escape, though, made the insides of the generatium intolerably hot. He did not know how the Mechanicus priests could stand it, and yet they were forever working, repairing, optimising and testing machinery amongst the long ranks of the generators, all the while still wearing their heavy robes. Were they even human?

Dostoyakev always watched them when he had the chance. As an artifex, his realm was the routine blessing and maintenance of much of the machinery aboard the ship, and yet, for all his experience, whenever he worked alongside a Mechanicus he felt as an infant might before a grand master. Their innate understanding of the machines, their communion with them, their ability to create anew and not just to restore was a wonder.

Out of the corner of his eye, he noticed that another one of them had wandered in. He turned to greet them, but they did not move. They simply stood there, side-on to Dostoyakev, staring down the long chamber of generators.

Dostoyakev was about to take a step towards the priest, but stopped short. The robe the priest wore, it was not a design he'd seen before. It was ragged, ripped and stained in a way that none of the fastidious Mechanicus could have borne. Beneath the priest's hood, Dostoyakev could also see that there was something wrong with his face. His jaw looked as though it hung low, stretched forward, far more so than should be possible in any human.

The priest turned from the door and the hood fell back. Dostoyakev choked. One side of its face was human, its eye blank, its nose and mouth fused together, bulging out into a muzzle. Its lips met on one side as normal and then skewed out, stained black. Human and animal teeth jutted out from behind, broken and clustered. The other side was the face of a beast, with layers of matted white fur grafted on as skin, the eye cream-green with the pin-prick pupil of a wolf. This could be no man. It was a monster.

There were more, others behind him. Their twisted limbs grasping, split faces twisted in grins and snarls. They had found their precious heat and the rage boiled within them.

WARD WAS SHOUTING, demanding an explanation for the invasion. Guir was shouting, his pistol pointed straight at the commander. The bridge officers were cowering behind their consoles, and Guir's bodyguards were shouting at them to raise their hands in the air. More of Guir's men were moving quickly through the command deck, shouting at the officers with the arrays, clusters and pits to come out. The officers, confused, shouted back. Some of the artificers slaved into the consoles began to panic and started trying to rip free their connections, but the mind-wiped servitors and logisticians had no reaction, their only existence tied inexorably to the sensors and data of the machine.

Bedrossian saw that their coup was working. They had caught Ward off guard. He just needed to get up there and formally remove Ward from command, but something was wrong. Bedrossian looked at the bridge officers again. There was something wrong with them. He shoved a crewman out of the way and got a good look. They were strangers. He didn't recognise any of them. They were fakes. He drew breath to shout a warning to Guir, but it was too late. Ward had already gone for his gun.

'STAND DOWN, COMMANDER! Stand down!' Guir pointed his gun steadily at Ward.

'Don't be such a fool, Guir!'

'Under battlefleet articles, I hereby remove you from command of–'

'Battlefleet articles? What charge?'

'Conspiracy and murder! You will be held within the brig until such time as a battlefleet panel can be brought to–'

'You are an idiot, Mister Guir.'

'Commander Ward, you will stand down or you will be taken down! If you do not stand down, you will be shot! Any officer or crewman who obstructs us in our duty will be shot!'

'I'm so sad to see you fail so completely, Mister Guir.' Ward reached down to his sid earm.

'Take your hand away, commander!'

'But alas, not surprised.' Ward finished, closing his hand around his weapon's grip.

Guir fired. The shot was dead-centre, straight at Ward's chest. There was a blinding flash. For a moment, Bedrossian thought that Guir had supercharged his pistol and obliterated Ward. Then he blinked, and saw Ward still standing, a sparking aura of light around him: a conversion field! Ward had a personal conversion field! Ward had his pistol outstretched and there was a deafening shot. Bedrossian opened his eyes again in time to see Guir falling back, a neat black hole through his left temple. The body hit the deck and sprawled over the dais. Commander Ward stood over him, pistol in hand.

Behind him, along the ranks of the logisticians pitted up
and along the wall, armsmen emerged, their guns ready,
pointed straight down at the intruders spread across the
command deck. Guir and Bedrossian had brought their best
men with them, experienced, veteran warriors. They reacted
at once, diving for cover in the pits and arrays where the
command officers and crew were already drawing pistols
that they had kept concealed. Every station on the deck
instantly erupted into bitter close-quarter fighting as the two
sides grappled, kicked and punched at each other, bringing
their weapons to bear.

On the bridge, arching over it all, the fire from the
ambushers blew the front ranks behind the commissar to
pieces. With nowhere to hide, Guir's men jumped from
the side, even as they were peppered with fire. Some
rolled and scrambled for cover, some landed hard and
screamed until they were caught by the bullets, and some
fell as a dead weights, their momentum carrying them
over the edge even after their lives had been plucked from
them.

With shots ricocheting around, no one was watching
the auspex sensors. In particular, no one saw the engine
readings from the *Piadore* flux, distort and coalesce into a
strange, alien signature.

Ward seized the commissar from the floor, knocked the
gun from his grasp and dragged him up to his hands and
knees. He held his pistol behind the blank mask that
reflected everything he did not wish to see. The air was
split with gunfire, crashing alarms, ringing and sirens,
shouts and screams. Nevertheless, the commander made
himself heard.

'This is how much you wanted to be free of me?' Ward
hissed, the commissar's eyes shaking behind the slits in
his mask. 'You're about to get your wish.'

At that moment, the dark eldar ship opened fire.

FOURTEEN

THE CORRIDORS OF the Perga, normally a place of silent horror, rang with the sounds of battle. Shroot, like a whirlwind, disarmed the foe before her, breaking its bones in the process. The operators of the Perga, men who had had all human compunction and feeling burned from them, were too used to facing opponents who were already strapped down. They were weak, spindly and awkward, once separated from the equipment implants within the cells where they operated. The cumbersome instruments they wielded proved less than effective against a target that was moving and hitting back.

After the Perga's gates opened to the disguised captain, Shroot and the rest of Ferrol's crew had moved in. They began with clinical efficiency, moving as quickly as they could to find Master Ferrol. That changed once they had broken into a few of the cells. Seeing what was inside changed them, driving a new desire to annihilate the operators of the Perga from existence.

Shroot had been at the forefront from the start. Becket had got them inside, but she would be damned if he was the first person Ferrol saw coming to his rescue, if he was still alive.

She slammed into a door and knocked it open.

There, there he was.

ARCHON AI'ZHRAPHIM HAD waited patiently for the Imperial warship to draw closer. Its crude construction and ugly lines disgusted him. Its design was little more than an angular ram, a drifting block compared to his elegant, refined, most deadly Slaver.

The Imperials' auspex technology was the equal of their aesthetics. The kabals had practised the arts of trickery and deception for aeons. Deceiving the Imperials' crude sensors to masquerade as one of their victims was a work of childlike simplicity. The *Relentless* had come at them initially with caution, but even as they had drawn closer, when there had been a small chance that they might notice an inconsistency, they had borne straight on the course that would take them alongside the *'Piadore'*.

The barbarians had sensed nothing. Ai'zhraphim had waited until the perfect moment, out of the direct path of their prow armament, but before they entered the arc of fire of the massive starboard batteries that could tear apart even a ship such as his. His plan of attack was classic, perfectly poised to take every advantage at his disposal.

The moment had come. The attack had commenced.

UPON THE COMMAND deck of the *Relentless,* the sudden energy spike set off an alarm that went unheard in the din of the crossfire. What was once a humble Mule freighter was revealed as a xenos raider, and the cogitators whirred into action, searching their ship records for a match. There was nothing, however, that could be done to protect the *Relentless* from the Slaver's first volleys.

The Slaver's gunners had every opportunity to pick their target, and all their fire was focused on the starboard broadside batteries that they feared so much. Their own batteries fired, and the unprepared energy shields around the *Relentless* collapsed in an instant. Deep inside the ship, the enginseers, clinging to their consoles as grotesque monsters rampaged around them, registered the shield collapse. They awaited the balancing coordination from the scutatum cluster on the command deck, but the officer responsible was locked in a life or death struggle with one of Guir's veterans who was trying to twist off his head.

In that critical delay, the Slaver's gunners did their work, landing shot after shot against the *Relentless*'s battery. They crippled the Imperial cannon, and smashed open the gunnery compartments behind, tearing through the gun crew's bodies, and blowing the remains out into space.

Ai'zhraphim allowed himself a small smile. The *Relentless* had bared its throat, and it was time for the Slaver to sink her fangs in.

The Slaver swept past the starboard side, taunting the damaged guns, before flitting away and disappearing into the gloom, leaving a trail of glittering stars. Each star was an individual assault boat, crammed with eldar warriors eager to make their journey worthwhile.

The main guns of the *Relentless*'s starboard battery had failed to fire, awaiting orders that never came, and had paid the price. The far smaller point-defence turrets needed no such authority, and opened up as soon as the attack craft burned towards them. The starboard side of the *Relentless* became a tapestry of criss-crossing turret fire. Half a dozen craft were hit square on, the energies focused on them bursting their boats apart like overripe fruit, leaving their debris to patter harmlessly off the *Relentless*'s hull. Two were knocked off their trajectories. One managed to right itself and continue, but the other, its steering destroyed, tumbled away into the void, far beyond any chance of recovery. More craft took minor hits, but survived and continued on, even though their craft stood no chance of making the journey back. These tiny losses, however, were trifles to the swarm that enveloped the *Relentless*, latched onto the hull and started to burrow their way in.

WARD PULLED HIMSELF unsteadily up onto the side of the captain's chair. The alarms blared in his head. The blasts had knocked everyone off their feet, and some were thrown clean across the deck. The arrays were smashed, and the pits were dark. Some of the ranks of logistician pods hung, broken off the wall, empty; their occupants torn forcibly from their installations and tossed down to the deck. Where was Bedrossian? He had been a moment away from ending the coward's life, and now he was nowhere to be seen. This was intolerable. He called for his bridge officers to report, and only then noticed the rubble that had fallen upon the dais and smashed the consoles. The debris was fragments of the mighty aquila that was sculpted across the command deck, centred above the dais, an aquila that was now fallen. Ward checked his conversion field, but it had blown too.

He staggered forward a few steps towards the consoles, and then dropped flat as shots from below ricocheted around him. More shots were fired in response, and then, haltingly, uncaring of the greater danger, the fighting began again.

Ward crawled back to the captain's chair.

'Mister Vickers!' he cried, and, as if by magic, the faithful senior armsman was there.

'Mister Vickers, secure the area!'

'Aye, sir!'

'And bring me some damn officers!' Ward wrenched the displays in the captain's chair so that he could view

them while sheltering behind it. He pulled out the vox.
Officers be damned, he would win this battle himself!

CREWMAN DJOL WOOZILY picked himself up from the floor.
His tub of slop had gone flying when the ship had
bucked, and now it was splattered across the corridor.
Djol staggered over to it, and was taking a grip on the
handle when he saw the small bug that had crawled up
and had begun to eat. Djol crushed it under his boot.
They couldn't allow an infestation on the ship, but no
matter how hard they screened the foodstuffs they
brought aboard, a few always slipped past.

Suddenly, with an awful screech, a blade carved
through the corridor wall. Djol tripped back, his heart
leaping into his mouth. The blade, bristling with energy,
cut clean through the wall to the deck. Another two
swipes, and a section of the thin, internal wall fell
through.

Djol was frozen with fear. Something stepped through
the gap, man-shaped, but not a man. Its chitinous
armour was segmented and spined like an exoskeleton;
the hooked mandibles around its mouth twitched and
beckoned him in; its helm rose up into a crest like a scor-
pion's tail; but its eyes, its red eyes, Djol felt them burn
into his soul.

It brought its halberd sweeping around, slicing Djol's
tub in half, and then held it over the crewman. Djol,
shaking, raised his hands. A noise came from its mouth.
It was saying something, but not to him. Another one
appeared at the gap behind him, a spiked rifle in its
hand. Its head darted left and right, and then it dashed
forwards, down the corridor. Then another came after it,
and another and another. One appeared every second,
helmet-plumes streaming behind them, flitting through
the breach and taking after the first. There was a
moment's pause, and then Djol felt his terror redouble its
grip. One more, taller, its armour ornately decorated with

scenes of pain and torture, stepped through. Djol felt his heart about to burst.

Dracon Ysubi glanced down at the petrified human, and then nodded to the incubi who captured him, allowing his warrior to ensnare his captive.

'Let the hunt begin.'

THE RAIDERS' FIRST insertions into the *Relentless* were met by limited resistance. Without coordination from the command deck, each section's defenders were on their own. In many cases, the first warning they had of an assault craft cutting through to them was the final explosion as the hull was breached and xenos warriors came pouring through. In many other cases, the raiders' entry was completely unopposed, and so the crew of the *Relentless* lost its best chance to keep the invaders bottled up in their boats.

Deck 202: mid-section.

Raiders on bladed sky-boards raced ahead so quickly that off-duty crewmen were still stumbling out of their barracks as they struck. This sudden strike effectively sealed off one of the primary cross-ship transit passages, keeping many work-crews pinned down while the following raiders consolidated their entry.

Deck 77: aft-section.

The raiders' scouting operations met so little opposition, and advanced so quickly, that the responding crew squads came under a withering crossfire and were put to flight in seconds.

Deck 111: fore-section.

The attack craft attempted to grapple onto one of the destroyed gun battery compartments. Debris in the area continued to foil their attempts to gain a solid hold. Instead, the raiders exited the boat through side hatches and used their smaller munitions to gain entry through the *Relentless*'s hull maintenance access points.

Deck 250: aft-section.

An assault boat latched on and burned its way through the hull, disgorging the raiders straight into the heart of the ghost-decks. The boat was chanced upon later, still attached, but there was nothing left of whatever boarding party it had held.

BECKET AND HIS men saw it all on the monitors within the Perga. They had found the surveillance chamber just before Shroot had discovered Ferrol strapped onto the interrogation slab. Ferrol was free now, but he couldn't stand, and could barely talk.

'This is our chance!' one of Ferrol's crew erupted. 'Let's take a launch bay, let's make it away from this blasted ship.'

'And go where?' Becket said firmly. 'We are dead in space. There is nowhere a transport will take us.'

'Then down, back to the ghost-decks,' Shroot said. 'We have Master Ferrol, we have what we came for. Now's our chance to get out ahead of the game.'

'Look at them, Shroot,' Becket said, pointing to the monitors where the xenos raiders were advancing on every front, with crewmen fleeing before them. 'It does not matter where you hide, they will find you. What they do not take they will destroy. This ship is life for us all. Without it, nothing matters.'

'Maybe so and maybe no, Vaughn. I know your story. The ship may be everything to you, but for us it's nothing more than a prison. You're gonna tell us you want to take the command deck and put yourself back in charge. It don't matter if the ship's going down and gonna take you with it, it's just got to be yours again.'

'It never stopped being mine.'

'It's not your decision to make,' Shroot rebutted, frustrated. 'I have to do what is best for my crew.'

'So do I, all of them.' Becket made to leave, but then turned back to the woman. 'Shroot, making a choice, ignoring what's right, just because you think that is what others want, it doesn't make you a leader. It makes you a servant.'

ACTING SUB-LIEUTENANT Baisan hugged the wall even closer and the splinter shots splattered around him. Emperor's Breath, the fire was murderous. Already, a score of crewmen had fallen. The raiders shouldn't even be here. Baisan had heard word that they were still two sections away when he gave the order for his men to fall back. There hadn't been a vox order, but then he didn't need one, it was common sense. The crewmen hadn't even been issued with their shot-guns and rifles, and were still clutching whatever machine tools were close to hand when the sirens began. All the real firepower they had were the officers' side arms, and they could not repel the raiders' attack. So, he had given the order to fall back. Any officer with a gram of sense would do the same, except that, somehow, the xenos warriors were on the flanks as well. He could see the silhouettes of their bladed, high helms through the smoke.

'Baisan!' the shout came from behind him. Baisan looked back and saw Lieutenant Aryll approaching, crouched over like a crab. 'Get your men back here! Get them– Aghh!'

Aryll jerked back, blood splashed across his uniform.

'Lieutenant? Lieutenant?' Baisan cried, but Aryll didn't move. Baisan realised that this was his chance. If he could make it over to Aryll then he could haul his body to the medicae decks and safety. He gripped his pistol and broke across the first gap between them, spraying fire liberally at the raiders. He dived and rolled, the impact knocking the pistol from his hand, and over to a crewman who snatched it up. There was no time to go back, he had to get to–

Baisan could not believe it. Sub-Lieutenant Ortus was already there, crouching by Aryll's side. The lieutenant was alive, talking into Ortus's ear. Another crewman took Aryll away, and Ortus ran over to Baisan.

'The lieutenant's left me in command, Baisan. Hold your men here until I give you the order.'

Baisan swore under his breath. Where were those cursed armsmen?

CROUCHED BEHIND THE captain's chair, Ward shared Baisan's concerns. All across the ship the *Relentless*'s armsmen were already deployed, not against the xenos attackers, but against each other. Below him, he could hear Vickers starting to root out Guir's men from the wrecked command deck, but it was slow. The mutineers knew they could expect no mercy if they were taken prisoner, but, worse than that, they had faith in their cause to depose him, and still believed they could win. Guir had sent men to the port landing bay, where the first officer's squads were beginning to get the upper hand. All contact with the starboard bay had been lost the instant the Slaver had attacked. He had voxed down to the generatium repeatedly to restore the power feeds, get some thrust to the engines, anything that would allow him to change the ship's vector and surprise the Slaver still lurking somewhere out there. He had voxed and voxed, but had received no reply. No one from the Mechanicus was responding to him, and he had no spare armsmen to send to investigate.

Ward's first order as soon as he saw the assault boats deploy should have been for the general arming of the crew. It was normally only authorised in such perilous situations as these, but he had hesitated. He who controlled the guns controlled the ship, and if he allowed the crew to arm themselves indiscriminately, who knew what they would do with the weapons when the danger was over. No, this was the right decision. His officers and armsmen would defeat the mutineers, see off the raiders, and finally root out the traitors for good. He had to keep control and maintain the strength of his command. It was in the most glorious traditions of the *Relentless*.

FIFTEEN

AFTER THE FEROCIOUS initial rush to gain a foothold on the ship, the raiders pushed more steadily into the depths of the vessel. They deployed heavier weapons: dark lances, firing beams of energy that burned straight through the crewmen's cover, and splinter cannon that scoured entire corridors of life in a few bursts. The crew of the *Relentless*, with few arms and no armour, fell back further and further. The raiders, emboldened by even weaker resistance than they had anticipated, pushed them even harder.

Deck 332: mid-section.

A raiding party destroyed an atmosphere reclamator complex with demolition charges, environmental systems being one of their priority objectives. Their ultimate goal was to cripple the ship and force the crew to escape to the sanctuary pods, where they could then be collected. The party, having achieved their primary target was then allowed to run loose with electro-nets and other non-lethal weapons, to take their haul of slaves back to their craft.

Deck 402: aft-section.

Raiders were confronted with several conscript shifts all still chained together. The conscripts' crewbosses fled at the sight of the alien warriors, and left the conscripts behind. Unable to resist the temptation, the raiders spent some time herding the conscripts back into the assault boats. They completely ignored the gunner silo for Turret 500-A18. As a result, the turret continued to fire throughout the length of the battle, and crippled several boats as they clung to the side.

Deck 53: aft-section.

A party of raiders was, in turn, ambushed by a squad of crewmen and enginseers led by Artifex Pierce. The enginseers had converted a crude but murderously effective flamethrower that scattered the survivors and left them vulnerable to the enginseers' charge and cutting tools. With the xenos weapons they captured, Artifex Pierce and his squad were able to effectively strike back at the invaders.

Deck 264: fore-section.

Sub-Lieutenant Zandrahan and a squad of petty officers attempted to lure a boarding party into a well-prepared ambush. Zandrahan acted as bait, drawing the attention of the raiders, and managed to get them into the kill-zone. It was only then that he discovered that the concealed petty officers had already been taken by the xenos scouts that continued to haunt the cargo bays. Zandrahan was presented as a gift to the boarding party leader, who slit his throat and consumed his soul right there before the eyes of his men.

WARD BLINKED THE sweat from his eyes as he focused on the data flying across his displays. Reports were coming in of raiders stalking the upper decks in small groups, selectively targeting officers, pouncing on them and hauling them away, or killing them where they stood, while ignoring common crewmen. At last he saw the pieces falling into place. The last few weeks: the dead ship that haunted them, the distress signal that led them into this trap, the surgical attack of the Slaver, and the headhunting squads, it was all becoming clear. This was not a simple hit and run raid. They were after something specific. They were after him.

They had been working him for weeks, stretching him and taunting him. They had planted the *Arc of Elona* in his path to ensure that he investigated, and then they had used the Slaver, able to mimic other ships even while active, to try to drive him out of his mind with terror. Well, of course, they had to do such a thing. With a ship such as the *Relentless* at his command, he would have been their most terrible foe. He would have burned them from their hiding places, and so they had to strike first. It was all so obvious. They expected him to hide, to cower and to be taken without a fight, but he had seen through their scheme. They expected him to baulk at the action he must take, to save himself, to save this beautiful ship from becoming an alien's prize, but he would not. The glorious traditions of the *Relentless* would keep him true.

Ward voxed again to the generatium, but there was still no response. He would have to go down there himself. He called Vickers back, and took most of his impromptu squad from him as a bodyguard. He contemplated bringing Vickers too. It would be strange to go into danger without him at his side, but ultimately he decided against the idea. The man's love for the Emperor had become fixated on the *Relentless* as a fetish, no doubt as the result of the heresy that he had been born into. It had made him an invaluable servant for all these years, but it might prove inconvenient for this particular occasion. Instead, Ward left him with a handful of men and bid him continue with his work, even though it would no longer make a great deal of difference.

* * *

IT HAD BEEN a quarter of an hour since Acting Sub-Lieutenant Baisan had last seen the raiders. Evidently, his men were not guarding anything that had caught their interest, and the raiders had been enjoying themselves attacking other areas. Baisan knew they were enjoying it, because he heard the echoes of their alien laughter and their captives' screams. At least, Baisan thought, it wasn't him.

Deck 26: aft-section.

After defeating the last of Guir's men in the landing bay, the armsmen squads were instantly redeployed from the untouched port side of the *Relentless* against the raiders on the starboard side. A quarter of their number were caught at a cross-junction on Deck 26, and were pinned down. Concentrated fire from the raiders' heavy weapons finally destroyed their last cover. They were enslaved and removed back to the assault boats shortly afterwards.

Deck 349: mid-section.

Deck-crews had been staging their own hit-and-run raids against the invaders, which although the toll was high on the work crews, at least allowed them the chance to get close enough to use their hammers and drills against their tormentors. The raiders finally realised that the deck-crews were using the gaps and crawl spaces in that area to surprise them and then escape. The raiders pumped gas through the system and, although it was designed to render the victim unconscious and ready for transportation, the prolonged exposure that many of the crewmen suffered, trapped in that confined space, proved fatal.

Deck 127: Armoury.

Protected deep inside the heart of the *Relentless*, the armoury remained sealed. Orders had yet to be received from any command-level officer to authorise the general arming of the crew. Lieutenant Commander Guir had been reported dead, but Commander Ward was still active, and his last instructions had been to refuse any additional issue. The only man who could have overruled him was Commissar Bedrossian, and his whereabouts were still unknown.

As retreating crewmen in desperation lay siege to the armoury, the trusted men sealed inside waited patiently for orders.

CADET-COMMISSAR KOSOW instinctively ducked down even further as the spray of weapons fire peppered the console he hid behind. This entire assault on the command deck had been a disaster. He had seen the man before him torn apart by the ambushers, who were suddenly everywhere on the walls. He had dived for cover and hid there until the shots and the shouts of the two sides blowing each other to pieces had finally quietened. He had dared peek out then, but another burst of gunfire had made him hunch back down. He was pinned down, the party was scattered, he could not see anyone but the bodies of the armsmen still out on the deck. It felt like an age since he had seen the commissar.

Kosow pressed harder against the side of his head to help staunch the bleeding. A fleck of metal had caught him, tearing off part of his ear. He was not hit badly, he kept telling himself, but he found it hard to ignore the blood spreading across his hand and down the side of his neck.

He knew that, sooner or later, the ambushers would tire of waiting and flank him, or maybe they had already called for reinforcements who would appear behind him, and that would be it. The coat and cap of the commissar were no protection in this madness. Who would notice another man dead?

As though the fates had heard his thoughts, there was a *kerrchunck* from the door-seal beside him. Someone was opening it from the other side. The cadet took hold of his pistol and held it up, his hand shaking with the adrenaline.

The door swung slowly open and a man stood there, dressed as a cadet, but with a face that was back from the dead.

'God-Emperor…' Kosow whispered in disbelief as he saw who stood there.

'Not quite, cadet… I'm the captain.'

THE COMMAND DECK was unrecognisable. Becket had known there had been fighting here, but he could not have expected such devastation. What had been the living, thriving nexus of the *Relentless* was now a wasted battleground, dead and dark. His party moved inside. Its numbers had swelled as they had raced here. There were not only the conscripts and those of Ferrol's crew who had followed him, but also others who had been left without leaders and had been swept up in the progress of the one unit that seemed to have a purpose. They were following him because he was giving the commands. Sundjata had quickly disarmed the cadet they had almost tripped over when they had entered, and he and the others fanned out around the entrance, arming themselves from the fallen. There were men still alive out there: the two sides had fought each other to a standstill, and Becket needed to force them apart.

'I am going up to the bridge,' he said to Sundjata by his side.

'It's your life,' the conscript replied. Becket could have laughed at the insubordinate tone in his voice, even as he prepared to follow him. Insubordinate? It was the tone the condemned man always took with him, but now their roles were changing.

Becket stepped out cautiously, but thought better of it. If the Emperor meant for him to be shot down then so be it, but he would not sneak up his own bridge like a thief come to steal back his command. The bridge was his, the command was his, it had never been otherwise.

He climbed up to the dais boldly, past Guir's body, across the pieces of smashed aquila, and, in the middle, there it was: the captain's chair. Now was not the time to retake it. Instead, he doffed his cadet cap and jacket, and stepped to the front, standing upon the aquila's broken head so that he could see and be seen by all on the command deck.

'Hear me!' he shouted, his voice echoing in the quiet space. 'I am Captain Becket of the *Relentless*. You were told I was dead by men who were traitors to the Fleet and to the Emperor, yet here I stand! You here have been fighting over a lie! A lie created so that a few may profit even as you spill your blood in their name!

'I am the captain, and I am ordering you all to stand down. My men will be coming round, they are the captain's men. If you touch them, you touch me. If you harm them, you harm me. If you wish to kill them then kill me now!'

Becket waited. He could hear his heartbeat. It was slow, he was calm. Once, twice, three times it beat.

'Good,' he said to them all in their hiding places. 'The *Relentless* is my ship and you are its crew. You are mine, and I am yours. It is not too late, not too late for any of us.'

Becket turned around. Yes, now the time was right, and he sat back in the captain's chair. Beneath him, his men were moving through the deck with caution, but the survivors were already standing up and coming out of hiding. None of them had expected to live for much longer, but the captain had set them free.

Cadet Kosow had come up to the dais as well. The young, frightened face he had worn before was now a mask of stone. A commissar of the Emperor could show no emotion, certainly not fear, and he had smothered his outburst of panic and relief. Becket could not look at him. Instead, he read the data streaming across his displays and reached for the vox.

'Armoury. Armoury,' he said. The armoury acknowledged. 'This is Captain Becket. I hereby give the order for the general arming and mobilisation of the crew. Authorisation Janvius Iro Ultima. Confirm.'

The voice on the other end spluttered.

'Listen to me! You will open up and arm my crew. You think I'm dead? You are out of date! Authorisation Janvius Iro Ultima. Confirm, or I will come down there and drag you out!'

The armoury confirmed and, decks down, their gates opened to the flood of men. Becket keyed the vox again.

'All decks! All personnel! This is your captain. Now hear this!'

Across the ship, from their cover, from their hiding places, from their holes, the crew of the *Relentless* looked up and listened.

'COME ON, BAISAN. It's time to push them back!' Ortus stood in the face of the enemy fire, sword drawn, looking ahead. 'Come on!'

Baisan muttered something under his breath, and levered himself out of his alcove. He dragged his sabre from his belt and followed.

WITH THE GENERAL mobilisation order given, the armoury raced to distribute arms to crewmen down the length of the ship. The armourers' greatest pride was the speed at which such a grand task could be completed and they had been drilled incessantly since Becket had first arrived on the *Relentless*.

Shotguns, lasrifles, pistols, ammunition and armour were shunted through their distribution network, and into the hands of the hard-pressed crew. With this equipment, crewmen and officers were able to hold their ground and start pushing back. The raiders, who had expected to hit their targets and then withdraw, had been lured deep into the ship by the crew's long retreat. Their ambition had driven them to chase on the crewmen's heels and grasp for a prize, the ship itself, that was no longer within their reach. When the crew struck back, the raiders found themselves exposed and far distant from the safety of their boats. They fell back and fought all the harder. Now their focus was to kill.

Deck 289: aft-section.

A band of raiders on a rapid strike into the ship was halted by squads of newly armed crewmen. Reinforcing units were quickly coordinated to surround the aliens. With their retreat cut off, the raiders turned on their attackers with an awful ferocity, as the flanking units advanced around them. No quarter was asked, and none was given.

Deck 156: aft-section.

Retreating raiders cut oxygen lines running through the section, turning the air within the area into a powder-keg. Thirty crewmen and a dozen of their own were killed.

Deck 397: fore-section.

Encountering increased resistance, one raiding party commander ordered his warriors to hold their ground. The armed crews prepared to attack his position, only to have the raiders withdraw before them. Encouraged by their success, the crews charged forwards and were torn apart by the splinter-traps and munitions that the raiders had left behind. The resulting explosions were enough to collapse the deck sections immediately above and below, and cause a significant risk to the *Relentless*'s structural integrity in that area. No further pursuit of the party was permitted.

Medicae deck.

For all the fighting to this point, the medicae deck had been relatively quiet. A small number of casualties from the Slaver's hits had trickled in, but most of the injured had been in sections that were being invaded by the raiding boarding parties, and rescue was impossible. A few more arrived as the retreating crew left their injured behind. The issue of arms, however, turned the situation on its head. Instead of running, crewmen were standing, fighting back and being hit. The number of casualties sky-rocketed, and more and more of them were being saved. Suddenly the medicae was awash with men with every manner of injury inflicted by the evil weapons the raiders carried: scarred by energy burns, riddled with splinter shots, cut by blades and broken in the mind. The med-icae's battle had just begun and, if they survived, it would carry on for days after the last shot had been fired.

Across the board, the outnumbered and outgunned raiders turned tail, many of them dumping some of their prisoners to slow their pursuers and ensure that they could escape with the rest. Dracon Ysubi, in overall com-mand of the boarding parties, realised that discipline had broken down amongst the foremost units, and their war-riors were streaming back with captives, declaring victory even though they had passed over their priority objectives in the easy hunt for slaves. The dracon caught one partic-ularly egregious offender with his agoniser-whip, and shocked the life from him, taking the slaves as his own. He then ordered his special reserves forward. They would hold the Imperials at bay, while his warriors sowed enough explosives throughout the starboard hull to blow it clean off the *Relentless*.

BECKET CLICKED THE intravox off. There was still no response from the generatium gallery.

'What bloody fool let you up here?' Ferrol shouted at him. Becket looked across. He was standing just off the dais. He was upright, attempting to hold himself up, though he was leaning heavily on Shroot standing beside him.

'Ferrol, I am glad to see that you're back on your feet.'

'And I plan to stay there, but I won't get the chance if you carry on the way you've been doing. I've been listen-ing, and I think that maybe you've forgotten–'

'Captain!' the shout came from below. Becket stepped to the edge and looked down. They had found Senior Arms-man Vickers. That was the man Becket had been waiting for, the man who would take him to Ward. He was being led out onto the command deck by Ah Dut and a few others. Becket saw the look in his eyes, and felt his blood boil. He swooped to the deck, and crossed the distance between them. The conspiracy against him had fallen apart: Guir was dead, Ward was gone and Bedrossian had disappeared, but Vickers was here. Vickers was here and he had known. He had stood over Warrant as Ward shot him through the head. He had been a part of it!

His men backed away as they saw the captain storm forwards. The anger burned in him. It was a physical thing, inside him. He could feel it pushing through his face, through h' hands. He smashed Vickers across the face with the back of his fist. Vickers saw the blow coming and took it. He went down. Becket pulled him up. His pistol was in his hand and he stuck it in Vickers's face.

'Was this what he felt, Mister Vickers? Do you think this is what he felt?'

A crowd was gathering around him, not daring to intervene. Becket knew that they did not understand, but let them watch. Vickers was looking up at him, his gaze serene. No, that was not good enough.

He tossed the pistol away and took hold of Vickers with both hands. He leaned in and whispered fiercely in his ear.

'Tell me what it was, Vickers. What was your price? How much did he have to promise you to betray your captain?'

Vickers did not speak, but Becket could see the look of indignation that flashed across his face. If not a bribe, then what?

'What did he have on you, armsman? What was he going to say?'

Vickers's serenity was shattered. He had expected death, but not this. He panicked and seized the captain back. He tried to throw him off, but the onlookers intervened. They raised their rifle butts to club him.

'Wait!' Becket ordered. Vickers was saying something.

'The test,' Vickers whispered. 'He was going to tell them about the test.'

Becket had read the files on Vickers when he arrived. He had read the files on all of them, but Vickers's file had a special note attached: a medicae report that had been formally deleted. Becket found a copy that the old captain had hidden away. Vickers had been a conscript, dragged on board from a primitive world as human fuel, but he had been tough enough to survive and prosper, so tough as to attract the attention of the old captain and Commander Ward. He had been through the cursory medical scrutiny when he had been brought on board, but they used the opportunity of his promotion to armsman to run him through another test, a genetic one. He had been one tick outside the acceptable range of genetic deviation. He was a mutant.

It was a tiny amount, but it was one notch too far. He should have been instantly exterminated and incinerated, or handed over to an Inquisition station on a planet for examination. He wasn't. Instead, they put Vickers on their leash, and they advanced him, confident in their control over him.

'I know, Mister Vickers, I already know.' Vickers sagged back down and put his head in his hands, but Becket could not relent.

'Where has Commander Ward gone?'

'He went… to the generatium.' To bring the power feeds back, Becket wondered? No, he would not have left the bridge for that, and why didn't he take Vickers with him?

'What is he going to do?'

'He didn't say. He just said it was in the finest traditions of the ship.'

Now Becket understood. He backed away, helped Vickers up from the deck, and cleared a path for him through the crowd.

'Mister Vickers, I know your love for this ship. I love it too. We will fight for it, and we will die for it. Its enemies are close. They are running through its veins, hurting it, killing it. You show them. You show them what a son of the *Relentless* can do.'

FERROL WATCHED BECKET stride back to the dais after letting the big thug go. Ferrol had flopped down in the captain's chair, perhaps this at least would get his attention.

'You listen to me now! You concentrate all you like on kicking those blasteds off this ship, but it won't do you any good. That Slaver's still out there, and as soon as it realises that its little boys are coming home, it'll be back to finish the job. You've got to get your engines back. You've got to send a squad down to the generatium–'

'I am leading a squad down to the generatium,' Becket said distracted, checking the displays for the final time.

'Well, good! Wait a minute, you can't lead it.'

'Ward's down there. He's going to destroy the ship.'

'That don't matter. You've got to stay here. You've got to let someone deal with Ward, and you've got to stay where you're needed. When you get your engines back, you've got to be here to command this ship. This retribution of yours, let it go. For the sake of the ship, for the lives of the crew, for the life of me, let it bloody go!'

'Know anything about space faring, Master Ferrol?'

'More than you ever will,' Ferrol snapped back instinctively.

'Good. The ship is in your hands. Keep it safe.' Becket said, striding away, and calling a squad of his men after him.

'Bloody blasted! That bloody blasted is going to get us all killed. Shroot, get Affa and Tonk back here. There's no point stopping us blowing ourselves up if that Slaver out there's just going to finish the job. Any of these Navy types still breathing, get 'em up and back to their posts. Doesn't matter which side they were on, we're all in it now, but make sure you keep a gun on 'em. If any of 'em give you any trouble, just say… Just say–'

'Say what?'

Blow their blasted balls off is what he would say, Ferrol thought, but these weren't like his men. What would put the blasted fear into these men like nothing else?

'Just say, "Captain's orders" all right, Shroot? "Captain's Orders".'

VICKERS PLACED HIS palm flat upon the deck. He could feel the rough texture, the firmness of the metal, the warmth of the ship's life. It was solid, something real, something that one could believe in, a foundation for a faith even. It gave him comfort at times of great stress.

He had not come to this place by chance, but by an instinct, built up from years of violent experience. Instinct had told him that here was where she needed him most.

The crewmen had recognised his powerful frame as he approached, and they had almost cheered. He was a terrifying beast of a man, but he was theirs. Vickers knew that these were his people, not the officers whose only use for him was as a machine to execute their orders, but these crewmen who accepted him completely as one of their own, irrespective of what he was inside.

The raiders had fallen back to their beachheads. No one knew why they were still there. They should have been gone already, and yet they were clinging onto their hold on the ship. They were well dug-in, but the crew were determined to force them off, and this position was opposite their strongest defences. One squad, approaching cautiously, had already been torn to pieces by their fire, and the survivors were cowering in the tunnel ahead, burying themselves behind what scant cover they could find. The reinforcing units had seen them go in, and the pieces come out again. The crewmen were tired. They were scared. This was how Vickers knew he was needed.

He felt the strength of the ship flow up from the deck, through his palm and into his core, and then he rose to his feet. The young midshipman nominally in charge gave the order to advance, but all of them knew that it was the Senior Armsman that they would follow.

Vickers kept a measured pace for the first section, keeping the crewmen together. He began to mutter 'Relentless, Relentless, Relentless' to himself, and the others caught the word and joined in. He rounded the corner and saw the barricade at the far end, the flickering angular silhouettes of the xenos warriors behind. He heard a cry of alarm, high-pitched, inhuman, and he started to trot. The first splinter, snap-fired, sailed high over his head, and he broke into a run, dodging as he charged.

'Relentless. Relentless. Relentless!'

A splinter-shot caught his brow, but it glanced away. One caught his thigh, but he didn't break stride. One zipped straight through his shoulder, but he ignored the pain, he couldn't even feel it. The Emperor had given him his body the way it was, and it was time to test how much His work could truly endure. Shots scored marks down his side, and he grimaced. They buried themselves in his gut. They would kill him, but not quickly enough. They fired straight into his chest, and the armour held.

'Relentless! Relentless! RELENTLESS!'

He burst through the barricade, every weapon pouring shots into him. His shotgun fired once in return, and two of the spiny alien warriors fell back. He fell, bloodied, through the gap, and thumped against the deck. Hooked bayonets stabbed to ensure that he stayed there, into his back, his side, once, twice. They came for a third time, and he felt the power run through the floor into him once more. He rose, and pulled the rifles from their hands. The shotgun fired again, and xenos blood splashed across him.

He could see the entrance to the assault boat, and in front of it a xenos officer, richly adorned and garbed, with a bodyguard of armoured raiders with halberds glowing with energy. His legs were heavy. Fire poured into him, knocking the shotgun from his hand. He still had a splinter rifle in the other. The spirit drove him one leaden step further, and he threw the bayonet like a spear at the xenos officer. A halberd swept, and the bayonet fell from the air in two halves. A laser shot blasted through Vickers's armour and scored a hole into his chest. The senior armsman fell to his knees, and only then did the fire finally relent. His head drooped, his body, scorched black, streamed with blood. It didn't even look like his own any more. It slowly sagged as though the air whistled through him.

He felt himself sway, and his one good hand swung behind him. He could sense that the officer was in front of him, watching him. His one good hand took a grip, and with one last effort he drew the knife and raised it high above his head. For that one moment, he locked eyes with the xenos. This was one officer who would never forget him.

'RE–!'

The shots tore through him again and did not stop.

DRACON YSUBI TOOK a step back as the human's bloody carcass smacked down onto the floor. He could not believe that, for a moment, his heart had been in his throat, that his eternal existence might be cut short by this barbaric creature. Now, following his path, a herd more stampeded towards him, howling and baying that chant of theirs. Ysubi had had enough. He was not going to have his life put at risk by Ai'zhraphim's folly. His warriors had plunder enough. This human-built scow was best destroyed at a distance in any case. His incubi bodyguards closed around him, and he called the last of his warriors back to their boats.

As the xenos departed, they left behind a rearguard to cover the vulnerable moments of their retreat. They were twisted monsters, the cast-off results of their torturer surgeons' experiments, pumped with chemicals to send them into battle-rage. They were aggressive, indomitable and expendable.

THE MAIN HATCH to the generatium stood open as Becket approached with his men and a band of artificers. He could feel the heat radiating out. It was hot, hot as that day in the pipe room. Were the men he had with him, Sundjata, Kimeal, Papeway, Fidler and the rest, thinking the same?

He gazed along the long gallery of generators that cut up through the decks above. Nothing was moving, but the generators were thrumming quietly. In battle, this chamber should have been a tumult of noise and motion as the Mechanicus and the artificers scrambled back and forth, driving the engines to the utmost, straining every unit of power they could at the bridge's command, and then pulling them back at the edge of overload.

Nothing was moving, but that did not mean that the chamber was empty. Becket stepped inside and something dropped in front of his feet. It was an armsman's helmet. The owner's body was hanging by his armour straps from the rail of the mezzanine above them. His death had not been quick or easy.

'I suppose it's too much to hope that Ward's already dead?' Fidler said.

'Would you wager your life?' Becket replied. Maybe he was dead, but he had to be sure. He started to the ladder.

'Captain!' Kimeal warned. 'The power-feeds, the engines, the Slaver!'

Becket stopped and turned back. 'Get the artificers working on the repairs. Make sure you keep them alive. When Ferrol calls, this is what you tell him...'

'HE SAID WHAT?' The vox-line didn't conceal Ferrol's tone of disbelief.

'Do you need me to repeat it, Master Ferrol?' Kimeal replied earnestly.

'What does he think this crate is? An interceptor?'

'He has faith, master.'

The vox crackled and squealed over Ferrol's reply.

'Sundjata! Sundjata!' Fidler was shouting in the distance. There were the sounds of Sundjata running, and then a blast of his shotgun.

'Apologies.' Kimeal left the vox hanging and grabbed his weapon. Now there was something moving.

FAR UP ABOVE, Commander Ward stood watch while Adept Tertionus worked nervously. Something was preying on the tech-priest's mind.

'Commander, you will assure me that this will only be used as the very last resort.'

'Of course, adept.'

'To do such a thing, to murder the spirit of such a great and ancient machine...' Tertionus shook his head. 'Even derelict, a spark will live on, can be rekindled. It is only if these filthy xenos can do as you say...'

Trap the spirit and torture it to madness. Could it be done, Tertionus wondered? Yes, it could. He had seen a few of the living examples of these aliens' work, which the Mechanicus kept secret and hidden even from the officials of the Imperium, damned souls bottled up within engines of destruction, xenos captives that could drink the spirit from a man. If a man, then why not a machine? Yes, if that were the case then the commander would ensure that the *Relentless* met a noble end.

Tertionus uttered a blessing of good purpose over his work, and then over himself for good measure. He so wished he could have consulted with the magos before coming here, but they had been...

The commander suddenly stepped away. Tertionus turned and saw him signal to keep silent. Ward had heard someone coming.

* * *

THE FIGURE WHO had approached, hidden, watched the Mechanicus adept turn back to the open regulator panel. The first officer was nowhere to be seen, but he had to be close. Surely he would not have left the adept here, and then made a run for a sanctuary pod? He deserved not only to be killed, but to be expunged from battlefleet memory, and here was the chance to avenge every treason, every degradation that Ward had inflicted upon them all.

He eased another step forward, and sighted his pistol at the back of the adept's head. The *Relentless* came first. It had to come first. He slid his finger onto the trigger, and then he felt the cold metal of a gun-barrel against his throat.

'Welcome to the end, Mister Bedrossian,' said Ward in his ear, and fired.

TWO SHOTS RANG out from above. Becket looked up towards them, and then carried on climbing.

KIMEAL, SUNDJATA AND Fidler fired in unison at the warped monsters that shambled towards them. Fragments of skin and bone blew off, but it did not slow them down a step.

'BRING IT DOWN! Bring it down!' Sub-Lieutenant Ortus called, but Baisan and the squad fired and fired to no avail.

The hulk stood over three metres tall and nearly as wide. What kind of creature it had been before the xenos surgeons had laid their knives upon it, was impossible to say. It was built like a bulkhead, its neck so thick that it had become a mere extension of the body, and muscled tubes writhed under its skin, struggling like snakes. Its fingers had been replaced by sheaves of razor-edged tendrils that it coiled around crewmen, flaying them alive.

The hulk bellowed as the shot bounced from its carapace, and swung its arm around again. Baisan dived forwards into the dirt as the tendrils lashed over him, ignoring the shrieks from behind him of those who were not so quick. The hulk stomped forwards a step, trying to smash Baisan under his foot, but Baisan yelped and hid in the side of the tunnel.

'Bullets are no use against the creature,' Ortus was shouting, a little melodramatically, Baisan thought. 'Close with it, men. Cut this monstrosity to pieces!'

Ortus waved his sabre in the air and led the charge. The hulk kicked out, and knocked him back hard into the wall. Not hard enough, in Baisan's opinion. More of the crewmen raced forwards, chopping at the hulk's midriff. It tore them to pieces, but then staggered, crashing straight into Baisan's hiding place. Baisan tried to shrink away, but there was nowhere to go. His gun was gone, dropped somewhere. The hulk's noisome flesh was mere centimetres away, and the thick snake wriggling under the skin was right in his face. In terror, he grabbed it, digging his fingers deep into the soft flesh. The hulk pulled away, but Baisan held tight, and yanked back with all his might. The snake snapped in his hands, the skin broke and purple fluid sprayed out over Baisan. He fell backwards and banged his head hard against the wall. The hulk stormed away, blaring in pain.

'Courage, men. Courage prevails!' Ortus was there again, sabre in hand. The hulk was sluggish, and Ortus easily caught the tendrils with the sword edge and sliced through them. The hulk stumbled back. The idiot, Baisan thought. Couldn't he see that it was already dead? Ortus struck, cutting once to the knee, and bringing it down. Then he struck it in its other arm, before finally burying the sabre through the hulk's chest, and dancing back out of range of its death throes.

Baisan, covered in the hulk's ichor, head aching, got to his feet, and saw the crewmen running forwards to congratulate their champion, chanting his name.

'Ortus! Ortus! Ortus!'

* * *

FERROL WATCHED THE tiny specks of the assault boats as they departed the crippled *Relentless*. They burned their way into the darkness in the direction that Ferrol knew the Slaver had to be hiding. Its attack run, and the subsequent boardings, had destroyed every cannon the *Relentless* had in its starboard arc, and there it had been skulking, in the blind-spot. Ferrol had never encountered one of these vessels, but he had survived as long as he had by learning as much as he could about what was out there. He had heard of these creatures before, and the reports had made him wake in a cold sweat for nights afterwards. Even if the *Relentless* was at her best, he knew that the Slaver was able to dance around her at will. With the starboard guns gone, the Slaver could hug that gap, and no matter which way Ferrol tried to turn he would never be able to bring the mighty cannon on the port side, still untouched, to bear.

They had no chance at all, except for the captain's plan, which, Ferrol confidently expected, would leave them more crippled than ever. If he could think of anything else, then, dust and vapours, the captain could go swing. However, he couldn't think of anything, and so that was that.

'Whatever starboard turrets we have left, target those boats,' he ordered. They all knew that crewmen from the *Relentless* would be prisoner slaves onboard them, but no one questioned the order. It would be a mercy.

'Can we map the boats' trajectories? Get a fix on the Slaver's location that way?'

There was a yell from the auspex array from both the officer and Ferrol's crewman who were stationed there.

'No need,' Shroot reported, 'we have it.'

'Where?'

'It's coming straight for us!'

Ferrol had wished, had prayed, that the xenos captain may have been more concerned to recover his own assault boats before turning on the *Relentless* again, but

evidently he had expected a little too much compassion
from this soulless alien butcher.

'Do we have power?'

Shroot checked the data.

'Not yet.'

'Not yet? Not yet? It's at our throats, Shroot, if not now
then when?'

Shroot didn't reply. Ferrol felt himself about to
explode.

'Now,' she cried.

'Then do it!'

The order went out. The power flowed from the generators towards the main engines, and then diverted away
and to the side. The full force of an engine burst roared
into the small manoeuvring thrusters dotted across the
ship.

Ferrol stared out of the main view-portal at the
starscape beyond. Nothing moved.

'Thrusters fired, master,' Shroot reported, and then,
with a pondering, inexorable sloth, the starscape started
to roll.

The curatium pit sprang to life as reports came back of
the small thrusters blowing apart, overloaded, but Ferrol
didn't care. They wouldn't be stopping.

'Incoming!' the shout went up.

The Slaver saw the *Relentless* begin its roll, saw its port
cannon batteries rotate towards them, but even it could
not manoeuvre that fast. Its guns fired. Its dark energy
beams lashed out and scoured lines across the undamaged dorsal hull, trying to carve the *Relentless* into two.
The *Relentless* survived.

'Fire as she bears!' Ferrol cried, and the gun crews of the
portside batteries did just that. The timing was calculated,
compensated for the rotation, and the deflection was
minimal as the Slaver was barrelling towards them. The
gun-crews lived for this moment, when, in the service of
the Emperor, they could strike out at His foe.

The decks fired one after the other, the gun-crews of every level firing almost as one, throwing an inescapable barrage of plasma shot, graviton pulses, magnetic cores and fusion missiles into the face of the closing ship. Its prow cracked as the payloads struck true, and then it shattered into pieces, the following salvoes exploding layer after layer.

'It's gone! We've lost it from our scans.'

'Find it! Find it!' Ferrol bellowed, trying to stand on his still-numb legs. 'Has it disengaged? I said, has it disengaged?'

Ferrol's crewmen and the officers were all intent upon the unfiltered data streaming across their screens, trying to sift through the information pouring in, and make some kind of sense of it.

'One of you blasteds talk to me!'

ARCHON AI'ZHRAPHIM did not look at his display of the battle any more. There was nothing to see there in any case, just the assault boats, which had escaped with fuel enough to return to safety, and behind them the *Relentless*, bloodied and gouged, but unbroken. No, the battle in space was no longer significant. Instead, his attention was fixed upon the bridge and every action of his subordinates there.

By any objective measure, he knew that this expedition was a success. Their holds were still full with their Pontic slaves and, despite their failure, the returning boarders would have brought more captives: Imperial officers that would add spice to their bounty. The damage to the ship was not critical, and could be repaired even as they went. He knew, though, that his subordinates would not be in an objective frame of mind. They would not see the archon's orders to retreat from battle as plain sense, rather that he had displayed a vulnerability. No matter how ill-founded, his subordinates had the excuse to strike. All he could do was deny them the opportunity.

He kept his personal force-sphere strong and opaque from the outside, so that no one would be sure if he were in there or not. The splinter cannon concealed within the throne's ornate design were fully loaded and sighted. He had double-checked the other, more devious, security devices he kept around him, and ensured that they were all functioning in their various ways. As his ace, his personal incubi bodyguard were ready to descend in an instant, should there be any direct assault upon his person. He could have had them deployed constantly around him, but he did not. To show strength, to show your hand in such a situation, was a beginner's mistake, as it as good as showed your weakness.

No, absolute confidence was what was required and, of course, a culprit to focus the blame upon. The navarchos, alas, was too valuable for the kind of public demonstration that the archon had in mind. Dracon Ysubi, commanding the boarding parties was a likely candidate, if he survived to make it back. If not, a more general example may have to be made on the surviving warriors of his sect. Retribution on this scale required either quality or quantity to be truly satisfactory. Yes, the path was clear to him. He needed to take action, and a firm display of his displeasure would allow him to keep control of the game.

Ai'zhraphim touched his sceptre to start the engines, and to raise himself once more above their heads. The familiar hum did not emerge. He tried to activate them again, more firmly this time, but there was no sound, aside from a tiny susurration somewhere behind him. For a split second, Ai'zhraphim heard the voices from the maelstrom. His father, and the others, had reached him even here. Then the reality struck him. It was gas. They were striking at him now!

He looked quickly around, but there was no movement outside, nothing to show that anyone beyond knew what was happening within. Nothing that could be seen, at least. He had to escape. Dropping the sphere would leave him without its protection, but he could compensate for that. He pressed the signal for his incubi to appear, and waved the sceptre to dispel the sphere. The sphere held. He gestured again, but to no avail. Nor had his incubi guard appeared. He touched the sceptre again and willed the sphere fully transparent. It remained defiantly shaded from the outside. Ai'zhraphim felt the strange sensation of his own terror rising high. They had turned his shield into his prison. His face crawled with pain and began to blister. His eyes burned. He hammered on the wall of the sphere and cried plaintively for help. Through his blurring vision, he saw a shadowy figure approach his throne, and he shouted his throat raw to be heard through the barrier that he had soundproofed to ensure his secrecy. The shadow did not move.

Ai'zhraphim fell back from the sphere onto his throne, clawing his agonised face with his hands, eyes weeping uncontrollably. This was it. They had hooked him well, and for all his precautions he had not heard a whisper of it. He had only one chance left. He clutched inside his chest as his breath drew short, and his long fingers closed around the icon he sought. Let them have thought of this, he laughed with glee. Let the clever ones have predicted this!

BECKET FINALLY HAULED himself up to the top level, and then he saw the corpses. The first was a Mechanicus priest, slumped forwards over an open regulator station. The second was at his feet, wrapped in a black coat, the blood pooling out from behind a silver mask.

'He came after me, you know.' Ward announced. 'He trailed me all the way down here. He avoided the men I left down there to those monsters. All the way here, and all he took was my little adept. He probably thought that that at least would stop me, but I was able to finish what he started. I was disappointed in a way. I would have thought that the commissar would have understood better the necessary execution of a failed servant, but he didn't.'

Ward was behind the console, the dangling pipes and supports make the floor a jungle. Becket could see that he had a pistol.

'I thought you might come.' Ward continued. 'The confessor told me once, when he was still new to us, that when the end came, my ghosts would come back to me. I never believed him, but this is the end, and here you are.'

'I am no ghost,' the captain replied.

Ward fired. The shot ricocheted off the girder by Becket's head.

'I think you are,' Ward concluded.

Ward was ranting. His reasoning had gone, and his judgement was horribly skewed. Worse, he still thought himself sane. Becket peered through at the open station. What could the tech-priest have done there? It could be the master, he could have stopped the coolant pipes, overridden the fail-safes. Would there be a delay? It would take time for the excess in the first to build up, but then the first would go, and the second, and then on and on. The noise of the generators had risen a few minutes before. His men had succeeded, but their success was going to trigger the chain reaction that would tear the ship apart from the inside.

'What are you looking at, captain? You're looking at the station, aren't you? Trying to work out what I've done.' Ward contemplated the thought. 'Why don't you know already? If you're in my head then you should know what I've done. Perhaps you are real after all.' Ward felt the sweat pour down him. 'If you are real, how did you survive? The raiders, yes, of course, you've been in league with them all along. You led them here, and you're going to give them the *Relentless* as your prize!'

'The raiders are beaten. They're gone. There is no need for this any more.'

'Then you have come here to save her! You arrogant...
She was mine for two years, two years! And for a long
time before that as well. You came here. You barely ever
left your quarters. Papers, that was all you were interested
in. Papers! Data! You never felt her. You have the pre-
sumption to know what's best for her? It is I who love
her!'

'I have been through its thoughts, Ward. I have been
through the flesh, the veins and the bowels. I do not love
the ship, I am the ship. I am *Relentless*.'

'Then prove it, captain,' Ward spat, as he stepped away to
the side. 'Is she worth your life? Prove it. If you make a dash
for that station, maybe you can figure it out, and stop what
I've started. I'll run you through, but maybe I'll give you just
long enough. Or maybe I'll believe everything you've said
and stop it myself. Or maybe it's already too late.'

Ward began to wander back. He shifted the pistol into
his other hand and drew his sabre.

'I did not come to save the ship, Ward.'

'Oh? Why did you come then?'

'I came to revenge the murder of Officer Samuel Warrant.'

'And who is he?'

Becket attacked. Ward raised his pistol, but Becket fired,
shooting the pistol away, and most of Ward's hand with
it. The commander reeled away, raising the sword, but
Becket blocked the shaky swipe. He grabbed Ward
beneath the shoulders, lifted him, and slammed him
back against a pipe. He wrestled the sword from his grip,
reversed it, and slid it deep into Ward's body.

Ward's eyes bulged and rolled up.

'Only through the shoulder,' Ward gasped. 'What kind
of captain are you? Don't you even have the courage to–'

Becket squeezed Ward's shattered hand, and he
squirmed in pain.

'You are right, Mister Ward. I was too interested in
papers. Papers tell you a lot, but no paper anywhere told

me of the manifest delusion you carried in your head that made you a traitor and a mutineer.

'But it was a piece of paper that briefed me on the operation of the vessel. It was a piece of paper that showed me the vital flows of the generatium, and it was a piece of paper that taught me that this was the pipe I needed to pierce to release that excess.

'The sword did not need to go through your shoulder. It only needed to cut through the insulation.'

Becket smashed the handle of the sword down, slicing through the insulation of the pipe, and into the super-heated flow inside, letting it out. The blade glowed red, and then white hot. Ward was transfixed, face stretched in silent agony as the plasma escaped from the pipe, shooting up and out along the sword blade, through his flesh. The *Relentless* roared out through his body, and burned him up from the inside out.

EPILOGUE

Captain Becket stood quietly in the antechamber of the Navis Nobilite. The stars looked down on him through the sky-dome, but he did not look up. The Navis knew of his return, of course. This was a necessary formality: a personal visit to demonstrate to them that he was formally back in command. It was as necessary as the extensive repair work that was still being undertaken throughout the ship. So far from a battlefleet dock, even making makeshift repairs was difficult. The Mechanicus had been at least cooperative, if not enthusiastic, in the work. Any time they were not needed, though, they remained sealed in their enclave. What they were doing there, Becket did not know, and did not have time to discover. Things needed to be done, further explanation would come later.

Further explanation would be needed, too, for battle-fleet. He had sent a message back by astropath as soon as he could. The complete report would take longer to reach them, but they would doubtless have many questions, when their schedule allowed. It had been two years between the old captain's death and his own arrival, and only part of that delay was caused by Ward's stalling. The wheels back at Emcor were creakingly slow, except in the face of the most dire emergency, but they would turn upon him in time.

Evidence and samples enough of the xenos raiders had been kept, secured away, and the rest had been destroyed. Their bodies were ejected into space, as Becket could not stomach to have them reclaimed. They could not be allowed to pollute the ship any more than they had already. The retention of xenos artefacts was a crime, and armsman squads had the authority to destroy any they found, but there were precious few armsmen left to fulfil such duties. It was not only xenos items that crewmen might have hidden away, but their guns as well. The armourers had recovered what they could, and estimated the amount destroyed, but the remainder was, even now, stashed away somewhere below decks. He could look, but as Becket had learned, anything the crew wanted to hide badly enough, an officer would never find.

He considered himself lucky that, for this time at least, there had been no hint of unrest amongst them. The stories of his return to them at their time of peril were embellished further each day. The edge of devotion that they carried almost troubled him as greatly as any discontent might.

The confessor, though, was not questioning the tinge of apotheosis. On the contrary, he had been most solicitous to the captain's every request. He even suggested renovating one of his own private rooms to become a new sanctum to commemorate the fallen of the engagement, engraving their names onto the wall. Becket appreciated the gesture, and had spent several hours there since it had been consecrated. The names he most wished to see, however, were not there. He would remember Warrant, Ronah and the rest in his own way.

One name, that of Cadet-Commissar Micael was there, however, joining those of the other cadets who had lost their young lives as part of Guir and Bedrossian's ill-fated grab for power. Micael's death had been an accident, but he was no less worthy of being remembered. The one surviving cadet, Kosow, had taken the responsibility of the disposal of Commissar Bedrossian's effects. His official trappings of office were retained to be returned to Emcor in due course. The rest he had sent to reclamation, save for the silver mask that had covered the commissar's scars from another battle long before. Kosow reported that it had not been recovered. The confessor and the cadet, two more to add to the legion of officers that Becket had to watch.

Back to the business at hand, and finally the face of Principal Menander appeared before him, nearly as strange and as alien as the xenos bodies that he had flushed away a few days before.

'Speak,' it said.

'Lord Menander,' Becket began, 'I am sure you have been made aware of recent events, and that I have been indisposed for some time. This is a formal notification that I am fully undertaking the role and responsibilities of the captaincy.'

'Your message has been received.' The face said, and then faded.

Becket shook his head and turned to leave, but then, unexpectedly, the face reappeared.

'Better luck, captain, for the future,' it said, and was gone again.

'Is he awake yet?'

'Shortly, captain,' the chirurgeon replied. The chirurgeon was another officer who was nervous around Becket, another one to watch, another one too valuable to lose. 'I cannot say how long he will live after we revive him, however. It was all most difficult. We were very fortunate that his body was so robust and his mind so used to such treatment. Their work upon him was far more recent than the others, far more recent.'

Becket looked down at the body in the bed.

'We have removed what we could, what he might find most disturbing, and we have covered what we cannot.'

There was a tech-priest not far away, face hidden within his hood. The chirurgeon saw Becket glance over.

'They wished to observe, captain, and requested to take custody, as they consider that he is one of them. They have been very good in assisting me with the more specialised aspects. You did say to take all measures.'

'They will have to wait until I am finished,' Becket said. 'The raiders have disappeared, vanished. Yet this man spent months upon the Slaver. I need to know what he knows. I need to hear anything he can say that might help me find them.'

For of the casualties of the battle there was not one list, but two: one, engraved in stone within an Ecclesiarchy sanctum, the list of the dead; the other, one that Becket had compiled: the list of the taken. They were alive and they were still his crew.

'Proceed with the revival,' the captain ordered, and the chirurgeon did so.

The auditor awoke.

ABOUT THE AUTHOR

Richard Williams was born in Nottingham, UK. He has written fiction for publications ranging from *Inferno!* to the *Oxford & Cambridge May Anthologies*, on topics as diverse as gang initiation, medieval highwaymen and arcane religions. In his spare time he is a theatre director and actor. *Relentless* is his first full-length novel.

Visit his official website at
www.richard-williams.com